THE BEACH CAVES

Trevor Shearston is the author of *Something in the Blood*, *Sticks That Kill*, *White Lies*, *Concertinas*, *A Straight Young Back*, *Tinder*, *Dead Birds*, and *Hare's Fur*. His novel *Game*, about the bushranger Ben Hall, was longlisted for the Miles Franklin Literary Award and shortlisted for the NSW Premier's Literary Awards, the Christina Stead Prize for Fiction, and the Colin Roderick Award. He lives in Katoomba, in the Blue Mountains.

Trevor Shearston

the
beach
caves

SCRIBE
Melbourne • London

Scribe Publications
18–20 Edward St, Brunswick, Victoria 3056, Australia
2 John St, Clerkenwell, London, WC1N 2ES, United Kingdom
3754 Pleasant Ave, Suite 100, Minneapolis, Minnesota 55409, USA

First published by Scribe 2021

Typeset in Adobe Garamond Pro by the publishers

Printed and bound in Australia by Griffin Press, part of Ovato

Scribe Publications is committed to the sustainable use of natural resources and the use of paper products made responsibly from those resources.

9781925849868 (Australian edition)
9781950354405 (US edition)
9781925938531 (ebook)

A catalogue record for this book is available from the National Library of Australia.

scribepublications.com.au
scribepublications.com

for Kerrie and Paul
sister, brother, oldest friends

Part One
May 1970–February 1971

Wray began by pointing their eyes to the door. It wasn't closed to keep things out, he said. It was closed to keep things in. The site was unlike anything he or Dr Herr — he nodded towards his wife — had ever stood at, or found in the literature.

'You will shortly understand why. But please — I repeat, please! — keep to yourselves what I'm about to tell you. I did weigh up saying nothing, just letting you see when you got there. But on site you'll be my colleagues as well as my students, I'd prefer that I can trust you. So return that trust. Yes?' The room murmured *yes*. 'Thank you. Now, how many of you have driven to the coast from here?'

Three hands rose.

'Is that all?'

He strode to the board and snatched up a stick of chalk, slashed two north-south wriggles — river and coast — made a cross on the coast and jotted *BB*, and, inland, another cross, *C*. He joined the two with a horizontal, then used the chalk as a pointer, left to right.

3

'Canberra, Clyde River, Batemans Bay. The highway crosses the river here —' he made and labelled a cross, *N* — 'at a village called Nelligen. The site's a mile upstream of the bridge.'

That made it sound like civilisation, he went on, but it wasn't. The site was on the other side of the river, in the state forest. Everything would have to be ferried across in dinghies, hence his stipulation of no non-swimmers. He'd arranged outboards and dinghies with a local boatshed. The camping would be rough, washing in the creek, a spade for a toilet. No days off and, once there, no leaving. He had use of a university Land Rover, but anyone with a car should bring it. Departing on the Saturday after autumn break began, ten days from now.

'Which should be enough notice to cancel other plans, and to find a sleeping bag.' He flashed them a grin that didn't bare his teeth. 'Sleeping bags not, I see from your faces, uppermost in your minds, but the larger question, i.e., if this site has gone undiscovered for so long, why now the urgency?' The best answer, he said, was to recount its discovery.

Monday morning of last week, a call had been put through to him by Jan the secretary from a Mr Hendy, who lived in Queanbeyan. On the Sunday, Mr Hendy and a mate had been fishing for bream off the mouth of a creek flowing into the Clyde from the eastern, state forest, side. The mate was hit by a need 'perilous to perform from a dinghy', so they pulled to the bank. As they in the room would soon see, the bank at that particular point was unusual in being two flood terraces, one

4

above the other, and both old. There was no sign that they'd ever burned, but they were almost treeless, just native grasses and bracken and a scattering of casuarinas and spotted gum so stunted they looked like different species from those on the bank proper. The explanation was that, under a skin of silt, the terraces were almost pure sand.

There were other boats on the river, so the man with the call of nature waded up through the bracken to the higher terrace. While squatting, he spotted what he thought was the remains of a stone chimney. When he'd finished, he went to look, believing he'd found all that was left of some sad little settler's hut. But it wasn't a chimney, it was a dry-stone circular wall, or, rather, three-quarter circle, largely intact, waist high, some three metres across, and heavily encrusted with lichen.

'Any guesses?'

'An old well?' one of the boys said.

'Yes, that was his next guess.'

But a well made no sense, either. The diameter was too great, and five minutes away was a creek fresh above the tidal reach. Then he spotted a second circle. That was when he called to Mr Hendy. They abandoned their fishing and went bracken-bashing. All up, they found seventeen of the circles, in three clusters, and a sandstone boulder with hatchet-grinding grooves. Fortunately, Mr Hendy had seen hatchet grooves before.

'He rang the university first thing on the Monday. I dropped everything, including your lecture — for which, again, I apologise, if not entirely sincerely — and drove over to Queanbeyan. He wasn't free to come with me till the Friday, so I got him to mark the creek on the map and I drove down there that same afternoon. I went again with Dr Herr on the weekend, and we did a little digging. Which is why I'm describing the place to you in — I must admit — a state of some "animation"! The reason being …?' He beckoned urgently with both hands. 'Anyone?'

'They're houses,' someone behind Annette murmured.

'Precisely! Having sat in one. Thank you. Stone houses! In this "land of the wandering nomad".'

The two young women sprinted against the lights across Barry Drive, then, needing to earth each other's excitement, linked arms and walked in fast lockstep the ten minutes to the house in Masson Street.

They were twenty years old. The blonde one, and the taller, was Annette Cooley. The dark one was Susan Klima. They'd met in their first prehistory tutorial, where each quickly learned, to her annoyance, that the other, too, had read *Prehistoric Societies* from cover to cover. No one else had ventured beyond the prescribed chapter one. In the Union afterwards, over bad coffee, Susan had put bluntly to Annette that friendship would be more advantageous to them both than competing.

They were then living on campus, in different colleges.

Already each was sick of the institutional food and the constant partying. Sue found the house, a tiny mock Californian bungalow with mustard-yellow stucco walls and surrounded by dead lawn. The science boofhead then vainly pursuing Sue, Vince, declared it the ugliest house he'd ever set eyes on, thereby endearing it to them both. And ugly meant unwanted and unwanted meant cheap. They'd been its tenants now for two years, and the rent hadn't budged. Annette covered her half with weekend shifts in a patisserie in Civic, Sue waited tables in a nameless laneway restaurant known to its patrons as 'the Slav's'.

The team meeting had been held after last lectures, and they were home later than normal, the autumn dusk beginning to soften the starkness of the house. Annette checked the letterbox while Sue walked on and opened the door. They stepped into the residual warmth of the water stored all day in the cast-iron coils of the heating. Sue had spotted the system instantly when she'd first inspected the house, remembering it from childhood, her grandmother's house in Prague. Old-school, but the best, she'd informed Annette. And she'd been right. On the coldest night, even the bathroom was snug. They dumped their rucksacks in the lounge room, shed their parkas. Sue went to the laundry to fire the boiler, Annette to the kitchen. The freezer always held an unsold quiche. She sparked the oven and slid their dinner onto a shelf. Sue came back, took two tumblers from the drainer and plonked them on the table, and went to the dresser for the current flagon. Other than at parties, neither drank, but Sue's lamb *guláš* demanded lashings of red. She filled the tumblers, handed one to Annette, and raised her own.

'To the Clyde — and to a pair of First Class Honours!'

'And, I think, to Mr Hendy.'

'Indeed! To Mr Hendy!' Sue hooted. 'And his caught-short mate!'

They were giggling wine over their hands and the floor. They stood their tumblers on the table. Sue calmed down first. She licked her fingers and picked up her tumbler, nodded down at Annette's that she do the same.

'Again. Two great theses.'

They clicked tumblers and drank.

'So, you seriously reckon we'll be allowed to use stuff. Whatever turns up's his.'

Sue shrugged. 'You heard him — going's in our "interest". What else would that mean?'

Two days ago Wray had broken into their tutorial to announce that 'a site' had 'come up' and that he needed volunteers, ten if possible. An awkward time, he'd agreed, so close to end of term. He wasn't calling for a show of hands, he would pin a sheet on the noticeboard. He'd then asked their tutor, Patricia Meylor, if he might see Miss Cooley and Miss Klima outside for a minute.

He'd led them away from the door and asked what their plans were for the break — because it would be greatly in *their* interest as well as his own to have them on-site. Was an answer today, even right now, possible? They looked at one another. They'd booked the train to Sydney to stay with Annette's parents. A lift of the eyebrows, answered by a nod, killed that. He was her supervisor, Annette spoke. 'We're in. And thank you.'

When they'd re-entered the tutorial, Annette had been fascinated, then more than a little smug, to see that Patricia Meylor was as much in the dark about 'the site' as they were.

'That reminds me — I still haven't rung my folks.' She pointed towards the oven. 'Could you check that and maybe spin it.' She took a gulp of wine and went to the nook in the hallway where the phone was.

She got her father. She apologised, told him they weren't now coming, she'd be at the Clyde River for three weeks with the head of department, Professor Wray, at a site he'd found.

'What — this has just come up?'

She'd hoped to get her mother, who wasn't so demanding of details.

'Pretty much. A day or so ago.'

'I know the Clyde. Whereabouts?'

'I'm not allowed to say, that's a condition of going.'

'For goodness sake, darling, who would I tell? I'm a bloody solicitor!'

'We gave our word.'

She knew how to silence him. Invoke his own codes.

'All right. Just, I never knew archaeology was such a secretive affair. Not in this country, anyway.' She heard his mind ticking. 'This Wray's also your honours supervisor, isn't he?'

'Yes.'

'I take it, then, he's anticipating finding faunal remains.'

She'd told him the title for her proposed thesis — *Reading the Bones* — and that it had come from the professor.

'We're assuming there'll be stuff for both me *and* Sue. Her supervisor's Professor Wray's wife.'

'Well, it sounds like the Clyde is where the two of you need to be, rather than sleepy Gymea.'

Sue had set out plates and cutlery, and also the cutting board, with crackers, paprika salami, and a bowl of the dill-pickled gherkins she'd introduced Annette to on the day they'd moved into the house, telling her, 'You live with me, you eat reffo food.' Sue had a cracker and salami in her mouth and another in her hand. 'It's only just warm — I turned it up. But I'm starving.'

Annette popped a gherkin whole in her mouth and sat and reached for the knife and the salami.

'So, they okay about it?'

'My dad, anyway. He got there wasn't really a choice.'

'You want to know something weird? About Wray and Marilyn? I checked. She's contributed to four of his papers, and he hasn't contributed to any, not one, of hers.'

When alone, they used Dr Herr's first name, as she'd instructed them to do whenever they worked at her current site, a complex of hearths on a sand ridge in the confluence of the Cotter and Murrumbidgee rivers.

Annette had been about to drink, but lowered the tumbler.

'Really?'

She knew Sue's thoroughness. And what was behind the checking. Sue had cooled on their professor when he'd persuaded each of them to do an honours year, then chosen Annette to supervise and steered Sue to his wife.

'Remember I asked her that time, out the Cotter, and Marilyn said he'd never been there? Not even for a look.'

'So … what is it you're saying?'

'That it's all a bit one-way, yeah! Like today. She's been to this site, too. I wanted *her* opinion.'

'Maybe she's okay with it being like that.'

'Would you be? She's not exactly a nobody.'

'Sue, can we drop this? We're supposed to be celebrating.' Annette stood. 'That's smelling cooked, can you get a mat.' She went to the stove, pulled on the oven mitts, and bent to the door — and was relieved when she heard Sue's chair pushed back, then the sound of the drawer.

Annette's other third-year subject was Applied Mathematics. She had an assignment on approximations due by the end of the term, and which she'd barely begun. In whatever time she could spare from that, she was in the CSIRO library making sketches of the mammals and fishes whose bones she expected to find in a riverine hearth. Still, the days crawled. Or stuck in her craw — for when nearly all she could think about or, when with Sue, talk about, was the Clyde, it was galling to have to read up on the Māori *pā* for their last tutorial.

Patricia Meylor had clearly now learned something of the site's features. She picked up, too, on Annette's and Sue's prickliness in class. As they were leaving the room, she called them back. She *was* aware, she said, how difficult it must be to feign an interest in the *pā* when they were chafing to be off to their own 'walled' city. But theirs would not be examined on.

The descent of Clyde Mountain ended with the xylophone music of a trestle bridge, then the Land Rover's stressed brakes fell silent, and they were coasting through a narrow valley, tidal flats and a creek to their left. But before they got even a glimpse of the village that Wray had chalked on the board — Nelligen — he turned off the bitumen onto dirt. They crossed the creek, climbed briefly into tall, straight gums with mottled grey and white trunks, then dropped again into a tunnel of casuarinas, which emerged at the back of an unpainted weatherboard shed. Past the shed, Annette got her first view of the river, its far bank dark with mangroves.

An hour passed before she was seated in one of the two dinghies rather than watching them head upriver and disappear. Between her knees were the last of the food cartons, stacked three high. At the outboard's tiller was a student from the other tutorial, a bearded surfer named Dan. They rounded the bend, and she saw figures on a beach still piled with gear and someone struggling up the bank with a tent bag on his shoulder.

She was assigned a carton of beef and vegetable soup. A path had been trodden uphill through bracken. Just when she thought she'd have to set the carton down and get her breath back, the path began to flatten out, and she heard voices.

The camp was at the edge of gum forest, in a circle of freshly slashed bracken. There was no sign of stone houses. Two tents were already up. Wray saw her and pointed towards the gear piled on a green tarpaulin. Annette added her carton and headed back towards the river.

By one o'clock the encampment was seven tents ringing a firepit. She and Sue had claimed the tent nearest the trees. She'd assumed — as had the others — that as soon as camp was made they would head to the site. Instead, Wray called lunch. They ate in bad humour, exchanging glances but no one daring to ask. Finally he flicked dregs from his mug and stood.

Firstly, protocol. Titles were clumsy so for the next three weeks it was first names. He turned and pointed, the site was a hundred metres that way. 'I trust no one needs enlightening as to why we're not camped closer.' There would be one track between camp and site, and everyone would kindly stick to it. A short recce, then they were going exploring. The only ones on site today would be him and Doctor Herr. He corrected himself as Marilyn began to.

They walked in single file, through bracken that was up to Annette's chest. When the ground underfoot softened to sand, Aled halted them.

'Okay, we're on the upper terrace. You'll see from the trampling where our discoverers have been. We, though, are going only to the first huts. No talk, just use your eyes. Observe, interpret.'

Aled led them out to where the bracken was flattened. Annette saw a curved wall. A shiver ran through her, as if two fingers had been laid lightly on her nape. Tears were not far away. She couldn't have said why, knew only that if she'd been alone she'd have permitted them. She swallowed the tightness in her throat and walked to the wall. It came to just above her hip. Encountered in an old garden it would have been unremarkable, neither well nor poorly made, but still standing, which was its own proof. The stones were not river stones, they were black and pitted. Annette laid the backs of her fingers against one. It was cold. Would they have lived here through winter? Compared with Canberra, the air was warm. But not if you weren't wearing clothes. She followed the wall's curve and found the entrance, its raked right side intact, but the left tumbled, the spilled stones heavily lichened. She stepped in, trod a nest in the grass, and sat. With a bark door, a roof of branches, and a fire, the hut would have been snug as a cubby. She closed her eyes.

'Hey.'

Her eyes flew open. Sue hooked a thumb, *we're off.*

Back at camp, Aled told them to sit and took up a stance at an invisible lectern. A site, he said, was always bigger than its seeming boundaries. The people who used these huts — certainly for hundreds of years and possibly longer — these people would have left in the surrounding landscape many signs of their occupation, once very visible, but even after all this time still visible, if one knew what to look for. He would, therefore, describe what — here — that might be. Basically, anything that looked unnatural. Sometimes the unnatural occurred naturally, but in the vicinity of a sedentary population the unnatural was more likely to be the product of human intervention.

They were to go exploring in pairs. One pair upstream and another down to do a careful survey of the bank in a fifty-yard-wide strip, not hurrying, and checking every tree of any girth. These were people who made extensive use of the river, they needed bark for canoes. Creek mouths should be checked for congregations of stones that might be the remains of fish dams.

The three remaining pairs were to work at right angles to the river, as far into the bush as they felt comfortable with, then turn back — he didn't want to have to send out a search party. They were looking for clearings, in particular where burrawangs — macrozamia — were growing in pure groves. It might be natural, or it could indicate cultivation by burning.

They were looking also for the source of the stone the huts were constructed from. It was volcanic, his guess a basaltic tuff, so there was possibly an old dyke eroding into a creek bed. If they penetrated as far as the foot of the ridge, they should keep their eyes open for anything that might be a quarry. For those who remembered their high school geology, the surrounding ridges were predominantly Ordovician metamorphics high in silicates, with associated basaltic intrusions. If they found a dyke, tool-quality silcrete might not be far away. And a *quarry* would offer a strong explanation for the huts being where they were, and not on the more spacious flats further downstream.

Any clearing that looked old and deliberate they should examine for human bones. Keep in mind they would be tan or orange, not white. A sedentary population required a cemetery. The importance of *that*, if found, couldn't be overstated.

'Take a notebook and pencil, don't rely on memory. And don't make just notes — anything you find sketch it, plot it against landmarks! And take matches in case you *do* get lost. Light a nice smoky fire. And please, treat this seriously. It's not just to fill time, you're *reading* this place. I'll leave you to decide your pairings, but Roger be scribe would you — who goes where and with whom.'

He ignored the questions in their faces and spun and strode towards the store tent, where Marilyn Herr was laying out surveying gear.

Sue wanted to find the quarry. She announced to Roger that they — she and Annette — were heading into the trees straight behind camp. Annette reminded her that they needed matches.

'Crap,' Sue snapped. 'We're not going to get lost.'

Navigating was easy. The further from the river they walked, the purer the mix of forest — towering spotted gums with burrawang understorey. They could see for fifty, sixty metres in any direction. East had to be the direction in which the slanting bars of sunlight pointed. Walk far enough, Sue said, and they'd hit the foot of the ridge. They came to a creek, just a crease in the forest floor, but running strongly. They agreed it had to be coming from a spring, they should follow it to the source. But after what seemed a long time, they were still in the cathedral gums. The compass bars of sunlight had disappeared. Annette was more spooked than she would admit. Finally, she halted, said they'd gone far enough. They should follow the creek back out, it obviously ran to the river and was probably the creek that came out beside the camp. Which, after joining with another, and cutting itself a gully, it proved to be.

They met Roger and Val, who were crossing on a log after exploring downstream. They hadn't found anything of interest either.

Dan had lit a fire. Aled and Marilyn arrived back at dusk. They carried the surveying gear to the stores tent and returned to the fire with two casks, white and red.

'To wet the site's head,' Aled said. 'Then we're a dry camp.'

When they all had mugs in hand, he asked each pair to report, beginning with the pairs who'd gone east, wanting to know if any had reached the ridge, which none had. He asked then of the pairs who'd followed the bank, how far they'd got. Till they were stopped by understorey too thick to enter, probably at a creek? Yes. And had that not struck them as odd, that what had been till then a stroll had ended so abruptly? Again, yes.

'Good. Because you were walking along a human artifact, a corridor. Created using fire and so thoroughly maintained that it's still there.' He swept his hand in an arc. 'The same as this clearing we're sitting in.'

Later — Sue arguing with Val the morality of bringing kids into a shit world — Annette got talking to the dreadlocked and bearded Dan, who was seated at her other side in the circle around the firepit. They'd seen one another in lectures, but had never been in the same tutorial, where they might have spoken. The dinghy's outboard hadn't allowed conversation. Guessing that, like her, he wasn't originally from Canberra, she asked where he was from.

'Wollongong. You?'

'The Shire. Gymea.'

'Ah, right — I've surfed all up your way, Cronulla, Wanda.' He grinned, had read what she wanted to ask, and the hesitation. 'Yeah, same question the bloke over there asked when I first walked in with my bleachy locks. Actually, through surfing. I used to camp out in the dunes down Lake Illawarra, Shellharbour, Seven Mile, kept finding signs that other people had been there before me. A *long* time before me, you know — burned shells, tools. Same story on all the beaches east from here, middens everywhere, tools blowing out of the sand. Bit hard not to start seriously wondering who left them.' He dipped his head, took a sip of wine. 'How about you?'

The grunt of amusement she made was directed at herself, the picture she still carried of the younger self who didn't outgrow her obsession with dinosaurs, and which in high school she disguised as an interest in how the bone structures of modern animals evolved from long-extinct relatives.

'I was set on being a palaeontologist, can you believe. At Gymea High. Anyway, in Year Eleven I had to have another humanity, so I chose Ancient History. Our teacher knew someone at Sydney Uni and took us to Curracurrang.' She paused and looked at him.

He nodded. 'Royal National Park. I've read about it, haven't been there.'

'Okay. So then you've heard of Vincent Megaw. He had a team of first-years doing the digging, mostly girls only a couple of years older than me. One of them put a bone point in my hand with the pit dirt still on it, and that was the end of palaeontology. Well, not entirely, I still get to dig up bones, just not as old. And hopefully not human. I'm a lot more comfortable with animals.'

'Why didn't you enrol there? Sydney.'

'I wanted to leave home.'

He swapped hands with his mug, put out his right. She didn't, for a second, understand, then did and laughed and gripped his hand, and they did a single, hard up-and-down.

He said quietly, 'And so here we are.'

'Yes.' She turned from him, spoke at the fire. 'I'm … assuming you've turned twenty.'

'Yeah. I was balloted out.'

'Was … that a relief?' She risked a glance at his eyes.

'It was for my mum. But yeah, rather be learning to handle a trowel than a rifle.'

Next morning they cleared bracken, then, under Aled's and Marilyn's supervision, pegged and strung six test pits — metre-square pits in two of the huts, targeting the probable position of their hearths, and two-metre pits on four activity areas tentatively identified the previous day. Mortars and pounders for crushing bracken roots still sat in a food-processing area where left by their last users. In a fabricating area, Marilyn had found tools and waste flakes of a distinctive red-brown silcrete. A hearth complex lay between the second and third cluster of huts. And at the terrace edge, overlooking the river, was a sprawling midden, with fire-blackened oyster shells protruding from the sand.

Annette and Sue automatically paired up, and Aled separated them. They'd worked at the Cotter with Marilyn, he wanted each with a novice. For Annette, he chose a second-year named Stuart, and gave them one of the huts. Annette had barely exchanged a word with Stuart, had no idea how he would take to instruction. But he sat where she pointed him to, and leaned

to watch when she picked up the trowel. She loosened round
the base of a cut bracken stem at one corner and drew the root
slowly from the sand, placed it aside. Then the next. Near the
centre of the pegged square, the plugs began to come up black.
She tried to speak calmly, but couldn't mask her excitement, this
being, after all, the first time she'd opened a pit. They had their
hearth, she told him.

'Cool!'

He jumped into a crouch.

'First, though, we clean the whole square.'

She reversed the trowel, proffered the handle. He took the
trowel as if it might be enchanted, sank to his knees.

As Aled had warned, all days were work days. Out of their
sleeping bags with dew still on the tent canvas. A short walk into
the burrawangs, or deeper in with paper and spade. Annette
began to enjoy squatting in the smell of leaf litter and earth,
blue wrens or flycatchers flitting fearlessly around her. Instant
oats or Weet-Bix, with tinned fruit and powdered milk still
frothy from the fork. Then the walk to the huts in a babble
of jokes and banter, all of them high on anticipation and the
promise of another day under a cloudless autumn sky a world
away from books and the lecture room, and the nightly footage
of the Vietnam War. News of any kind had been banished, as
had music. Aled had banned transistor radios.

Boats appeared on the river on weekends. Their occupants, often two men, stared — or the opposite, pretended not to see. A few gave a hesitant wave. None came ashore. On weekdays, the only traffic was birds — shags, wood ducks, pelicans, noisy flocks of black swans. Annette couldn't conceive of eating a swan or a pelican, but they were big birds, and she fully expected to find their bones.

She and Stuart were down thirty-five centimetres, the square now a shallow pit. He was quick on the uptake and now deft with a trowel. And beneath the carroty hair was a sense of humour. He'd christened the hut 'Number 3 River Street'. The hearth was an undifferentiated mass of charcoal on charcoal, indicating almost continuous occupation. Stone flakes were few, but they'd found, sorted, and bagged much charred bone — fish, bandicoot, native rat, all far outweighed by possum. Stuart rechristened the hut 'Possum's End'. When, though, she unearthed at the side of the hearth a pocket of blackened husks and a wizened kernel, she sent him to fetch Aled.

He confirmed her guess at a glance. 'Lovely. Expose the rest of what you've got there right down to the base, then come and get the camera and photograph it please, plan and profile, before you remove anything. I'm sure they won't be the only macrozamia we find — they're probably in all the hearths — but here's the first, so I want a full record.' He rested a hand briefly on her shoulder. 'Also, I might need you elsewhere. But I'll see.'

When he'd gone, Stuart burst out, 'He can't! Tell him!'

'Sure, our professor. Anyway I don't know yet what it is.'

But she did — or believed she did. Aled wanted her on bone ID.

Next day he moved Dan into the hut with Stuart and placed her on roving duties. She spent time in the adjoining hut, and with Sue and Val at the midden, but for much of the day was with Aled at the hearth complex, where every scrape of a trowel seemed now to turn up bone, the majority macropod — eastern grey kangaroo, wallaroo, and wallaby — but with the finer swan and pelican bones she'd anticipated, and the occasional giant otolith or vertebra of a fish she was able to identify as mulloway. In a break for a drink, Aled asked for her thinking on what they were finding. She was seeing the bone coming from the huts, and what was coming from these hearths. How did she interpret the strangely rigid dichotomy that was emerging?

He didn't need her opinion. This role he'd given her of roving bone 'expert' was, Annette knew, for her benefit, not his. Still, she had been silently asking herself the same question. The only explanation that made sense, she told him — to her, anyway — was that fish and smaller game like possums were cooked in the huts and eaten as family food, and roos and wallabies and fish too big for a hut fire — and, for the same reason, pelicans — were communal food, cooked in these open hearths.

Aled studied her a moment, nodded.

'Thank you. That's the only one I see, too.'

*

As she walked to the huts next morning, Annette felt a touch on her arm. She stopped and began to turn, and Marilyn placed a hand in the small of her back that they keep walking. 'So how are you enjoying your first extended fieldwork?'

'A lot. It's fantastic.'

'Oh, I hope it doesn't prove to be *that*.'

Annette felt heat suffuse her face. Marilyn laughed.

'But yes, it is looking good. And you've impressed Aled, not an easy thing to do. I left out the dinosaurs, I just mentioned that I'd observed at the Cotter that you possess an unusual ability to differentiate species, and that he should have you doing IDs.'

'Thanks.'

'Simply making the best use of you. And, speaking of the Cotter, I hope my sand ridge doesn't now strike you as a bit tame compared to here.' Her hand fell quickly onto Annette's forearm and squeezed. 'I'm just being mischievous. But I'd be grateful if you and Sue could come out there again after we're back, if you're free one weekend. I had to leave a quite tricky profile under plastic, and it'd be good to have some help exposing it.'

'Um — well, I'd be more than happy to. But it'd be better if you ask Sue separately.'

'You don't pass on messages to one another?'

'Yes. But she wouldn't be thrilled with me passing on this.'

Marilyn was silent for a couple of steps.

24

'But not the other way, I sense.'

'I tend not to be so touchy.'

'That's a good trait to have. I wish I could say the same of myself.'

Annette didn't know her well enough to reply, then didn't have to when the woman disarmed the words with a smile.

'Same as last time, I'll leave a note with Jan.' She raised a hand in mock farewell, 'I'll zoom on ahead if you don't mind, I want to take another look at something that's bothering me.'

On the Wednesday of their final week, Aled was gifted the source of the hut stone. Stuart and Dan, they now learned, had been doing private expeditions at night, with torches, and again at first light.

The two led them all to what looked like a sinkhole, now filled with ferns.

'That's a shitload of boulders to lug,' someone muttered.

'Yes,' Aled said, 'but they're *Homo sapiens*, not ants, they had your brain. Vine nets. Slung on poles. The same as you or I would do.'

That night he emerged from the stores tent with another two casks.

'I was saving these for our last night. But we've had a day worth celebrating.' When each had a filled mug, Aled lifted his towards Dan and Stuart. 'Thank you, gentlemen. A big question answered.' He swung his mug to encompass the ring of faces. 'And thank *you*, all of you. We've been a productive and harmonious team.'

For their last night Aled appointed himself chef. He cooked rice and lentils, and a curry from a frozen slab of mulloway presented to him by the owner of the dinghies. He was almost manic, laughing, throwing his arms around people, even dancing a jig with Sue when Stuart inverted the frying pan on his lap and began tapping a beat with knives.

After curry, they glutted on apricot halves drowned in condensed milk. Val made a vat of cocoa.

Seated with a mug, Aled became calm. He lifted his hand for banter to stop. They wouldn't, he warned, get too gluttonous. All leftover cartons would be going into the boatshed. Because, if they hadn't already guessed, they'd be returning here. He didn't need, he said, to dwell on the importance of the site — it was self-evident. He did, though, wish to take them back to their initial meeting, to the closed door. That door was still closed. It would remain closed until they had dates, and those depended on the lab. At the moment, charcoals were taking about two months. So, could they stretch their patience? They would, he promised, be present at any announcement. They deserved their share of the limelight. And there *would* be limelight. Stone huts were mentioned, yes, in explorers' journals.

'But for the last three weeks we've been walking every morning into a stone *village*. *That* will make headlines, I assure you — and not just in archaeological circles.'

He spoke for ten minutes. He reiterated his and Marilyn's hypothesis that the site was a trade centre, that men from surrounding tribes came here for the silcrete so much in evidence. There was probably a separate site where visitors had camped, more than likely on the other side of the creek. That, too, they'd make time for on their next trip. He preached once again, as he had in lectures, the value of working in the Holocene rather than fall prey to the lure of 'chasing the oldest'. Here, after only three weeks, they had so much more than just stone and charcoal — all that usually survived in Pleistocene sites — they had opened the window into a society! They could *see* how people had lived here, could *feel* their presence! Rarely did a site yield so much information in such a short time. And they'd barely scratched the surface.

There was a note addressed to her and Sue in the undergraduates' pigeonhole. She found Sue, and they read it together. Were they free this Sunday? Sue asked Jan, the department secretary, could they use the internal phone to ring the Research School, Dr Herr. After giving Sue time and place, Marilyn asked to speak to Annette.

'I'm wondering, would you have time to pop into CSIRO

and take a look at their holdings on red-necked wallaby? You might already know, it hasn't been seen since the fifties and is likely extinct, but I think I might have it in a hearth. Thanks if you can. If not, don't worry.'

Annette went straight from her last lecture and spent three hours making sketches of the animal's skeletal structure and species markers.

Sunday was clear, and very cold. The pick-up was at eight, the car park behind the tennis courts. They left the house in coats, beanies, and mittens. Lawns and verges were white, even the concrete path had a skin of ice, forcing them to walk on the road. Despite what she'd so adamantly stated a month back, Sue began speculating on whether Marilyn would be alone or might Wray be with her.

Marilyn drove in alone. Annette would never have asked, but Sue was more forthright. Did Professor Wray ever assist at her sites? They were crossing the lake. Cars were chopping and changing lanes around them, the Kombi labouring, and it was a moment before Marilyn answered. Yes — if she turned up something more interesting than charcoal and flakes. Such as what? Well, for one, to a site at Uriarra when she struck a burial. They'd excavated it together — her — it was a woman. Where were the bones now, Annette asked. It was her silent fear, how she would react the first time a bone under her trowel turned out to be human. In a box on a shelf in the Research School, Marilyn answered, unaware of, or ignoring, the tremor in Annette's voice. Sue leaned forward, asked what the odds were of a burial at the Cotter.

'Always a possibility in sand. Easier to dig.' She glanced at Annette, returned her eyes to the road. 'But I don't expect a burial in a hearth, and hearths are mainly what I'm chasing.'

She'd noted the tremor.

It was freezing on the sand ridge, a strong southerly funnelling along the Murrumbidgee, low cloud scudding overhead, lower at times than the trees. They left coats and beanies on. The pit was twice as deep as the last time Annette had seen it, the previous hearth now just a faint grey stain, and a new, older, hearth in the corner. The complication Marilyn had mentioned was what appeared to be a second hearth intruding from the side, and a scatter of blackened stones and bone that she was postulating might have come from an oven. While the other two trowelled, Annette examined the bone. The few wallaby bones were all rock wallaby.

Marilyn had brought pea and ham soup in a thermos, and mugs. As they broke and dipped bread rolls, sipped, she talked about where they were sitting — keen, Annette thought, to make the point that the Clyde, despite its uniqueness, was simply one more in a web of sites, and did not lessen in importance what she was finding here. She pointed past them, up the ridge. Pits One and Two, now backfilled, had each gone down a metre, Two giving a basal date of 3350 BP. So this spit of sand in the junction of the rivers was not a transient campsite, it was returned to. The question was why. That was the question she was asking of all her occupation sites along the Murrumbidgee, why this place and not another? Wanting to keep her talking, Annette asked how many sites that was.

'Nine so far, including here. Not all dug, four are just surface scatters. Along about ten miles of river. So, as you'd imagine, I'm kept very fit hiking up and down riverbanks. One of the side benefits of our profession.'

'It seems to have bypassed Dr Sieglitz,' Sue said.

Marilyn roared laughing. Tom Sieglitz was a jovial, huge-bellied American also working in the Research School. He'd delivered two guest lectures, on Hawaii and the Marquesas. None of the undergrads could believe he'd ever done fieldwork, but the papers existed. Marilyn subsided to chuckles, gave Sue's wrist a playful smack.

'I'll have you know that Dr Sieglitz is an eminent prehistorian and a very good colleague.' She grinned. 'But no, he wouldn't make it up this sandhill.'

They worked till the points of the trowels began to blur and they couldn't feel their fingers.

When they hit the city, instead of crossing the lake Marilyn drove into Manuka. She took them to an upstairs grill with a blazing open fire. All three had the bangers and mash she recommended, and shared a carafe of red. Annette's first glass went down like raspberry, burned beautifully in her gut. They didn't talk archaeology, but about Canberra. It wasn't a city,

Marilyn agreed, but as a place to pursue an academic career it was perfect, something they should seriously consider. When their plates were empty, she excused herself and walked to the payphone in a booth by the toilets. Sue watched her begin to dial, then looked back at Annette and arched her eyebrows. A little drunk, Annette didn't catch on.

'What?'

'Reporting in.'

Sue's interest in Aled and Marilyn had always been more than 'academic'. The first day she and Annette had seen them together, on the library steps — Aled and a woman who, from his manner, was clearly his wife — Sue had stared, then muttered, 'Wow. Don't people look in the mirror. He's married his sister.' The truth of the observation had stayed with Annette, recurring whenever she saw them bent over a feature in a pit, heads almost touching, or Aled whisper some remark that made Marilyn smile. Both had the unusual pairing of black hair and blue eyes. But whereas Aled was merely good-looking, Marilyn was beautiful. A week or so after the library, Annette and Sue had seen them again, on the Barry Drive oval, stripped to athletes' silks and singlets and doing sprint-starts. After standing for a minute, Sue had murmured, 'They'd be something to watch in bed.' She'd turned and seen Annette's face. 'So? I've got a dirty imagination.' Her imagination was at work as she watched Marilyn at the payphone.

'He's suspicious of her, you're saying?'

'No. Wanting to know how long she'll be. Sunday night, he's been on his own all day. You wait.'

When Marilyn came back to the table, she didn't sit, couldn't quite meet their eyes. She asked would they mind if they skipped coffee. Not at all, Sue said.

'Thanks.'

She turned to go to the register, and Sue gave Annette a wink.

At the end of a tutorial, Patricia Meylor detained her and Sue. Annette guessed before the woman spoke what she was going to say.

'I've been asked by Professor Wray to inform you that he has some lab results he's sure you're keen to hear.'

The woman's face betrayed nothing, but Annette heard in the carefully neutral tone that she herself was not yet a party to the dates.

'The lecture room at twelve.'

Roger and Val were the last to enter. Wray asked Val to close the door. He acknowledged the puzzled faces.

'My wife won't be joining us, she's at a conference in Auckland. I phoned her yesterday, and she agreed I should meet with you rather than delay till she's back.' He continued to speak as he delved in his briefcase and drew out what he was after, a fat pouch of photographs. 'You've been told I have dates, which I do. But before that I'll give you an equally exciting piece

32

of news — which I *have* been sitting on.' He looked up, let the tension grow, broke into a grin. 'We have our quarry.'

He raised an imaginary mug, and they whooped. He tapped on the pouch. 'I'll pass these around at the end, but right now I'd prefer you listened.'

'So who found it?' Stuart broke in.

Wray gave him a mock-incredulous stare. 'I *have* been known to go for a stroll myself, Stuart.'

Before the laughter quite stopped, Dan said quietly, 'How close to the hut stone?'

The levity left Wray's face. 'You didn't miss it by much, a hundred metres. I walked past the opening myself — twice. It was only that I saw what was obviously a core lying in this little gully I'd already crossed, as I say, twice. The quarry's actually *into* the ridge. There's a pool and a little waterfall, a very lovely spot. And at one time a very busy one. They've quarried out what's almost an amphitheatre. The photos will give you a sense. And there's the real thing for those of you who can make it back. I'll keep you informed.' It sounded like a conclusion. He saw the frowns, and mouths opening. 'Don't panic, I haven't forgotten. But — please?' He gestured towards the closed door, then spun, pulling from his coat pocket a sheet of paper, and went to the board.

The dates from the lowest level of each of the two huts were so close as to be archaeologically identical, 820 ± 80 BP and 870 ± 110 BP. The pit in the communal hearths yielded an earliest of 3940 ± 130 BP. It was possible, he said, that extending the pit might yield an even earlier date. But even without it, his initial hypothesis had proved to be correct, the hearths substantially predated the huts, demonstrating that people had been camping at the site for at least three thousand years before societal changes and a growing formalisation of trade links led to the building of permanent structures.

'*Organised* permanent structures. By anyone's definition, a village.'

He put the same proposition even more forcefully to the journalists and television cameras gathered the following day in the small courtyard between the department and the library. That it was a village in every sense of the word — with well-constructed huts of stone disposed in clusters, clearly defined communal areas, evidence of the cultivation and processing of macrozamia for food, and a quarry yielding a distinctive and high-quality silcrete that was certainly traded up and down the coastal fringe and probably onto the Monaro itself, perhaps as far inland as the site of this university.

'And all this in the land of the wandering nomad, on eternal walkabout in search of the next morsel to put in his mouth.'

He gave the dates for the hearths and huts, stressing that the importance of the site was not in its dates, which weren't, compared with other sites, especially old, but in the level of social organisation the village clearly demonstrated. That this was such a village as our Neolithic ancestors in Europe might once have occupied. It was entirely possible — hypothesising further — that if whites had not arrived on the continent, many or even most Aboriginal societies might have become sedentary or semi-sedentary as populations grew and tribal boundaries became more fixed.

'Who knows? Coming a hundred, even fifty years later, Cook and Banks might have found villages of stone huts at Botany Bay. And how different would our history have been then?'

That night Annette experienced the thrill of seeing herself on television, kneeling with 'the team' behind the display of tools Marilyn Herr had laid out on an ironed white cloth.

Four nights later, Wray was on *This Day Tonight*.

The village had been judged sufficiently newsworthy to have drawn the host presenter, Bill Peach, down to the Clyde. He explained to camera why there were no location shots, that the man who had discovered it, Professor Aled Wray of the Australian National University, had requested that they not reveal precisely where on the river the site was. Annette and Sue looked at one another. Would Aled correct him, honour Mr Hendy and mate? He didn't.

Wray led Peach and the camera on a tour of the huts. He gave his hypothesis on why the village was situated where it was, the trade in stone. He displayed points and scrapers in the distinctive silcrete, but apologised for not being able to conduct the viewers to the actual quarry, it having been found only in the last month and not yet properly assessed. Peach asked — the question clearly coached — how the site changed the picture of pre-colonial Aboriginal society, and Wray was away, his eyes ablaze, the now-practised phrases tumbling from his mouth. Sue said, without taking her eyes from the screen, 'Getting good at this, isn't he. And getting off on it.'

A month later, he found a second village.

The team this time was smaller, handpicked. Annette travelled down in the Kombi with Marilyn Herr and Sue. Clyde II was a mile upstream of Clyde I, but the same triangulated distance from the boulder dyke and the quarry. Only a person with Wray's eye and ruthless persistence could have located the site. The bank was forested to the river's edge, none of the walls was intact. They exposed fourteen huts and sank test pits in three. Wray postulated that this second village predated the first. The bank was lower than at Clyde I. The hut walls had been toppled not by time and tree roots, but earlier, by a flood. The people had moved downstream to the higher terrace at Clyde I and rebuilt. The dates, when they came in, proved him right.

In October his preliminary paper was published in *Mankind*. The editor also ran a rejoinder. Annette and Sue read both standing at the Current Serials rack.

The tone of the rejoinder was academic sarcasm. The writer, a professor named Horlick, accepted the Clyde sites as evidence of sedentism. But where was the evidence that these people on the Clyde were *wholly* sedentary, living in their stone huts year round? The seeming unbrokenness of the stratigraphy was just that, 'seeming'. One could depart a hearth protected from the elements by stone walls and return the following year and kindle a fire on the same hearth and it would *seem* to the archaeologist a thousand years later that one had never been away. Professor Wray was advancing a negative argument. The writer granted that the Clyde sites indicated a strong degree of sedentism in one Aboriginal society during the late Holocene. But to inflate the evidence from this one site into evidence of increasing sedentism in Aboriginal societies *as a whole* during the late Holocene — stone huts at Botany Bay, for example, as Wray had envisaged to the press and public — was to draw too long a bow. The bow might break and the arrow strike the author in the foot.

Wray called a meeting. He asked Stuart to close the door, told them Dr Herr knew they were meeting, and plucked up *Mankind* from the lectern.

'You've no doubt all read these, mine and his.' He didn't wait. 'Don Horlick and I have crossed swords before — or should I say bows — in print and in person, and he has always come off second best. My friend Donald has done what he does with any paper that doesn't fit into his own particular little wheelbarrow, he ignores what he can't attack, and misrepresents what he believes he can. When have I ever stated that people lived at the Clyde year-round? That they were *wholly* sedentary? He ignores completely our hypothesis on the bone points we found in huts three and five and which eluded us till we got back here.' Wray lifted his hand towards Annette. 'And they were, Annette? Remind us all.'

Caught on the hop, her mind blanked. 'What? Oh — muttonbird. Shearwater.'

'Thank you. And again for the ID.' He smiled, then it was gone. He again took in the rest of the room. 'Which could only have come from a beach. Traded in, possibly, but more likely brought back, the coast being only a good day's walk away, a couple if you're not in a hurry. Words our friend ignored.' He slapped the journal down on the lectern. 'Well, I've done that walk. And I wasn't in a hurry.'

It had, Wray said, since day one, been on his mind to explore whether there was a travelled route from the Clyde to the coast, and if so, where — 'on which bay or beach' — it came out. A fortnight back he'd gone to the Geography department and obtained aerial photographs of the strip of state forest between the river and the coast. Two possible routes stood out, one more promising than the other, which he pencilled onto the topographical map. Only then did he reach for his hiking boots.

Wray turned to the lectern and picked up one of the envelopes they'd used at the Clyde and tipped into his hand a tool, held it up between thumb and finger. It was a scraper, the stone the familiar grey-flecked brown from the quarry.

'This was part of a surface scatter. I found five open sites. All had our silcrete, along with worked pebbles from the local creeks. A firetrail brought me out on the Princes Highway about a half-mile from the top of Teapot Lake. I hitched to the Bay and caught the bus. Dr Herr and I drove back down the following weekend. The lake's tidal. Horror of a road in. Halfway along the beach there's a cave.' Wray lifted from the lectern a sliver of worked bone. 'This we found in the cave. The dunes are full of their skeletons, and when we were there the shore was actually littered with drowned birds, and more washing in. It's a seasonal event, I'm told by Dr Yallop at CSIRO. If muttonbird's your fancy, all you had to do — still do — is walk to the edge of the surf and pick them up. It must have been a quite pleasant sojourn for our Clyde friends, all the muttonbird you can eat, mussels, fish, pipis, crabs — and wombat for dessert. We saw one toddling along the beach.'

He passed the bone point to Annette. It was light as a toothpick, its tip dulled by use or blown sand, traces of what might have been gum still visible at the hafting end.

'The cave is our immediate objective. We find our silcrete there, we've joined all the dots, conclusively established that littoral people and coastal people can be the same people.

My plan is mid-January into February, so it's a bit of an ask. I'm aware, too, a number of you will have actually flown the university coop, so it's my intention to put up fliers in other departments as well as Prehistory. We *might*, therefore, have "foreigners" in our midst.'

They laughed.

The assembly point behind the tennis courts was now so familiar that Annette and Sue had 'their' wattle. They were sitting in its shade. The boys were out on the oval with a bat and tennis ball. Annette had very much hoped Dan would be one of their number, had even, before third term ended, put herself through the exquisite torture of waiting for him outside a tutorial to ask. He'd told her he'd deferred honours, was driving to Western Australia straight after his last exam to work for a year on oil rigs and to surf. He'd given her an embarrassed hug. She put the memory away, looked at her watch. Aled and Marilyn were late. As she had the thought, she heard a car. It wasn't, though, the distinctive clatter of the Kombi, or the Land Rover's rattle. What rounded the hedge was a Ford Anglia, two-tone blue, not a car she recognised. But the driver waved and steered into the bay nearest their tree.

The driver was Vicky Leavitt. Near term's end, she'd searched out Annette and Sue. She was desperate to put her name down for North Teapot, but was worried about what it was like 'for girls' on a dig. Well, at least it wouldn't be like the Clyde, Sue had told her, shitting in a scrape and washing from a bucket. The colour had drained from Vicky's face. 'It won't be anything like that,' Annette had quickly interjected, 'we're going to be in cabins.' Always ahead of the game, Sue had asked did she own a car. No, Vicky had answered. Yet here she was in a shiny two-tone Anglia.

She joined them under the tree. 'Whose car?' Sue said.

Vicky reddened. 'Mine. From my dad. To go down in.' She gestured towards the car Brandy — Henk Brandjes — drove, a green FJ Holden warpainted with maroon undercoat. 'Do you … already have a ride?'

Sue looked at Annette. The Anglia's seats would be a lot more comfortable than the Kombi's or the Land Rover's. They stood and carried their rucksacks and sleeping bags to the boot.

Marilyn arrived in the Kombi, the university Land Rover on her tail. Aled pulled up in the centre of the car park. Marilyn waved to them, but walked to the Land Rover and got in the passenger side. Still talking to do, Annette decided.

'Who's that?' Sue said.

Annette spun, but the question had been addressed to Vicky.

The two were squinting into the glare off the oval. The figure they were watching spotted the Land Rover and changed direction. The boys had paused in their game. The figure nodded, but kept walking. A wide flat-brimmed hat and the glare made it impossible to see his face. Dig uniform was shorts,

T-shirt, and sandshoes, but he was wearing a checked shirt with its sleeves rolled to mid-biceps, green work trousers, and boots. Projecting above his left shoulder was the point of what was, Annette saw when he reached the kerb, a dun sausage half as long as his body, tied with rope and worn diagonally from shoulder to hip.

'It's a jolly swagman.'

Sue grinned and Vicky giggled. He walked to the driver's window and spoke. Annette saw Aled nod, then offer his hand. He introduced Marilyn, and the stranger shot his hand across the cabin. Aled gestured towards the cricket game. The stranger shook his head. Marilyn pointed him towards their wattle.

He removed his hat to introduce himself, but remained standing. Brian Harpur. '*U-r* not *e-r*,' he added immediately. Annette wondered why the spelling mattered. They gave their names in turn, reaching up to shake hands. When her palm met his, Annette almost recoiled, the skin reptilian. He seemed not to notice. When his gaze shifted back to Sue, she snatched a look at his hands. The backs had scars and half-healed nicks, the nail of his left thumb was ridged like cowhorn. They were the hands of a much older man, not one she judged to be her own age. His hair was normal, a coarse curly blond. His eyes were not. They were blue, but the left was speckled brown, as if someone had flicked a loaded paintbrush and caught the lid open.

He'd been talking as she studied him. He was in engineering. All he knew about archaeology, he said, was how to spell it.

He hadn't been able to get to the meeting. He'd spoken to 'the professor' on the phone, but hadn't met him till just now. He still made no move to sit, or to dump his swag. Its cover, Annette saw, was the same oiled cloth as the raincoat she'd worn in primary school. Vicky looked at her and Sue. Sue shrugged, *your car*.

'Has Professor Wray offered you a lift?'

Brian Harpur looked across at the Land Rover, spoke into the air. 'Don't think so.'

'There's room with us.'

The scan he did of their faces felt to Annette like a test. Which, apparently, they passed, for he nodded. 'Thanks.' He lifted the swag over his head by its rope and dropped it on the ground, crossed his legs and sat. He'd no sooner settled when Aled did a double-beep on the horn, started the Land Rover's engine.

Sue claimed the Anglia's front seat, Brian Harpur and Annette shared the back. He seemed relaxed at being in a car with three young women — and a woman driving. *A sister, or sisters*, Annette decided, *probably older*. His hands lay open in his lap. Whenever he looked out the window, she stole glances at the palms. Where hers had lines, Brian Harpur's had cracks. It was too soon to ask how he'd got hands like that.

'So, Brian ...' She waited for him to turn. 'How come you put your name down for this?'

Sue heard and swivelled on the seat.

He asked if they'd heard of a poet named Charles Harpur.
Like him, *u-r*.

'The name, that's all,' Annette said. 'In high school.'

'I'm off a sheep farm. About due south of here — Numeralla
— out of Cooma.' Harpur the poet and his son were buried on
a hill overlooking the Tuross River. For three weeks in January
every year Brian Harpur, his parents, and his sister — *Got that
right,* Annette thought — used to leave the farm in the hands
of his father's brother and drive down to somewhere on the
same strip of the South Coast, Harpur country. 'The connection
being, my father fancies himself a bit of a bush poet.'

He told them of being dragged by the hand when small
across a paddock and up the hill to the graves. The family
had gone to North Teapot first in 1958, when Brian Harpur
was seven, then for the next two years. His father had hit it
off with the owner of the cabins there, another friendless man
named Artie Gorman. The man had a crippled left arm from a
sawlog, was probably still there. He had a two-man prawning
net he only got to use when a man like Brian Harpur's father
stayed at the cabins. 'Dad can still lift a big ewe straight up
out of the race.'

His mother didn't take to Gorman. 'I didn't much either, but
more because he grabbed Dad when I wanted him with me.'

Vicky butted in, asking where the lake got its 'weird' name.

Not so weird, he said placidly. If the lake mouth was closed, as
could happen after a big southerly, the water grew a pale brown

algae. It didn't smell, and you could swim, but the sediment looked like tea leaves. That was the story, anyway.

At Nelligen, crossing the bridge, Annette tapped him on the shoulder and pointed. 'About a mile up there's our site that was on television.' The grunt he made disclosed nothing. Did he not know? She didn't ask and perhaps embarrass him.

Aled had warned of the North Teapot 'road'. It turned out to be a track that snaked between trees too big to fell, with exposed roots, washouts, boulders. Vicky had never been off tarred roads in her life. The dust boiling up in clouds behind the Kombi soon had her driving at little above walking pace. The Kombi's brake lights disappeared. Brian Harpur refused to take the wheel. Only one way, he said, to learn to drive a track like this. But he'd come into the front seat and talk her along. Which he did, sitting with arms folded and advising in a calm, quiet voice when to brake, which side of a pothole to steer.

They emerged from forest into coastal scrub running along the back of a beach, with glimpses through foliage of breaking waves and, further out, water of a startling blue. Ahead was the glitter of iron roofs, but, before they reached the first shacks, Stuart stepped from shade and pointed them into a two-track through tea tree. The tea tree ended at a post-and-rail fence, and they passed through drawn sliprails into a paddock, on a rise to their left a weatherboard house, and ahead four identical cabins. A small mob of cows stood beneath a gum, its lower branches lopped.

Aled was standing by the bonnet of the Land Rover talking to a pot-bellied man in shorts and a faded green T-shirt. The others were wandering about inspecting the outside of the cabins and the dunnies and a wall-less structure with a water tank, which Annette guessed to be a laundry. Brian Harpur pointed Vicky into the thin shade of a wattle. She turned off the motor and sagged in the seat, close to tears.

'Hey,' he said gently, 'buck up, you did great. Got us here. Thanks, ay.'

Shamed by his generosity, Sue and Annette mumbled their thanks. They climbed out, Annette observing Brian Harpur over the car's roof. She saw him look at the row of cabins and nod, a private nod. His gaze shifted to the pair by the Land Rover, and his jaw hardened.

'Is that who you mentioned? Gorman?'

Brian Harpur didn't look at her. 'Yep. Just more of him.'

The three women carried rucksacks and sleeping bags, and he his swag, over to where the others were congregated around a brick fireplace and tabletop that obviously served all four cabins.

'So who's in which?' Sue said.

Brandy pointed towards the cabin closest to the sea. 'The prof and Dr Herr are in that one, and it's doubling as lab and storeroom. You girls've got one, we've got two. Up to us which.'

The cabins were identical boxes of unpainted fibro on stumps. Sue pointed to the next in the row. 'That's ours, then.' She set off towards it.

Three splintering steps mounted to a plank door. The key was in the lock, the duplicate hanging from it on a frayed string. Sue snapped the string, handed the second key to Annette, swung the door open.

The interior walls were unlined, there was no ceiling. Louvres were missing, splits in the flyscreen were sutured with fishing line. Old newspapers covered the shelves and dresser-top. Some time that morning, the man had evidently emptied a bucket at one end of the main room and broomed water and dust to the doorway and out. Vicky, though, was looking not down at the damp floorboards but up, and frozen with what Annette realised was horror. She, too, looked up. Nets of cobweb hung between the roof trusses, web craters filled every joint and corner. It took little imagination to picture the roof cavity at night.

'Don't freak,' Sue said. 'We'll find a branch.'

They claimed beds and went back to the fireplace, where Marilyn was laying out on the table pre-packed sandwiches and fruit. Aled asked the boys to boil the billy. The 'firewood' was a dumped heap of blocks and limbs, tangled in bark. There was a short scuffle over the axe, in which Briàn Harpur took no part. Brandy won. When its blade bounced for the third time from a branch, Aled called a halt before Brandy bounced it into his ankle. Brian Harpur quietly asked for the axe and in five minutes broke enough to fill the fireplace — breaking being what he did, with the back of the axe head. He leaned the handle against the bricks and took up his interrupted sandwich.

Aled asked him what he needed to put an edge on the axe, would a file do?

Brian Harpur angled a discreet thumb. 'Ask this one.' They turned their heads and saw Gorman. 'He'll have a wheel. Even if he reckons he hasn't.'

The man had done no more than walk down his paddock, but Annette could hear his breathing from twenty metres away. She judged him to be about fifty. He walked with a rocking motion, the left hip locked, and carrying the crippled arm out from his body like a bird with an injured wing. The sawlog had, she guessed, crushed the elbow. Two or three days of ginger stubble caught the sun as his jaw worked, hair the same ginger frothed from the throat of his T-shirt. He came to a halt, his blue eyes flicking round the circle. Annette saw them return to Sue's breasts as Aled spoke.

'I won't do introductions, Mr Gorman, too many names to remember, but everyone, this is Mr Gorman, our landlord.' The man nodded, nominally taking them all in, but his eyes flicking back to Sue, who folded her arms. 'I was intending to come up to see you shortly, but what can we do for you?'

His visit was to warn 'the young people — yous bein from the city' about the danger of fire. They were at the beach, but they were surrounded by national park and state forest. If they lit a fire at breakfast, could they make sure it was out before they left for the cave, and same at night, would the last ones to bed make sure the fire was out, not leave it to burn out. The request was reasonable, but after seeing their cabins, and now the axe, no one was feeling reasonable.

'What fires,' Stuart muttered, 'seeing we can't chop anything.'

The man's eyes narrowed dangerously. 'What's that, matey?'

Aled motioned to Paul to hand him the axe. 'Could you put an edge on this for us, please. On your wheel.'

'Wheel.'

'You're running a farm, I'm reliably informed you'll have a grinding wheel.'

Gorman gave Stuart a sour glance, then took the axe and let the handle slide through his hand, the head hitting the ground with a thud.

'And what I was coming up about, we've got a problem with the trestles you've supplied. Half of them are missing their ropes.'

'Ah — have to be later.' The man hefted the axe quickly to the shoulder of his good arm and rocked away as fast as his hip allowed. Stuart made a small mocking bow. Before they could break into sniggers, Aled put a finger to his lips, shook his head.

Gorman had, at some time, cut steps in the earth cliff that descended to the beach. Most were so eroded — boards retaining air — that other feet had worn their own steps. At the base of the steps was a grassed corridor that led them between huge, old coast banksias. Annette knew her birds down to their bones and identified lorikeets, rosellas, and friarbirds feeding on the brushes. The ten members of the team walked in a din of shrieks and whistles, and, below it, like a giant heartbeat, the boom of the surf.

The cliff became sandstone, they emerged from the corridor into dunes. To the north a massive headland, its sea-face sheer, walled in the beach. Sue touched her arm, pointed. In the hollow of a dune were the half-buried remains of a roo, just bones and scraps of hide, but enough for Annette to identify an eastern grey. Bound by the toughest sinew in the body, the tail was still articulated, rising like a beckoning finger.

They walked on the dry squeaky sand at the back of the beach, following the line of the cliff, the ocean a band of serene blue to their right, the breakers audible, but invisible below the shelf carved by the wash. Stuart and Paul, in the lead, sped up when they spotted a low arched opening, but Aled called, 'No, gentlemen — it's around the corner.'

They rounded Aled's 'corner' into a wide bay of low dunes and marram grass where the cliff curved inland. The cave was a dark hole in its far side. From a distance, Annette thought it too small to have sheltered the population at the Clyde, but it grew as they approached, and revealed additional ledges and overhangs. A deep, but dry, gutter cut through the dunes. The others crossed and kept going. Annette started down their prints, then, caught by the gutter's incongruence, halted and looked along it to find the source. A section of the cliff face was lower and darker, its lip fat with ferns. She turned a slow circle, silently rebuking herself for being in such a hurry to get to this cave that she was forgetting the basics. Fresh — if ephemeral — water, the ocean, a lake, roos, muttonbirds and their bones, stone. It was all here, the Holocene supermarket.

Aled had taken up a lecturing stance at the cave mouth. 'Okay — the red and purple markings you're all staring at and wondering, are they paintings, are iron stains. The cave itself is the result of wave action, fortunately not recent — the last few thousand years anyway — or we'd have nothing to excavate.'

Annette and Sue — veterans of these lectures — stood at the rear. Annette tilted her head, looked along the roof peak. A lot of fires had gone into giving the sandstone its dense black sheen.

Aled was pointing. 'The pit will be against that wall, but I won't invite you in. Marilyn and I need to do a thorough sweep of the floor. Anything obviously a tool has gone long ago to fossickers, but there are flakes and quite a bit of bone. But take a look over here.' He stepped to the base of the right-hand wall and waved his hand above a line of stones half-buried in sand and roof-fall. He flicked the sand from around one and picked it up, displayed it on his palm. It was no tool Annette had ever seen before, real or drawn — a pear-shaped rock with a rough hole through its narrower end. 'Can anyone tell me what this is? And why the arrangement?'

Wishing probably to be unobtrusive, Brian Harpur, too, was standing at the back. He'd changed into shorts and was

barefoot, but had retained the check shirt and hat, its brim
tipped up. He wasn't looking at the rock, he was watching the
sides of faces, a half-smile of disbelief on his own. He felt her
gaze and met it, arched his eyebrows. Annette shrugged. Brian
Harpur mouthed words she couldn't read. Aled was growing
testy. 'Come on! Someone!'

'It's a net weight. The net's rotted, but it hung on that wall.
Probably from a couple of sticks shoved in that crack.' Brian
Harpur carved in the air with a finger the crevice they could see.

'Sea or lake — the net?'

'Lake. Stones that size wouldn't sink a net in surf. Unless you
were up in the lee of the headland.'

Aled gave him a level stare. 'You're in the wrong faculty.'

Brian Harpur grunted, not so much flattered, Annette thought,
as amused at some private joke. His face, though, had reddened.

'Now, those of you familiar with my methods, please try
to contain your boredom.' There were to be two excavations,
carried out simultaneously, a two-metre by two-metre pit
against the rear side wall where the shell deposit was heaviest,
and a metre-wide trench, running from the entrance to — he
pointed — out beyond where they stood, to plumb where in
good weather people would have cooked and sat, and extending
for as far as cultural material was being found. Because it was
school holidays, he'd been given permission by National Parks
to erect a stringline in front of the cave and a tent on the
beach. The stringline had no legal authority, but would operate

successfully, he believed, on people's natural courtesy. The tent would house two of them each night to guard gear and the site. He'd leave it to them to decide their pairings.

Vicky had turned to find Annette and was giving her a panicked look.

'What?' Annette murmured, but Vicky was already turning back to Aled.

'What about ... you know ... toilet?'

One of the boys groaned. Aled flashed a warning look, then met her anxious gaze and pointed towards the dunes.

'It doesn't have to be seaweed, though,' Stuart said evenly, 'you can bring some paper.'

It was impossible not to laugh, even Aled needing to rub at his mouth.

He gave his 'explore' speech. Annette had heard it at the Clyde, but made herself listen, telling herself she was only a year or two away, perhaps, from delivering it herself, at *her* first site. See the place through Holocene eyes. Where are your food and tool plants? Where's your drinking water? What direction's the prevailing wind? You need a pebble to flake, where are you going to look? That rock shelf, what's growing on it? Wade in the lake, what's there for the taking? Up in the sky, out on the water, what birds do you see? A site isn't just the few square metres you dig. Go where there's no footprints and read the sand. You can't *interpret* finds until you know the place as intimately as did the people who left what you're finding.

'Questions?'

Greg — so quiet Annette hadn't yet heard his voice — asked about the tent. Did they need to fetch it?

'Not for just pegs and string. But I'll put you down for tomorrow, shall I?'

'With Vick,' Stuart muttered, loud enough to be heard.

Aled hushed the laughter, told them to clear out.

Annette wanted a clean, intact muttonbird skeleton. Sue wanted to be scouring the cave floor for stone, but said she'd come with her. Two of the boys were already climbing the cliff. Brandy was headed towards the exposed rock shelf Aled had pointed out. As she turned towards the dunes, Annette felt a hand on her arm. 'Could I … talk to you?' Brian Harpur's gaze excluded Sue.

'Um — we were just going.'

He nodded, but waited.

Sue gave her a wink. 'See you both later.'

With Sue gone, he became less mysterious. 'Actually it's something I need to show you.'

'And you couldn't show us both?' Brian Harpur didn't answer. 'So it's where, this "something"?'

He turned and pointed towards the headland, which, from where they now were halfway along the beach, seemed to shrink the sky. 'That rock sticking up? Just this side.' He read what she was thinking. 'We don't leave the beach, okay.'

Brian Harpur led her to the hard sand at the water's edge where their feet didn't sink. He walked watching the waves. His silence began to annoy Annette. She could break it, but he'd initiated this, it was up to him. He'd talked freely in the car. He felt her glance — he certainly had that knack — and gave her a quick nervy smile, but returned to watching the water. *Okay,* Annette thought. *But this had better be good!*

The rock had become a cluster, it being the tallest. Annette made out also an exposed ironstone platform some forty metres from shore and running parallel to the beach.

Brian Harpur finally broke his silence. 'That platform shows only at dead low — why we couldn't hang about.'

He steered her up onto a sand ledge. The headland blocked the nor-easter, the air in its lee calm. The water between the platform and the beach was a mirror of the sky, punctured by a curving wall of black oyster-encrusted rocks running to a few metres from shore.

'What — this's it? A bogey hole.'

'Well, it's that too — but it was built for them.' Brian Harpur pointed into the water. Five or six sleek silver-grey fish were swimming in a lazy circle. 'Sorry if I'm telling you what you already know — but they're mullet, sea mullet. A whole school if you look out further. There'd be bream, too. Probably chopper tailor and the stray big salmon. They're all what I saw people take out of here, anyway. Two days running.'

'What people?'

'Abos, blacks — whatever we're supposed to call them. With a net. It's a trap.'

Annette didn't believe him. On a beach. And the area of several tennis courts. But as he swung his arm to indicate where the other, shorter, wall ran — between the rock cluster and the start of the headland platform — then brought her gaze back to the wall that ran almost to the beach, pointing out rocks that had toppled, but once had capped an almost unbroken line into the shallows, she not only saw that he was right, but her stomach began to churn as it had the first day she'd stepped ashore at the Clyde.

She tried to keep the rising excitement from her voice. 'And … the people you saw … did they say if they built it?' If so, the trap was of little other than ethnographic interest, a few decades old at most. But if not … Unable to look at him, she stood very still and waited.

'Yeah, I asked the blokes that. They thought it was a huge joke, the clueless little gubba. Couple of the women called me over but, told me "old people" built it, long time ago, before whitefellas. They just came here to net themselves a feed.' He lifted his hand, let it drop. *What I was told.* 'I went along the inside of the wall one low tide. Tallest part was up to my chest — my chest then — about four foot. Looked old to me — she was welded solid with oysters, still is by the look — but anything in the ocean looks old. That's why I wanted your opinion.'

'I'm no expert on this stuff. We need Aled.'

'You don't reckon he'll think I was just being bullshitted?'

'Maybe — I don't know. But you *saw* Aboriginal people using it. Even if it's not old, he'll be pleased, it shows this is still a beach they come to.'

Brian Harpur made a low whistle and grinned. Only then did she realise how much he'd feared appearing a fool. Perhaps most of all to her.

On the walk back, he barely glanced at the ocean, he talked. His memory for the detail of things seen some twelve years earlier was astonishing. The women and kids had driven the trapped fish — slapping the water with their hands — towards the men, who had a gill net. Three drives cleaned the trap out. Little stuff and rubbish like toads they threw back. The fish were piled into big baskets, the proper cane baskets used on trawlers back then, and wet sacks thrown over. They left out about twenty mullet, wrapped each in bracken fronds, and buried them in the coals and raked the fire back over. Then they got stuck into a carton of beer, men and women. The little kids came over and asked his name, but the kids his age ignored him. He decided to leave. One of the men saw him going and called to the kids to fetch two mullet out of the baskets and give him. 'For your mum, ay!' the man yelled, when Brian Harpur had a mullet hanging by its gills from each hand. 'Tell her don't fry em but, ay budda.'

Next day he'd kept an eye on the tide and on the end of the beach. When he saw tiny figures, he walked up there again, but watched from a dune, worried they'd think he was there for another handout. After they'd gone with the baskets slung on poles, he followed their prints and found the track they'd used, down through the bush, the regrowth freshly slashed. They must have had utes or a small truck up on the road. They didn't come the next day, or the next. On the third day they didn't come, he knew they weren't coming again — or not in the few days more he had at the cabins — and that was when he'd gone up in his swimmers and inspected the walls. The story left on her the strong impression that even at nine years old Brian Harpur had been a very serious animal.

Aled and Marilyn were working with tape and dumpy level at the cave mouth.

Aled wasn't pleased by the interruption. 'What's the problem?'

Brian Harpur had asked that she do the talking. 'Brian's just taken me up to the end of the beach. There's a fish trap up there.'

'A fish trap.'

Annette saw him glance at Brian Harpur, then he returned his gaze to her. She read disbelief, and something else — disappointment? Her judgement warped by hormones in just one afternoon.

'It's still operating. It's full of mullet.'

Marilyn had joined them. She looked as sceptical as Aled. 'A construction, you mean? Or a pool?'

'A construction.' Annette stepped back, tapped Brian Harpur on the elbow. 'He's seen it used.'

He repeated what he'd told her on the walk back. Halfway through the account, Annette saw the two exchange a look she'd seen before. Excitement, deliberately muted.

'We'd better take a look. Can you come back in an hour?'

'No point,' Brian Harpur said, 'the tide's turned. It needs dead low.'

'In that case, we'll wait till tomorrow, then all go. Let's keep it a surprise, though, can we.' He held Brian Harpur's gaze. 'You sure you won't consider changing degrees?'

Again, his answer was to laugh. As he and Annette walked away, though, he muttered — to her or to himself — 'Yeah, I can just hear *that* at the dinner table, "Hey Mum, Dad, I'm ditching engineering, gonna be an archaeologist."'

On the steps up the cliff they met Greg and Brandy coming down with towels. The others were already in the surf. They'd see them there, Annette said.

Standing at her cabin, Brian Harpur was awkward. He wouldn't come to the beach, sorry. There was a sandbank in the lake where he'd caught whiting as a kid. He wanted to see if it was still there. Annette was sweaty, badly wanted a swim. But she found herself wanting also to go on being with him. He read the hesitation. It wasn't the surf, he said, but there used to be a channel near the sandbank. She could swim there and not disturb his fishing.

Annette had brought two costumes, her old black one-piece, and a pink bikini she'd owned for a month. She put on the bikini and pulled her T-shirt on over it and grabbed her towel. When she opened the cabin door, Brian Harpur was standing a few metres from the steps. She thought for a second he'd been there the whole time, then saw he was wearing a khaki canvas satchel.

He stopped at the forty-four-gallon drum that did as a bin. He peered inside, then picked up a stick and hooked out an empty baked beans tin and twisted the lid till the hinge of metal broke. He dropped the lid back in and peeled off the label and dropped that in, too.

Annette laughed. 'I hope they'll be bigger than that.'

'You good at putting your foot down?'

'What? Sometimes. What happened to my swim?'

'This's on the way.'

They waded across the lake entrance. The water was only up to her knees, but the weight of the incoming tide was palpable, each step creating a boiling in the lee of her calf. She thought it likely he'd be taking a swim on the return leg whether or not he wanted to. When they reached the sandbank, he drew the tin from the satchel and began walking the fringe, studying the skin of advancing water. Annette followed dutifully, a picture in her head of doing this a thousand years ago with a dillybag on her shoulder instead of a towel.

She snapped out of her daydream when he bent, pushed the mouth of the tin into the sand, and stamped on its base. Jets of sand and water erupted around his feet. Brian Harpur had taken a clear plastic box on a belt from the satchel. He stooped and picked up two writhing things and dropped them into the box, then held it for her to look. They were a species of legged worm, a pale but iridescent grey-green, with a bright thread of blood for a spine.

'Bloodworms,' he said. 'Original name, eh.'

He stooped again and grabbed a handful of wet sand and dropped it on the worms, then handed her the box. He jolted the plug of sand from the tin and repeated the stamping. Nothing had been said, but she understood her job was to pick up the worms. Three were rippling on the sand. Knowing marine worms could be soft, Annette lifted the first gingerly, but the bodies of these were as muscular as earthworms. He'd stamped twice more. He gathered up worms and dropped them in the tin. He said nothing, but again didn't need to. She was lagging.

By the time he offered her a turn, she'd worked out the physics. Place ball of foot squarely on base of tin and tread down hard, one movement, thus creating a sudden pressure, transmitted by the laws of hydraulics to all holes connected to the one targeted. Occupants shoot out, defeated by science and a baked beans tin. She evicted another ten or so, then refused, believing he was just letting her play God. No, Brian Harpur countered, he needed plenty, they broke on the hook. Any left over they'd return to the sand. They worked along the edge of the bank for a further ten metres before he declared enough. He pointed out the channel, gave her a brisk nod, and strode away towards a spit of sand running out into the body of the lake.

'Thanks!' Annette said softly at his back.

She sidestroked the channel to the beach side and left her towel and shirt above the tidemark. When she turned, she saw he'd waded out to his knees, the baitbox now strapped around his waist. He had a bright yellow caster in his left hand and his right outstretched. As she watched, he struck, then jammed the caster into his armpit and retrieved the line with both hands. A flash of silver flew up out of the water. He worked on the fish for, it seemed, no more than a second, then swivelled and pulled from the water a net bag tied by its cord to his belt. He thrust the fish into its mouth. Annette saw the flash of another already inside, decided to make her dip short.

The influx was so clean and cold she stayed in longer than she'd intended. When she joined him, he had nine whiting in the submerged keep net, sleek fish, with sloping foreheads, a pout, and bulging eyes. *Sillago ciliata*. She'd eaten them, seen them in fish shops and as a watercolour plate, but never live. Annette bent over the net, careful to keep her alarming shadow to the side. The nine were resting calmly on the meshed sand, gills and fins working, waiting until this inexplicable captivity ended.

He hooked another, brought it in fast, telling her over his shoulder the reason — so that the hooked fish didn't spook the school. He added it to the net and cast again, then told her to move slowly and stand beside him. The ripples some twenty metres away cleared, and she could actually see the worm lying on the sand, fish already circling. One darted in, shook its head. Brian Harpur struck and began hauling in the line, the nylon emitting a quiet *ping* each time he changed hands. Soon the whiting was cutting angles a couple of metres from her legs, its eyes, Annette thought, fixed on her in terror. Then it was in his left hand. He worked the hook from its lip, said to open the net. Again, the hunter's handmaiden.

Brian Harpur coiled the line, threaded a worm onto the hook, and said as he began swinging the sinker, 'You're catching the next one.'

'Me?'

He was already laying the line through her palm. He positioned it on her index finger, pushed her thumb onto it, then enclosed her hand lightly in his. Annette remembered the cracked reptilian skin. She didn't have time to be repulsed, he was chanting softly 'not yet, not yet', then he snapped 'yep!', and jerked her hand. A second later, she was joined to an animal fighting for its life.

Annette had seen the whiting in the net. How could this be the same size, it felt as strong as she was! Brian Harpur was trying to instruct calmly, 'Bring in line, hand over hand,' but she could hear his mounting exasperation. The wet nylon kept slipping through her fingers. She was beginning to blink away tears — of panic, yes, but also of anger, at him, and at herself. She gripped the line in both hands and waded backwards. Ten steps, and he was able to stoop and catch hold of the sinker and lift the fish from the water. Annette dropped the line in a way she hoped wouldn't tangle and returned. Brian Harpur tried to hand her her trophy, but she shook her head.

'Sorry, sorry.'

He thought she was talking to him and began to say something about lots of people, their first fish, but Annette shook her head again and pointed to the whiting.

'Ah — right. Yeah, well, my fault. I thought you wanted to.'

'I did, too.'

That night he wrapped the cleaned whiting in pairs in young bracken fronds and foil, with a dob of butter, and laid them on the grill. Annette believed she'd eaten fresh fish before, learned that she hadn't, not until she ate the whiting he placed on her plate.

They set up the sieve cradles at the north side of the cave mouth, which offered shade in the hottest part of the day. The first few spits from the pit were almost solid shell, with bone and charcoal, and Annette was soon flat out sorting, bagging, and labelling.

When the buckets slowed, which they did when the trowels began to expose the first tools — many, as Aled had predicted, Clyde silcrete — Brandy took over from her on the sieve, and she had a chance to more closely examine the bone. At that surface level it was mostly fish, well-preserved otoliths, mandibles, ribs, vertebrae. She set herself up on a sheet of plastic with her self-compiled bone 'bible' and her copy of *Fish and Fisheries of Australia*.

Brian Harpur left a bucket at the sieves and came and squatted beside her. After a moment he asked why she was working from drawings. Wouldn't real skeletons be more accurate? Yes, Annette said. But fish skeletons weren't exactly portable. He nodded, didn't reply. He rose and walked back to the sieves and picked up an empty bucket.

The cave was a hike from the lake and camping ground, but by mid-morning, families were wandering along the beach choosing their own little patches. Annette was working with Marilyn, who'd opened the outside trench. People came and stood at the stringline — kids in swimmers, their faces clowned with zinc cream, women in straw hats and towelling coats, men lugging furled beach umbrellas. Each new lot of gawkers asked where were they from, what were they looking for, what would they do with whatever they found? Marilyn answered each time as if it were the first. As yet another family ambled away, Annette asked wasn't she getting sick of the same questions.

'Well and truly. But they're paying for us to *be* here. *They* don't know that, but we do. Worth remembering.'

She winked to remove the sting.

Around two, Annette saw Brian Harpur deliver a bucket, then look along the beach. She caught his eye, and he shook his head. She kept a watch on him, though. Each time he emerged from the cave, his eyes went first to the sea. Finally he gave her a nod and went back into the cave empty-handed. Aled came out, followed by Sue looking puzzled. Aled called them all to attention. They should put tools, buckets, clipboards inside the cave and lay a sheet of iron over the outside trench. Just the iron, not the plastic. They'd be coming back.

Sue trudged along beside Annette, grumbling. There'd be other low tides, why had Aled chosen the hottest time of day to count mussels? It wasn't a pleasant walk and others, too, were grumbling, the nor-easter ripping at their hair and coating lips and lashes with salt. The grumbling stopped when they reached the trap.

The walls were more exposed than yesterday. An even larger school of mullet was swimming a slow circuit, almost to the shore, turning parallel, then out again. A knot of darker fish, which Brian Harpur identified as Australian salmon, milled about the green holes in the lee of the platform. Stuart strode out into the water to his knees, hugging himself at the sight of so many fish. He spun and yelled to Aled they should ask Gorman for a net! Aled deflated him. A gill net needed a licence.

'Unless you're black,' Brian Harpur said quietly.

'Even then,' Aled said. 'But I concede, less chance of the law being enforced. Which is your cue, I think.' He clapped for silence. 'Okay. The evidence of our eyes would seem to tell us that this is a fish trap. They're not uncommon in coastal northern New South Wales and Queensland, but I've never heard of one down here — which is *my* ignorance, because this has obviously been known to people for a long time, white and black. But as well as our eyes we have ethnological evidence.' He opened his hand in invitation. 'Mr Harpur.'

For whatever reason — not wanting, Annette's guess, to big-note himself — Brian Harpur gave a much truncated version of what he'd told her, then Aled and Marilyn, leaving out entirely the feast, the gift of mullet, his inspection of the walls. He caught her frown, shrugged.

Unprepared for the brevity, Aled quickly recovered. He warned them not to assume that cave and trap were contemporaneous just because of contiguity, the two fatal *c*'s. 'But we're permitted to imagine.'

One of Aled's gifts, Annette had learned at the Clyde, was peopling a site. In minutes they could not only see the original naked glistening women and children driving the fish towards the men, but hear their yipping and laughter, the flurry of water under their massed hands, the boil and surge of fish breaking sideways when they saw the nets, the teenagers leaping to head them off, turn them. Fires would already be burning on the beach. They would gorge. The rest they would thread through the gills onto poles and carry home. It was an attractive hypothesis, Aled said, that much of the bone they were already finding at the cave had its origin here.

For the whole time he'd been talking he'd held in his hand a large whelk, bleached to chalk, using its minaret as a pointer.

Now he leaned back and lobbed it into the greatest density of mullet, which opened like a suddenly wakened eye.

That night Gorman came to the fire. He wore padded rugby shorts and the same green T-shirt with its cotton dissolved in the armpits. Aled welcomed him into their circle, asked Paul to fetch a can. Annette had come to know Aled too well to interpret his effusive hospitality as simply that.

Paul returned and placed the can in the man's hand. After a long swallow and a lordly exhalation, Gorman lowered the can, glanced round the circle to confirm that he had their attention, and asked Aled if the cave was 'up to expectation'. Aled nodded as if to acknowledge a searching question. The indications were good, but it was too early to say more. And when might he know if it could be as big as the Clyde, how many days of digging? Aled explained that the process wasn't so much 'digging' as scraping, it was slow. The Clyde was stone houses — much more 'visible' to the public mind. Speaking of which, they'd located a stone fish trap up at the headland end of the beach. Why, Aled wondered, had Gorman not thought to mention something so obviously Aboriginal?

Annette watched the man's face twist into pained surprise. He was almost as good an actor as Aled. It was no secret, he said, he just thought they'd have been told by whoever it was put them on to the the cave. He never went up the beach any more, not in years. A storm could have knocked the thing to pieces for all he knew and he'd have given them a bum steer.

Aled swivelled in his chair, looking for Brian Harpur, who was hovering at the fringe of the firelight, wanting to hear but not be noticed. Aled spotted him before he could duck and waved him forward. 'You might remember this bloke, he stayed here as a kid. He saw the trap being used.'

Annette had thought it was a tenet of country manners that you shook a man's hand no matter what your opinion of him. Brian Harpur halted where Gorman could see him and nodded. 'G'day. Brian Harpur. My parents are Jim and Phyllis Harpur.'

Gorman had leaned forward, squinting against the flames. He rolled in the chair as if a sudden twinge had nipped his hip, then scrutinised Brian Harpur, before returning the nod. 'And how are they, your mum and dad? Your dad well?'

'They both are, thanks.'

'Still on the farm?'

'Yeah. Rain last year helped.'

'Thought we might've seen yous at Teapot again.'

'And Mrs Gorman? I think our last time, she was about to go into hospital for more surgery.'

Gorman stared at him before answering. 'Not much wrong with your memory, is there.'

Aled cut short the exchange. 'Brian's described for us seeing Aboriginal people taking fish from the trap. Some ten — eleven? — years ago, was it?' he said towards Brian Harpur.

'Twelve.'

Aled turned to Gorman. 'Do they still?'

Gorman was still staring at Brian Harpur. Annette had the strong sense he wanted to explore his memory further. But he changed elbows on the chair arm to bring himself round half-face to Aled, wincing as he did. Gorman was going to need surgery himself one day.

'Nah. Not for ages.'

How do you know? Annette thought. *You never go up there, remember.* She saw that Aled, too, had noted the contradiction, but he said smoothly, 'So where would they have come from? They local?'

'Used to be a reserve on the other side of the highway. About seven or eight families livin there.'

'Used to be.'

'Government took it back. You know what they do to houses.'

Aled didn't rise to the baiting tone. 'And moved them where?'

'Back up to Nowra's what I heard.'

'So they weren't *from* here. Originally.'

'Dunno. Could've been. They had stories about here. For one thing, they wouldn't use the National Parks track through to the beach, reckoned it went past where a clever fella was buried. They made their own, further up.'

The circle had frozen, except for their darting eyes.

'A clever fella. That they … knew?' Aled lifted his can to his lips. Annette was amazed that he could swallow.

Gorman laughed. 'The Gudgeon boys were clever bastards themselves, but I don't think even they'd figured out how to live three hundred years. That's how long they reckoned he'd been there.'

Aled smiled. Annette saw that, right now, none of them existed, there was only Gorman. 'And ... how precise were they — can you remember — about the burial place? Would you be able to take us to roughly where they believed him to be?'

'No — cause I reckon he was buried in their heads. No one round here'd even heard of him till the government told em they had to piss off out of the houses. Then out come all this stuff about how he used to have pelicans spot salmon schools for him, he could sing muttonbirds down. They had to stay and look after him, his bit of bush. I told the government fellas come here, "You believed all those blokes told ya, you'd be pannin the lake for gold!"' Gorman jerked back in the chair and gave a bark of laughter, but Annette didn't hear any mirth in it, and neither, it seemed, did Aled, because he let the subject drop.

She went to the toilet. When she came out, she found Brian Harpur and Gorman waiting for her. Gorman had him lightly by the elbow, as if for support.

'Mr Gorman wants a word. He was asking about stone tools, what they might be worth if someone had any. I told him I'm the wrong person.'

From this close, Annette could smell the man. He'd turned so the firelight caught his face. His eyes were a beautiful sea blue, but below them the cheeks were webs of broken veins. He gave her what he probably believed to be a disarming smile, but he was clearly unused to being so close to a young woman and kept darting out his tongue and running it along his lips.

'I'm not the tool expert. You need Marilyn.' Annette looked past them, hoping to spot her.

'I'm happy to speak to you, miss. Brian here tells me you know your stuff.'

Thanks very much, she glanced at Brian Harpur.

She explained the difference between collectors and archaeologists. That they were interested only in tools found *in situ*, that could be related to other finds, and, more importantly, dated. Then a shiver ran through her, he knew of another site!

'Have you found some, Mr Gorman? That you'd like to show us?'

'Nah, miss, nah — just curious.' He released Brian Harpur's elbow. 'I do a fair bit of diggin, fence posts and the like. Just interested in case I find any. But thank you, miss.'

They watched him rock away up the paddock towards his house. A dim light showed in just one window.

'Sorry. He didn't want Aled and he wouldn't let go.'

'He doesn't just smell, he's creepy.'

'You know why he's asking — he's got a shoebox full.'

'We won't get to see them.'

'Don't ever be alone with him, right.'

Annette gave a snort of laughter to say it was not something she planned ever to have happen. She saw Brian Harpur misread, even for a second thought he was going to take her by the shoulders and shake her. He dropped his hands.

'I'm serious. You see him coming, you make sure there's someone with you. And tell Sue and Vicky.' Still angry, he turned to go.

'Hey! — okay. Now tell me why. Apart from he's a creep.'

He took time with choosing his words. 'I wasn't told this, I overheard my mother telling my father. Some girls staying here got pawed. I think I said in the car, I've got a sister.' Annette began to open her mouth, and he shook his head. 'No proof at all.'

'But … did the cops, you know, question him or something?'

'Might've. How she heard. It wasn't any of the actual times we were here.'

'Has he got kids?'

'No. His wife's got something wrong with her spine. We came here three times like I said, and I only ever saw her the once. Mum took her some *Women's Weekly*s. She reckoned she spent most of her time in bed.'

It made no sense that two cripples would go on living for years on a joke of a farm so far from town and doctors, and Annette said so. Brian Harpur had been raised to harsher realities.

'They're not you. They don't see choices.' He angled a thumb towards the low roar coming from the darkness beyond the cabins. 'And she can hear that, even if she can't get there.'

Two evenings later, Annette was lying on her bed when Vicky came to the doorless doorway and said Brian Harpur wanted to see her. She was tired. They'd walked back from the cave in a group only half an hour earlier, he could have spoken to her then. But she got up and put on her shorts.

He hadn't showered or changed. He was holding in both hands what looked like two toy coffins of folded paperbark. 'I've got you something.' He knelt and found a patch of bare earth between the paspalum tufts and set the packages gently down. 'Could you hold the base. This stuff's a bit springy.'

Annette was expecting a bush food, elaeocarpus berries, or wattle seed. Not the clean perfect skeleton of a fish!

'This's your whiting, the other's your flathead.' Brian Harpur raised the flaps of the second package, the wedge-shaped body emerging first, then the distinctive blunt arrow of the skull.

Annette couldn't find words. The fins were brittle-dry, but intact, the ribs were still attached by scraps of ligament to the spine. He'd caught both fish, but she had no idea, none, how he'd rendered them into skeletons.

'They're beautiful,' she finally managed to say, and was instantly angry at herself for the birthday-present cliché. 'How

... I don't get how they're ... in one piece.'

'I can show you, if you want. You'll have a bream and a flounder in another couple of days.' He began refolding the bark over the flathead. 'Leave these under your steps. You'll need something on your feet.'

Brian Harpur led her out to the road. They crossed into scrub, which soon gave way to spotted gum and burrawangs. After some thirty metres, he halted and held aside a frond, and Annette stepped into a small clearing with, at its centre, the bald orange mound of a meat ants' nest. On top — a miniature barrow for a Celtic chieftain — was a slab of sandstone resting on squat rocks, the whole arrangement surrounded by a calf-high stockade of sticks hammered into the mound's hard clay. At the base of the stockade were deep clawmarks. A labour line was still in the process of carrying away the loose soil grain by grain.

'Hah — great! She worked.'

'Is that a ... fox?'

'They'd be around, but no, that's a goanna. Bloody big one.' Brian Harpur stepped delicately onto a patch clear of ants and crouched. 'Hah!' He was still delighted at how well his 'fortress' had withstood assault. He gestured for her to join him, pointed beneath the slab.

Annette saw the torn ends of another two paperbark trays and the forms of what she knew to be fish only because he'd told her, each rippling with pale orange bodies.

'Scale them, slit the skin, they do the rest.' He jumped up and back, flicking at his boots. 'Shit, they've found us!'

When the burrawangs swished closed behind them, she asked would he mind if she brought Sue here.

'No. I have to say, but, she strikes me as hard to impress.'

'She's impressed by anything she can use.'

He laughed, then glanced at her again over his shoulder — pleased, Annette saw, that she'd permitted him to know that her loyalties weren't blind.

At the cabins, he said he'd get her a tailor and a salmon when he could get a crack at the beach, but a mullet would be harder, they wouldn't take a bait. Annette waited, but no invitation came. Once was enough — he preferred to fish on his own.

She carried the bark coffins over to Aled and Marilyn's cabin. The door was open. Marilyn was seated at her trestle table washing the stone found that day. She glanced round, saw the coffins, and lowered her hands. Annette carried them over to the workspace she'd been allotted and put down the flathead, brought the whiting to show her.

'Oh my goodness!' Marilyn ran the tip of her index finger up the sloping forehead, as one stroked a cat's. 'Did you prepare this?'

'Hardly. Brian.' Annette explained that he'd seen her making identifications from drawings and asked why she wasn't using skeletons. 'I said where would I get them. I thought nothing more of it, then just now he turned up at the cabin with these.'

'From where?'

Annette described where she'd just been.

'He's off a farm, right?'

'Yes.'

'So am I.' Marilyn had leaned to look more closely at the skeleton. Even with gentle handling, already a few ribs had come loose. 'We brought poly. I don't say do it now, they're still too green, but in a day or so give them a couple of coats.' She looked up, the tip of her tongue impishly visible. 'This is a serious gift.'

Annette was on the sieve when Marilyn called to her from the trench, could she come and look at something. She'd spoken calmly, but wanted her *now*! Annette dropped the brush, stopped the sieve.

The first three squares of the trench had bottomed out at just over half a metre onto a sterile fine gravel. She was down to nearly that depth in the fourth. Annette knelt and looked at the trench floor below Marilyn's finger. The sand was the wrong colour. Marilyn took a shaving and handed up the trowel. Annette spread the damp sand with a fingertip. The grains were not just stained, she could see actual specks.

'It *is*, you can see it.'

Annette swung the trowel blade to Paul, who peered, then nodded. 'Yeah, tiny bits of red.'

'You'd better go and get Aled. We may have a burial.'

It was, but, to Annette's relief, not human. She made the identification as soon as Marilyn exposed the first bones — a hind leg. *Canis familiaris*, almost certainly dingo.

Aled's disappointment was palpable. He soon recovered, his mind leaping down another path. Why had a dingo been sprinkled with ochre? It was a rite associated with human burials. He'd never heard of an animal being honoured in such a way.

Perhaps there was a human beneath, Vicky ventured.

'Unlikely,' Aled snapped. 'Side by side.' He stood kneading his lower lip and frowning down into the trench. Then grunted assent to some question in his mind and held out his hand for the trowel. He'd take over, if Marilyn would go inside please and work at the pit.

'Aled — this is my trench.'

'And my site.'

'No.'

'I'm sorry, but I'm asking you.'

'And I'm giving you my answer. No. It's my trench.'

Vicky caught Annette's eye, *should we leave?* The two already speaking as if they weren't there.

'Your expertise, my dear, is in tools, not burials.'

'I'm perfectly capable of excavating an animal.'

'I agree. But perhaps not interpreting. And I wish to do it.'

They stared at one another. Then Marilyn pushed the point

of the trowel into the sand an inch from the toe of his right sandshoe. She placed her palms flat on the trench rim, sprang to clear the stringline, and strode away towards the surf, the sand squealing beneath her bare soles. Aled asked Paul to fetch his trowel from the cave.

He didn't want onlookers. Paul did buckets, Brandy worked the sieve, Annette and Vicky sat in the shade of the cliff. It soon became clear that the grave extended outside the stringline. He pegged a side square and called to her. When Annette stood, she looked towards the water. Marilyn was so far out beyond the breakers she thought at first the black dot was a cormorant.

By four, Aled and Annette had exposed the entire skeleton. The dingo was an old female. She'd been laid on her right side in a round hole, her spine curved to fit its wall and her legs crossed beneath her belly, the front lying over the hind. Her tail completed the circle, its tip resting against her snout. She'd been heavily sprinkled with ochre — most on the head. Granules had trickled into the skull cavity and were caught among the worn brown teeth. Beneath the skull, the sand was bright red.

Aled sketched and photographed her. Annette knew he wouldn't want to delay the removal till next morning and compromise another day. He asked if she'd mind staying.

The others almost slunk away. She thought that once the two of them were alone he might say something about the scene earlier, but his only talk was of the lady in the hole. She'd been a matriarch, borne many litters of hunters, and was certainly herself a great hunter. The ochre and the careful arrangement of the body said she'd been buried with reverence. What puzzled him was the siting of the grave, in a direct line from the cave mouth where people would have moved about and sat. By the time they began walking back — he carrying the bones rolled in a towel — he'd formed a hypothesis for the siting as well. Dogs, too, would move about and lie above her, be infused with her fecundity and hunting prowess. And don't discount sentimentality. Her owner can speak to her, invoke her to other dogs, she's right below where he's sitting. Annette answered yes and no as required, but her mind was far busier with the question of whether, when they arrived back at the cabins, both the Kombi and Marilyn might be gone.

The answer was waiting at the top of the steps up from the beach. Marilyn was barefoot, in jeans and a cheesecloth shirt. Her hair was freshly washed. She gave Annette a cool smile, signed to her that she take charge of the bundle. 'In the cabin, please — the door's unlocked. My husband and I are going for a walk.'

All of them, it looked to Annette, were gathered at the fireplace. Greg and Brandy should have been at the tent. No one called to her, but she felt their eyes all the way to the cabin steps. The work room was lit by the firelight refracted through the dusty louvres and flickering on the ceiling. In the air, mixed with the midden smells of drying shell and bone, was a faint scent. Annette stood sniffing, couldn't decide whether it was simply shampoo, or perfume. She left the bundle on Aled's table.

She wanted to wash, but knew she'd have to go to the fire. She was still five paces off when Sue barked, 'So what's happening?'

'They've gone for a walk.' The table was bare of plates or food. Annette looked at the grate, hoping to see a billy pushed against the bricks to stay warm.

'That's all they said?'

'That I got to hear.'

Brian Harpur had caught her look. He picked up both billies and set off towards the laundry.

Sue persisted. 'What about on the way back, didn't he *talk*?'

'Yes, but only about the bones.'

'Jesus.'

'So what do you think's going to happen?' Vicky said in a small voice.

Sue gave a harsh guffaw. 'Quite a bit I'd say, Vick.' There were smirks and stifled laughter. Sue's eyes didn't leave Annette's face. She wanted reassurance, at stake her honours supervision. Annette could only shrug.

The boys poured three cans of baked beans into a saucepan and filled the grill plate with chops. Vicky buttered bread. Greg and Brandy ate fast, then set off for the cliff edge and the tent, the beam of their torch tapping the ground ahead of them like a blind man's cane.

Sue sat in a chair at the edge of the firelight, no part of any conversation and her eyes fixed on the end cabin. Annette filled two plates, carried a chair over and placed it beside her, and came back for the plates. When she tried to put one in Sue's lap, it was pushed away.

'If I eat, I'll chuck.'

'I doubt it. Just try.'

Sue rounded on her. 'Don't fucking mother me, all right!'

'Okay, okay.' Annette swivelled in the chair and held the plate towards Vicky, who'd been watching. She darted over and took it. 'How about a tea, then.'

Sue was staring again at the cabin. 'Two sugars.'

When Annette reached the table, Brian Harpur had the mug poured, a spoon poised over the open canister. Annette carried the mug back.

'Here — no, by the handle, it's hot.'

Sue did as instructed, but without taking her eyes from the cabin. Annette picked up her plate and sat. Sue transferred the mug to her left hand and with her right cupped Annette's knee. 'Thanks.'

Annette quickly cupped the hand with her own. 'It's *them* should be apologising. They've *got* their bloody letters after their names.'

Sue lifted her hand and swiped a finger across each cheek. 'If I have to find someone else, then it's what I have to do. But there's not a huge choice, is there.'

'No. And you know one another. And she's approved your outline.'

Sue nodded and thrust the mug out in front of her, stared at the ground. 'Over a *fucking* dingo!'

Annette couldn't suppress a belch of laughter. 'Sorry. But yes, buried a yard either way and we wouldn't be here.'

Vicky said goodnight and went to their cabin. Annette saw the torchlight change to lanternlight, which became a glow where her head rested on the pillow. Reading her Bible. Brian Harpur came and took their mugs and Annette's plate, and a few minutes later they heard the sound of washing-up coming from the laundry. When the clatter stopped, Paul called to Annette that they were leaving to play cards, should he put out the fire? She lifted a hand, do it, and a second later came the splash and hiss.

'Sue?' Paul called again. 'It'll be all right, hey — my feeling.'

'Great, thanks,' Sue said into the air, 'just what I need, dumb cheerfulness.'

A low whistle from one of the boys cautioned Paul not to respond.

Sue said when they were alone, 'I can't go to bed. I need to see how they come back.'

'Well, let's sit on our steps. It's less obvious.'

They stood, and Sue reached for her hand.

Annette left her sitting on the top step and went inside to the room they shared and fetched Sue's sleeping bag. They sat hip to hip, the bag around their shoulders. They didn't talk. Sue wanted to hear any sound of approaching feet.

Annette woke with her head on Sue's shoulder. Sue was rigidly awake. The end cabin was still in darkness.

'I have to go to bed,' Annette slurred.

*

When she woke again, it was first light. Sue was on the other bed, staring at the iron roof. Sue rolled her head, looked at her. 'Well, she's still here.'

They were out of their cabins and gathered at the fire when Marilyn came down her cabin steps alone and walked to the table. She greeted them as on any morning, selected a bowl, and began helping herself to Weet-Bix.

Five minutes later, Aled appeared. He walked up behind her and placed his right arm lightly round her waist, left it there a moment, then gave her hip a pat and reached for a bowl.

Greg and Brandy were waiting at the cave, the trench open, tools and buckets laid out, driftwood collected and stacked beside the day fireplace. Aled told everyone to sit. Annette saw from the panicky flitting of eyes that they'd all had the same thought — the bad news was just delayed, now here it came.

He'd decided, he said, to ride their luck. They'd found one burial, why not two? He pointed to Paul, then Stuart. 'Gentlemen. Be upstanding.'

Looking as puzzled as the rest of them, the two got to their feet.

'You're going in search of our "clever fella". Mornings only, for the angle of the light, and for five mornings only.' Aled turned. 'But I'll explain the drill to you all. That scrub on top hasn't burned in years, so it'll be hard going and they may well require a swap.'

The base transect was the National Parks track. They would separate and walk transects on each side at ten-yard intervals, from clifftop to road, back again to the clifftop, as many as they could do each morning up to eleven o'clock. They were looking for carved trees — the least likely — a stone arrangement, or simply a human-sized depression. It was also entirely possible that 'our Mr Gorman' was right — that the grave was a fiction. But in his, Aled's, experience, only when Aboriginal people had been backed into a corner did the deep story come out. Then, because it emerged so late, and seemingly so conveniently, the story was labelled a fiction.

Paul and Stuart appeared back at the cave at lunchtime drenched in sweat and their arms and legs a mess of scratches. Aled sent them straight to the surf. That night they came to the girls' cabin to scrounge anything with long sleeves. Next morning, Stuart twisted his ankle. Aled replaced him with Brandy.

On the third morning the pair had been gone less than an hour when Brandy was back. He was excited, but tight-lipped. Fortunately, the cave was an echo chamber. They had found a depression covered with slabs of rock like a short, paved path. Aled yelled for Annette to replace him at the pit.

Those at the cave were too distracted to work. Marilyn asked Brian Harpur to make a fire and put the billy on. The bigger sticks were beginning to catch when they saw Paul jogging across the bay of sand.

Aled wanted brushes and pans. And they were all to come.

The school holidays were ending, the cave had almost ceased to attract gawkers. Still, from habit, Annette and Vicky picked up a sheet of iron.

'Leave it,' Marilyn said. 'Brian, sand the fire.'

Paul led them forty metres up the National Parks track. He'd marked the turn-off by breaking a branch. The scrub was thick, tea tree and coast wattle, lomandra, stunted gums. Annette peered ahead and caught movement, then the colours of Aled's and Brandy's shirts, low to the ground. When the scrub thinned, she saw the two were on their haunches and fanning the ground with switches of gum tips.

Aled heard them and shot to his feet, yelling to halt there! Marilyn was to come, then the rest of them, in turn, a pair at a time. And along the sticks! The panicky edge to his voice told Annette he believed he had indeed found, if not Gorman's 'clever fella', then certainly one of 'his' people, for whose cemetery, or even just a single grave, they'd searched in vain at the Clyde.

Her own heart was beating in her throat, and not with elation. Aled would almost certainly ask her to work with him. She'd handled a dingo without emotion. But these bones were once a human being. She'd always known this day would come. She faced into the bush and closed her eyes. *Apologise, then do it.*

Aled shouted, 'First pair!'

Sue jabbed her in the back.

They followed the line of sticks. The grave was as Brandy had described, like sunken paving. It was squeezed between a long-ago burned gum butt with a sapling springing from its base and two lomandra clumps. Nothing had, though, forced itself up between the slabs, which were heavy and overlapped.

Aled and Marilyn were crouched at the head, or foot, of the grave, Aled working now not with his improvised whisk, but with brush and pan. The two slabs he'd swept — what Annette could see of them for lichen — were a dark iron-red, like the headland rock platform. Surely they hadn't been carried all this way. But perhaps they had, proof of the occupant's importance. Her next thought came out of left field. Would Aled, as required by law, inform the police? He looked up to see who the legs belonged to.

'At last, eh? We get a look at one of our hut-builders.'

Marilyn proffered up to Sue what she'd been rubbing between her fingers — a small but perfect backed blade. Annette saw immediately that it was Clyde silcrete. Sue felt its edge and passed it to her.

'So you think it isn't Gorman's clever fella?' Sue said.

Aled didn't stop brushing. 'On the contrary, I think there's an excellent chance that's *exactly* who we have.' He sat back on his heels. His eyes had an almost roguish twinkle. He tapped the slab with the brush handle. 'They've gone to a great deal of trouble, wouldn't you say? I'm guessing as much out of fear as reverence. They wanted him to stay *in*.' He gave them a fierce grin, his teeth clenched. 'Brian's fisherfolk knew about him all right. *Oh* yes!'

He was not lidded by the slabs — beneath them was soil, dry and compacted. It took an hour to expose the first bones — and they were a bird's! Their size told her what they were. Pelican. His shroud was a wing.

'What else?' Aled said simply. 'For a man whose familiars they were.'

It was late afternoon of the third day before he lay fully revealed. Annette's qualms had been anaesthetised by the tedium of recording, removing from within the bones of his frame, and sorting into sequence the tinier bones of the wing. Fortunately, it was only one wing. But it was huge, had shrouded him from forehead to feet. He had been sprinkled with ochre, but, strangely, not as heavily as the dingo matriarch. From the wear of the teeth, Aled had placed his age at about fifty. His head lay to the west, the Clyde. A core and two points of quarry silcrete rested as they had in a vanished skin bag. At his nape he wore still a muttonbird skull on a necklet of vertebrae. A snapper otolith with traces of gum lay beside each temple.

Unique as they were, the grave goods and orientation fitted a pattern, were accessible to interpretation. The left hand wasn't. Annette had been the first to spot that the middle finger was missing. Aled had straddled the pit, his face inches from the hand and its stub. When finally he straightened, he told them, his voice breathy, that the finger had been amputated. With what, and why, he had no idea. But several times thereafter, Annette saw him interrupt what he was doing to stare at the hand, then off into the scrub.

Marilyn, the better artist, was sketching, he photographing. He shot a full roll. When he'd packed the camera again into its case, he stood at the pit, staring down and kneading his lip. Marilyn had stilled her pencil. He gave four emphatic nods.

'It was deliberate. He did it himself.' Aled raised his left hand, bent the middle finger into the palm. 'He gave himself a claw.' He raked the air. 'I think not a gentleman I'd have chosen to cross.'

When Annette stumbled down the cabin steps, Brian Harpur was already at the fireplace. They were joined by Stuart, yawning so much he couldn't speak. Bracken and twigs were burning clean and bright.

Brian Harpur, continuing to add twigs, hooked his head in the direction of the house. 'I'm wondering why he's up so early.'

Annette looked and saw Gorman at his yard gate. Brian Harpur lowered the grate and stood the first of the billies on the flames. As he lifted the second, they heard the car. There came a two-finger whistle that made even the cows stop tearing grass

and raise their heads. They heard the car skid to a halt, back up.
A slice of white roof appeared above the unpruned wall of coast
rosemary growing along the house fence.

Annette jumped when Aled said from just behind her ear, 'Is
that a police car?'

Brian Harpur shook his head. 'They'd know where he lives.'

'Oh? Why is that?'

Annette wondered what he'd say. He picked up a burning
stick that had fallen to the ground and slid it back under the
billies. 'Just country cops. They know their locals.'

The air was so still they heard the rattle of the chain. Gorman
ushered a man through the gate, re-chained it.

The man stayed behind Gorman, breaking stride several
times to bat dew from his trouser legs. He wore a camera bag.
Annette guessed him to be in his mid twenties. When close, he
lifted his hand in a wave meant to be disarming, but dropped it
quickly when it was not returned. Annette heard a sneeze and
glanced over her shoulder. The others were out of their cabins.

Gorman greeted Aled, ushered the man to him. Professor
Wray. Laurie Marr, the *Bay Examiner*. Aled ignored the man's
extended hand. The man reddened. He stumbled through a
prepared speech. Aled heard him out, then, without a word or
nod, turned to Gorman. 'And from where, exactly, have you
been spying on us?'

Gorman met his stare. 'People are on my patch, I like to keep
an eye on what they're doin.'

91

'I think you have an exaggerated notion of your "patch", don't you? A half-mile up the beach.'

The younger man interposed his hand. 'Professor Wray? If you'll allow me? From what Mr Gorman's told me, the grave's in the National Park, so it's actually public land.'

Aled swung back to him. 'Where I have all the necessary permits to work, did Mr Gorman also tell you that? And that you're a means to an end — publicity for his cabins? But to answer your point — yes, you can come and stand there, and I can't compel you to leave. By the same token, you can't compel me to remove the covers, nor can you compel me to tell you anything about what's under them. So where's your story?'

Making sure she was not observed, Annette found Sue with her eyes. Lying in their bags the night the grave was found, they'd discussed what Aled might do, given that he'd lectured on the legal and ethical obligations of the archaeologist. If the man had done his homework, he would know that the discovery of any grave, no matter how strong the evidence for its being old and Aboriginal, had, in the first instance, to be reported to the police. *They* might not mind if a reporter was present when the covers were removed. Sue looked past her and studied the man, met Annette's gaze again, and shook her head. Aled waited, his face a mask. The man didn't speak the magic words.

'Here's what I suggest,' Aled said.

The deal was simple. In return for an embargo till the end of the dig, Aled would conduct Laurie to the grave and remove the covers. He could take photographs. However, as guarantee, Aled would tell him nothing of the grave's meaning until the final week, when Laurie should come to North Teapot again, and Aled would give him a full interpretation — the probable age, the reverence reflected in the burial, the man's evident connection to the Clyde, and the significance of the discovery to the wider picture of Aboriginal life on the South Coast prior to Europeans. Without all that, Aled finished up, you have half a story. 'Less than half, in fact.'

Gorman tapped Laurie's elbow and lifted his chin towards the paddock, he wanted a word. Laurie turned to him. 'My decision, Mr Gorman, sorry.'

He asked Aled only the obvious question — when the dig would end. Three weeks to a month, Aled told him. Laurie considered, nodded, offered his hand. This time, Aled took it.

The three set off up the paddock towards the car. Sue didn't care whether they were out of hearing.

'That fucking creep hasn't been spying on just graves, he's been watching us women at the tent!'

'Not any more,' Brandy said softly. 'If he values his teeth.'

Sue wouldn't be mollified, was clumsy with anger, knocking over her mug.

'Sue — please — calm down,' Marilyn said. 'Even if it's true, he's just a sad voyeur, I wouldn't think he's a danger.'

Annette turned and found Brian Harpur. She'd neglected to, then forgotten to pass on his warning. This wasn't the time. She arched her eyebrows, and he nodded. She took the nod to mean he would tell Marilyn what he'd told her.

That night a massive electrical storm swept in off the sea. Each clap of thunder took the cabin in a fist and shook it. Pulling the sleeping bag over her head was worse, she got no warning flash. The boys, too, were awake. After one huge clap Annette heard above the rain's roar a half-scream of 'Jesus!' She didn't whisper across the few feet separating their beds. Sue — all of them — knew their visitor. *You've destroyed my sleep, now I'm destroying yours.*

They woke to a sky of rinsed blue. The sandy soil didn't retain puddles, but leaves sparkled, and bark and the raw fibro walls were leaking wisps of steam.

Stuart and Paul had a fire going. How, Annette asked. Brian, Stuart said. He'd stashed kindling in the laundry. She asked where he was — was he still asleep?

'No. Gone somewhere. Before we woke up.'

Annette walked as casually as she could to the gap in the trees that gave a view of the lake. His whiting bank was covered, its only fisherman a cruising pelican.

After breakfast the boxes containing the 'clever fella', his shroud, and the grave goods were loaded into the tray of the Land Rover, covered with a tarp, and the almost-weightless load lashed to the rings in the floor. Marilyn gave Aled a brief, formal, kiss — he'd be back next day — and they waved him off. They were free now to do as they wished. Aled had declared a holiday.

The storm swell was huge. They stayed close together in the shore break, being dumped, but clear of the vicious undertow. Annette couldn't have said why — he could have been anywhere — but each time she stood up from a wave and flicked the hair from her eyes, she looked along the beach in the direction of the trap.

Between one wave and the next a figure materialised. Annette said nothing, left the water and dried herself. She didn't hurry, she would be at the cabins well before him. But he didn't veer towards the dunes track, he kept coming along the wash. She saw the keep net hanging from his hand. Stuart, too, had spotted him. He sprinted to him, grabbed the net, and jogged back holding it aloft, as excited as if he'd caught the haul of bream himself.

Brian Harpur gestured to her wet hair. 'You're mad.'

'This's nothing to a Cronulla girl.'

He smiled, but he was waiting. The thought struck Annette, *You haven't just been fishing!* Before she could speak, Stuart pounded up the sand and flung the catch down at Brian Harpur's feet, and tore off back to the water.

'What've you found?'

He didn't fence with her. 'I reckon it's who really built the trap.'

'You're joking — another site?'

He made a damping motion and glanced past her, then looked at her again and flashed a quick, fierce grin.

'But you'll need your sandshoes.'

'Hang on, Marilyn's at the cave — you came right past her.'

'Yeah, she didn't see me.'

Annette began to say, that's not what I meant, and stopped. He'd said what *he* meant. He lifted the strap of the satchel over his head, held it to her to take, nodded down at the fish. 'They're cleaned, shove them in your fridge. I'll meet you at that dead roo.'

He walked them fast along the fringes of the wash, Annette having to keep breaking into a half-jog. Only when they were past the cave did Brian Harpur slow. She grabbed his arm to halt him while she caught her breath. He stood bristling with impatience. To keep him halted she asked was the site visible from the beach.

He turned and pointed towards the humpbacked ridge that climbed and swelled to become the headland. 'See that sort of stripe — where the trees seem to step up?' She couldn't, and he looked her along his arm. Annette saw then the line, darker than the bush above and below. 'As a kid I always wondered about that. Whether it was an actual thing, or just the light.'

'So, what is it?'

'See when you get there, won't you.'

Some forty metres from the fish trap, a gutter halted them. A massive volume of water had flowed down the gully, whose mouth she could see, and across the beach. Tan water was still running. Brian Harpur forded at his previous prints, and she followed. Once across, he turned away from sea and trap and led her towards coast banksias standing like sentries among lomandra clumps, marking the edge of the sand. He pointed her to a fallen banksia, its branches collapsed and its bark coming off in plates. They sat and brushed their feet, put on their sandshoes.

The gully mouth was crowded with light-starved sweet pittosporum, the heads featherdusters and the stems as dense as bamboo. Annette looked doubtfully at him, and he turned and plunged in, as if swimming breaststroke. The gully sides were glistening earth, the tread on her sandshoes was too fine. To let go of a stem was instantly to begin sliding. She tried stepping into his prints and it was worse, twice landing her on one knee. The pittosporum gave way to burrawangs and slender spotted gums, more like mottled poles than trees. Brian Harpur began grabbing hold of burrawang fronds and pulling himself along. Annette could believe what he was doing only because she'd seen his hands. Soon she was catching only glimpses of his hair.

She stopped and looked back along the gully. Not a speck of beach or ocean was visible. When she faced forward, the gully ahead was still. Panic spurted into her bloodstream. She fell to her knuckles and scampered beneath the arching fronds like a chimp.

She found him gazing up at a boulder shaped like a giant shaved head. She stood before he turned. He pointed his thumb towards the scar of his previous passage, up through ferns crowding the slope beside the boulder. 'First part's a scramble, then it levels out.'

The climb was actually easier than the gully sides, the soil firmer, with knobs of rock offering footholds. As he'd promised, the slope eased, and soon they were crossing patches of open ground under tall spotted gum and bangalay, the burrawangs growing singly, not massed. The climb, though, and her panic, had dried her mouth. Annette wished she'd insisted on a drink back at the creek. As if to mock her, she imagined she heard falling water.

She halted and looked at him. He grinned, nodded.

The water was falling over a sandstone ledge. Excitement overpowering her thirst, she scanned the walls and ceiling, before the realisation sank in that the ledge was too narrow to have afforded shelter, its floor too wet.

The water was so clean it was without taste. As she wiped her mouth, she studied the ledge. She could see no way up. There was a cleft, but choked with ferns.

'I can't climb that.'

'We don't have to.'

Brian Harpur led her to the cleft and parted the ferns at her feet to reveal, like a tiny stage, a flat-topped boulder. It took Annette a second to understand that it was a step! He invited her with a showman's flourish to mount it, then motioned *keep going!* She parted the ferns again, and there was another step. They were not spaced to a suburban notion of steps, but they were not rockfall. They'd been placed. The proof was a small square rock wedged into the angle where the lower boulder met the upper. It was a half-step. For shorter legs — a child's.

They climbed nine steps up to the ledge, he breaking stems so they wouldn't have to descend blind. From the top, she could see splinters of ocean. He'd walked to where the stream crossed the ledge, and she joined him. A skin of black algae said the flow was ephemeral, but millenia of storms like last night's had worn a channel.

Brian Harpur nodded at the spout leaping into space. 'It doesn't reach the beach. Must go down a crack.' He touched her elbow. 'Anyway, see what you reckon about these.'

He led her to where the water had eaten out a sore in the sandstone. Around it was a nest of hatchet-grinding grooves.

'Oh my,' Annette breathed, and crouched. They were far older than those at the Clyde, the grinding surfaces as scabbed with lichen as the surrounding rock.

The possibility suddenly hit her. That the men kneeling here had looked out over a valley running onto a plain, the ocean nowhere in sight, beyond the horizon. She resisted the impulse to blurt the thought, not wanting her grandiloquence repeated and laughed at if she was wrong. But something showed when she looked up, because he winked.

'This's only the entrée.'

Scrub and burrawangs crowded onto the ledge. Brian Harpur started along the only possible path, the creek, jumping from boulder to boulder. Annette followed, the water gurgling inches below their sandshoes.

He halted on a boulder just big enough for both of them and signed for her to join him, grabbing her elbow when she teetered, then, as quickly, releasing her. He pointed to a shelf exposed by the receding water. Five brimming hatchet grooves were small oval mirrors reflecting the broken sky.

'There'd be more I reckon — still under.' In the gaps between trunks, she could see a rockface. Brian Harpur saw where she was looking. 'No, where we're going's further up. Patience, mate. Things are running, but they can't run away.'

'What?'

He laughed and jumped to the next boulder.

Fifteen, sixteen more boulders and the bush on the left bank thinned, became a fern flat, a crease remaining where he'd walked before. They jumped onto a gravel beach. He made her go first.

When they were twenty metres from the rockface, she began slapping at the fronds obscuring her view. A sinuous red stain didn't make sense. Then she saw why — it had legs! She halted and stared. She'd seen paintings at Bredbo of tiny dancing men, and at Namadgi roos and emus little more than a handspan high. This goanna was life-size — and crawling up the wall!

She stepped over water lying along the dripline and only then observed how badly the goanna was weathered. She could see rock through the ochre. Also so weathered she hadn't spotted them till now were a double-line of three-toed tracks, and, at the height of her knees, a creature painted in ghostly white that appeared to be both reptile and rodent, and was no animal she'd ever seen, in life or in a book. Wanting to puzzle it out, she crouched, but Brian Harpur, gone past her and now standing where the rockface ended, called 'Hey!' and flicked fingers. As Annette joined him, he stepped aside and gave her a light push in the back.

It was the main shelter, ten feet deep, the ceiling blackened. At its far end was the dark mouth of an opening. He touched her arm, pointed down. In the angle of the wall was a grindstone. Wind had banked dust against its base, but a pass of the hand, a puff of breath, and the stone would stand ready to receive seed or ochre. A pace further on, beside perfect prints of his sandshoes, was a backed blade of milky quartz. He knew enough now to have left it in place, but an aureole of flattened dust said he'd blown it clean for a better look. From the blade the line of his prints ran along the centre of the shelter floor to the opening.

Aled would be pleased that he'd not wandered. He'd be less pleased by two sets of prints, Annette knowing better. She jumped to the dripline — and froze. Hidden till now by the wall's curvature, a slab had yawned off leaving a smooth panel — which was crowded with paintings!

She crept along the dripline. A fortuitous sunspot hitting the floor bounced light up the wall. At the centre of the panel, four hunters holding spears and waddies stood over a kangaroo with two spears in its side. Above the men — which she knew to interpret as behind — three more roos were hopping away. To the left of the hunting scene was a complex of painting and overpainting, much of it too faded to read. Annette made out, faintly, two more goannas and an echidna. They'd been overpainted with two larger echidna, and what looked like a clutch of eggs. An oval black disc with what she read as a string attached to its top corners was a dillybag, or perhaps a magnified pendant. The narrower space to the right of the hunters had been left almost bare. She made out what might have been footprints, and, more clearly legible, two small hatchets, their mulberry-red outlines still strong but the infill all but gone.

She heard Brian Harpur come up behind her. He said almost timidly, 'Only thing, there's none of those hands.'

She couldn't stop the scoffing sound she made, it burst from her. She turned quickly. Brian Harpur had reddened. She touched his arm. 'Sorry. They're uncommon this far south.'

'Oh. Right. But … it's good?'

'"Good" is *not* the word!' Annette felt her eyes brim. She swiped them with her palms, wiped her hands down her shirt in what she hoped was a brisk manner. 'And you know what else is missing? *Big* thing missing. Fish. Or have you seen some? What's round there?' She pointed to where the line of his prints disappeared round the far end of the shelter.

'Nothing. It's all here. And in the cave.'

'You ready for a pronouncement, then?' Her eyes were prickling again, but she didn't care. 'Whoever lived here didn't build the trap. They were here before the sea was. This place is o-old, Brian! It's Pleistocene! Has to be!'

'And Pleistocene's what?'

'Ice age! Before the sea rose.' Annette flapped a hand in the direction of the beach. 'Way before our cave down there.'

'And you need charcoal, right?' He nodded towards the opening. 'There's a pretty old fireplace in here.'

The cave was dim after the broken sunlight of the shelter. He had to point out the hearth, black specks barely visible through a blanket of roof fall. Annette didn't say — it was stating the obvious — *you've developed quite an eye in a short time.* She placed her feet carefully on his previous prints and squatted. To judge from the smoke-staining on the wall, the hearth probably ran deep. She straightened and studied the wall opposite.

'I thought you said there were more paintings.'

Brian Harpur pointed into the deeper gloom at the rear of the cave. 'Not animals — but they're painted, whatever they are.'

They were tally marks. In the textbook photograph she was recalling, the marks were engraved, but she knew, had read, they existed also as paintings, done with a finger or a twig brush. All the flatter part of the wall was filled with rows, from eye level down to her knees. The ones at eye level were black, with faint red streaks, iron aged to black. She dared to run a fingertip over two of the strokes. They had a light patina of age varnish.

'And there's these.'

He was pointing into a small alcove. The dust in the alcove was trampled. He'd not been able to stand still.

More tally marks, but this time engraved. What had grabbed him, though, were the circles, with a second circle pecked into their centres. A giggle squirted from him. 'Fried eggs.' They burst out laughing, then as quickly suppressed it, from the same impulse — that they'd laughed in church.

'They'll flip, Aled and Marilyn, when they see these.'

Brian Harpur smothered another giggle, and only then did she hear what she'd said and had to smother a second fit of her own. They were becoming hysterical.

There was a patch of sunlight just beyond the dripline. Annette flattened a fern and sat facing the creek to try to get her awed feelings under control. But she couldn't stop looking over her shoulder. This place would be her life for years! She couldn't guess what Brian Harpur might be thinking, an engineer.

He gave a light cough. 'So, where else have you seen those marks?' He wasn't in his own thoughts, he was absolutely with her!

'I haven't. Only photos.'

'Do you know what they mean? Because they're like sets. You know?'

She'd told him coming down in the car that her degree included applied maths.

'Which is why they're called tally marks. No one knows what of.'

'I'd bet our prof does.'

Annette was surprised to find herself bristling. 'He's got his limits, too. Not many people have been in a place as old as this, and that includes him.'

'It'll be over his head, you reckon?'

'Of course it won't! But he prefers to stay in the Holocene. After the sea rose.'

'Do we need to tell him, then? Either of them?'

She spun on her buttocks.

'Are you mad!'

He shrugged. 'I just thought you might want it. Change your honours to here.'

The surge of feelings brought on by his words made her speak roughly. 'Would you be given a bridge to build!'

She looked away to find the position of the sun.

'We need to fetch her up here. I'll go if you don't want a third trip.'

'No, I'll come. I didn't have breakfast.'

The descent was a blur, her mind running on all she'd seen, what it would become. When she sat on the log to remove her sandshoes, another thought hit — that already the place needed a name. The conventions of nomenclature would have it be North Teapot II. It deserved better, not second fiddle to a lesser site.

She said, when they stood, 'Would that little creek have a name, do you reckon?'

'Wouldn't even be on a map.'

He set off at a fast trudge towards the hard sand at the waterline, she skipping to keep up.

'You should get the naming right.'

'To the creek?'

'The site!'

'*My* name?'

'No, you dill! A descriptor name.' Annette burst out laughing, suddenly seeing in a journal heading what he'd said. 'Brian's Cave!'

He began to giggle, embarrassed, then snatched up a strap of seagrape and threw it at her.

Annette was glad to see Marilyn's head bobbing at the trench. She hadn't wanted the further half-hour to the cabins.

Brian Harpur slowed. 'Can you do the talking.'

'Me? Why? You found it!'

He took so long to answer she halted, halting him. He spoke looking towards the water. 'I don't want that stare.'

'What?'

'Please.'

Marilyn heard the squeal of their feet and stood up, alarm scrambling into her face when she saw theirs. 'What's the matter?'

'No! We've got another site! It's amazing. I've just been there. Brian found it.'

'Where?'

She looked dubious.

'Up behind the headland. You can't see from here, you need to come out on the beach.'

They walked her up a low dune. Annette pointed out the gully, then the ledge, glancing at Brian Harpur, who nodded. She described the shelter and the paintings, had barely started on the cave when Marilyn said, no longer hearing her, 'Jesus, it's Pleistocene.'

'That's what I think, too.'

Marilyn spun and fixed him with the stare he hadn't wanted. 'You're bloody uncanny. What on earth took you up there?'

Brian Harpur spoke looking at the sand and glancing at her from beneath his brow. 'Just a feeling. That slash always had a sort of pull.'

'You really are wasted in engineering.' She didn't wait for a reply, was suddenly all purpose. How far was the site from the gully mouth? Twenty-five minutes, Annette said, maybe thirty. Less, he murmured. Now they'd made a track of sorts.

Marilyn strode down the dune, 'Can you give me a hand with the iron.'

He wouldn't have told her himself, so Annette told her, that he hadn't had breakfast.

Marilyn gave a shrill, almost girlish, laugh. 'You're cheap to please.'

She apologised in advance for the peculiarity of her

sandwiches — mashed boiled egg and chutney. She gave Annette half of one, Brian Harpur both halves of the other. She'd also brought an orange, but saved it till they were walking, sending pieces of peel spinning towards the surf, then breaking the flesh into three.

Annette struggled to keep up with her on the climb from the gully. Her examination of the hatchet grooves was cursory. Brian Harpur looked his confusion at Annette.

She whispered, 'It's just, they're undateable.'

'Ah. Right.'

The paintings held her for some minutes, she squatted and studied the grindstone. But Annette saw that the magnet was the cave. Brian Harpur made to follow her inside, and Annette touched his elbow and pointed to the side of the entrance, where they wouldn't throw shadow.

Marilyn's lack of reverence shocked Annette. She blew dust from the tally marks, ran her fingers over the engravings. She lifted a loose flake of ochre and brought it on her palm to the broken sunlight at the cave mouth. The intensity of her concentration utterly precluded them.

A worm of irritation uncoiled in Annette's belly. Marilyn was crouched again at the hearth, sifting with her fingers. Annette glanced at Brian Harpur, hoping to see the same annoyance at being made non-existent. All she saw was admiration. This was a professional. His site was in good hands. *Fuck you too, then,* she said silently and walked out to the ferns.

She was, however, listening, and when she heard Marilyn come outside, turned — and saw they existed again. Brian Harpur more than she. It lessened Annette's anger, if only slightly, that he looked terrified at the sight of a beautiful woman advancing on him with gratitude filling her face. Marilyn pulled him into a quick hard embrace, then, still gripping his right arm, raised her right hand and cupped his cheek, which had flushed bright red.

'Thank you! Very much!' She gave the cheek a light slap — the strange reward meted out to those who've placed you in their debt. She released his arm but continued to look into his eyes. 'You truly *are* in the wrong profession if you can "feel" a place like this.' She turned to include Annette. 'Now, would you both mind leaving me here. I can find my way. And would you not say anything yet to the others — Aled needs to see this first.'

In the places where talking was possible, Brian Harpur grilled her about Marilyn. Where in the university she worked? What the Research School did? How well known she was as an archaeologist?

In the last half-hour, Annette had discovered another Marilyn, one she wouldn't have guessed existed, and didn't much like. It was difficult to equate this woman with the warm, generous person she'd worked beside at the Clyde and the Cotter. She had always thought Marilyn unaware of her beauty, but just now she had used it shamelessly. Brian Harpur was still in the throes of its effect. Annette couldn't refuse to answer, or answer churlishly, he wasn't a fool. But she was curt. He didn't hear.

His questions veered into the personal. What Annette thought of her? How long had she and Aled been married, did she know? He seemed to lord it over her a bit. Did it seem like that to Annette? That business with the dingo, for instance.

Annette was glad when they reached the gully, where the swish of the burrawangs and the risk of slipping ended talk. Soon she saw the pittosporum thicket that signalled they were near the gully mouth and heard the muffled boom of the surf.

Sue cornered her in the toilet.

'So where've you two been all day?'

There was no point lying about the direction they'd come from, they'd been seen. But Annette was determined not to disclose the site, at least not until she and Sue were safely in their sleeping bags. Annette knew her too well. Once told something, Sue rapidly convinced herself that the information was hers, to do with as she liked.

'We went over the headland to the next little beach. Brian knew a track.'

'And found what? You found *something*. It's in your face.'

'Yes, a beach.'

'Bullshit.'

The doorway was narrow, Sue was strong. Annette had no hope of pushing past.

'Could we have this conversation without the pong?'

'If I get a promise.'

'You'll blab. I know you.'

'And you know I'll keep *at* you. Simpler to tell me.'

'All right. But away from here. Come and get kindling.'

Sue had seen Brian Harpur arrive that morning at the beach with his bag of bream. Annette gave her the rest of the day from then, at the level of detail she'd have demanded if she'd been the listener. Sue asked only about the tool stone, was it solely quartzite. Yes, Annette told her. The place *way* pre-dated the Clyde. She begged her again not to say anything, not even hints. Aled was back next day, and they would all go up there.

'Okay. Now that I know.' Sue dumped her armful of sticks in a clatter. She bent a bracken frond to the ground and lowered herself onto it. 'You too. Sit.'

'What's this about?'

'Just sit.'

Annette laid her sticks down and sat.

'Different but related topic. You're spending a lot of time alone with him. So what's happening? Anything?'

'Not really.'

'How come?'

'I'm not even sure I want anything to happen.' *Especially after this afternoon*, she wanted to add. But she didn't want to believe, either, the change in the person she'd come down the gully with.

'Not the impression I got. From either of you. He wouldn't

be the worst you could find for your first, you know.'

Annette shook her head.

'Why not? You'd know when you're safe. And lots of nice places on a beach.'

'Sue, please. I know it bothers you. It bothers me, too. But don't push me, all right. I'll decide in my own time.'

'You want me to speak to him?'

'No!'

'Okay! I was just asking.'

Sue retracted her feet and shot out her arms to propel herself into a crouch and began shuffling her sticks back into a bundle. Annette's were still lying neatly. She gathered them into her arms, stood and waited. If she strode away, Sue would think her a wounded petal.

Brian Harpur arrived at the fire just on dark with two cleaned flathead.

Annette was surprised into hope when he came directly to her, the fish still hanging from his hand. But all he wanted to know was whether they'd eaten the bream.

She'd completely forgotten them. She lied, said she hadn't wanted to bring them out without his say-so. But everyone had eaten — apart from him and Marilyn.

'She still not back?'

'No.'

He helped himself to sausages and bread, ate fast, then vanished into the darkness and returned with young bracken fronds. He wrapped the flathead in fronds and foil and tucked the packages behind the fireplace.

The first they knew of Marilyn's arrival was when the lamp bloomed in her and Aled's cabin. Ten minutes later, she joined them at the fireplace. Her face betrayed nothing but the tiredness of a long day in the trench.

Paul and Stuart had gone in Vicky's car to the roadhouse on the highway and returned with a carton, to round off the 'holiday'. Paul asked her if she'd like a beer. Die for one, Marilyn said. He pushed the tab, put the can in her hand. She took a thirsty swig, then placed the can down and picked up a plate and the tongs. Brian Harpur jumped to his feet and blurted that there were a couple of fresh flathead already wrapped, they'd only take five minutes. That would be wonderful, she said. If no one else wanted them. They'd all eaten, he told her. He snatched the foil packages from their hiding place. But when he moved to lay them on the grill, Marilyn stepped in front of him and took them from his hands.

'I think you've done enough for one day.'

The others had returned to being raucous, she'd spoken in little above a murmur, but Annette — watching — heard.

Brian Harpur's face glowed.

*

Next afternoon Annette was with Vicky on the pit sieve, Paul on buckets. He put down the one he was carrying and leaned over the sieve. 'Hop to it, kiddies. Daddy's home.'

Annette stopped the frame and squinted into the salt glare. Aled was coming across the bay of sand. He saw he'd been spotted and raised his arm in a cheery wave. Paul called towards the trench, 'Marilyn?' Her frowning work-mask rose above the rim. 'Someone to see you.' She turned to look — and sprang from the trench.

They exchanged a kiss, then walked in lockstep back to the cave, Aled with an arm across her shoulders, she an arm about his waist. Her face, Annette saw, was the proverbial cat's with the cream, so close to being able to break the news. Aled detached himself and walked to the sieve, asked what had been turning up. Just the usual, Annette forced herself to say.

He looked satisfied when he came out of the cave, Brandy and Sue in tow. He fluttered his fingers for them to gather. The news was good. The lab believed they could have a date reasonably quickly. Palaeontology were *very* interested in an evident amputation. He grinned into their circle of faces. It was looking like North Teapot, too, would make a bit of a splash. Sue caught Annette's eye, *mate, you don't know the half of it.* Annette frowned and shook her head. Aled saw.

'What?'

Sue butted in smoothly, 'Just me giving her cheek.'

He waved them back to work, moved to go to the tools to

fetch his trowel. Marilyn intercepted him, took his arm. She spoke so low Aled was forced to incline his head.

He reared. 'What — now?'

Marilyn steered him out towards the dunes, but after some twenty paces released his arm, not wanting, Annette thought, to be followed by the prurient speculation of those who didn't yet know what this little walk was about.

Aled refused to go further than the first dune. Marilyn again took his arm and turned him towards the headland. She spoke using her hand to create the ledge and steps, the shelter, the cave. They couldn't see Aled's face, but his back proved eloquent — the hard set of his shoulders, the redness that rose up his nape — and not only to Annette.

'That didn't go down too well, whatever it was,' Paul said.

'Sure didn't,' Vicky murmured.

Aled pulled his arm free. Marilyn strode back to them.

'Ah, something's come up that Aled and I need to take a look at. We'll probably be a couple of hours. Leave the trench, just continue in the pit. First, though, you'd all better listen to Annette.'

She forgot only the engraved 'fried eggs', and Brian Harpur prompted her. By then, details didn't matter, she was a teacher trying to control a class of infants. Greg and Stuart grabbed Brian Harpur's arms and spun him in a mad Highland fling that ended with them all sprawled in the sand, he flushed and giggling with both pleasure and embarrassment.

'You're a bastard,' Brandy accused Annette gaily. 'But you're a bloody good actor.' He swung his finger to Brian Harpur, who was getting to his feet. 'You, too! You're both bastards!'

Paul, though, stalked past Brandy and planted himself in front of her. 'Fuck the acting, we could have gone up there yesterday.'

'She asked us not to say anything.'

'Yeah? Well, I'm sick of this mummy-daddy-and-the-kids shit.'

'Paul! Hey!' Sue pointed across the bay of sand. 'There's your answer! I'll drive you in, and you catch the bus!'

'Piss off. I want to see this place.'

'We *all* fucking do!'

Paul stalked away, but only to the top of the closest dune, where he flopped down facing the headland.

'Thanks,' Annette murmured.

'Yes, well, getting bolshie's the last thing we need.'

Annette felt a shy tap on the arm. Vicky was standing with a pad and pencil. 'I'm just wondering — could you draw it? What you saw.'

They walked into the shade of the cliff and she sat on a fallen slab, Vicky leaning over her shoulder. She began on the hunting scene. A pair of legs came and stood in front of her. Then another. Even Sue's.

Afterwards, no one wanted to pick up a trowel or bucket. They lay on the cool sand in the shadow of the cliff. Stuart fell asleep. But when Paul shouted from the dune, 'Hoi! They're coming!' they leapt to their feet and ran to join him.

Marilyn was in front, Aled following in a fast trudge, its intention, Annette saw, to keep up, but not catch up.

'What's that about, do you reckon?' Sue said softly.

'Ownership.' The word had arrived in her mouth without thought.

'What?'

Annette shook her head.

Marilyn halted at the foot of the dune, summoned them down. Her voice was flat and hard, and no one dallied. Aled had halted twenty metres away. Marilyn didn't look to see where he was. Her tone when she began to speak was dry, almost without inflexion.

She assumed the new site had been described. She looked at Annette, who nodded. She believed it too important to wait. She and Aled had been unable to agree on a strategy that would enable a rapid yet full assessment to be carried out simultaneously with the work remaining to be done here. She'd therefore informed him that as of today, as of right now, she would be leaving the beach and going up to the headland. She would put down a test pit by herself if this impromptu meeting gave her no other option. But anyone who wished to join her was welcome. They did, however, need to be crystal clear that choosing to join her meant leaving the cabins, the team, and this site. The camping would be primitive, to say the least, and the hours long. But she believed the importance of the new site demanded the decision she'd taken.

It was her role to speak, Annette knew, but she couldn't make her tongue work, the ultimatum so final, and so coldly delivered.

Vicky said, 'We couldn't do both? You know, roster ourselves differently?'

'No.'

The snap in that one word froze all nice notions of academic discourse.

'I fully understand the constraints most of you are under, some more than others.' The tone was softer. 'I won't be taking personally whatever decision any of you makes. So — anyone? I'm sorry to hurry you, but I want to be up there, have a camp of some sort, before dark.'

Brian Harpur's hand rose instantly. Then Sue's. Annette slid hers into her pockets and made fists.

'We done?' Marilyn's eyes flicked over their faces. 'Okay, thank you. Three of us will be enough. But if any of you has second thoughts, Annette can give you directions.'

There were mutters of 'see you', 'bye', but they were too confused, on both sides, by the suddenness of the split and the vagueness of its conditions, to know whether formal goodbyes were what the moment required. Sue looked at Annette, lifted her shoulders, *what can I do — my supervisor?* Annette nodded. Brian Harpur brought his hand to his chest, bent his fingers. It was a child's wave, and she refused to return it.

Marilyn had moved away so as not to cramp the lame, and largely dumb, farewells. But when they looked like dragging out, she clicked finger and thumb and pointed along the beach in the direction of the cabins.

It was weird — those remaining being in the majority — but when the three passed the tent and headed out across the bay of sand, the sight of their backs gave Annette — and not only her, she saw — a feeling of terrible loneliness, as if they at the cave were a lost expedition sending out a rescue party and knowing in their bones that the three would reach safety and they would die. Their figures grew sparkling haloes as Annette watched them diminish.

Greg cut short her wallowing. 'This is fucked.'

'Sure is,' Brandy muttered. 'We can do both!'

Aled had walked to the dune hollow. The mutterings stopped. Annette saw him glance down to find the exact spot where Marilyn had stood. He flashed them an angry smile.

'My apology to you all for being forced to be part of a most unpleasant debate. As you've guessed, this split was *not* at my suggestion. I'm very aware that by thanking you for your loyalty, I risk insulting you, but thank you. We're a smaller but still perfectly viable team.'

Annette thought when Greg cleared his throat he was going to say openly what she was thinking — that 'loyalty' had nothing to do with it. Aled was head of a department from which they all hoped one day to graduate. But Greg said, 'Why's it even necessary? There's enough of us.'

Aled didn't look at him, as if they'd all spoken. 'Possibly. Perhaps even probably. But there's a big difference — which I hope you'll grasp when you've given it thought — between being flexible and losing sight of one's priorities.' Annette heard in the straining for evenness of tone just how angry he was. Aled lowered his head and gave an ugly, strangled cough. Vicky broke away to go to the soak. 'No, Vick! But thank you. I'll finish what I'm saying.' He waited for her to return. 'What do I mean? This. I'm not for a second saying the place I've just been isn't important. It is. Or will be. Immensely. But not *more* important than where we're standing. Yes? As I've been at pains to both state and demonstrate throughout my career, the age per se of a site is not the chief measure of its worth. What and how much it tells us is! And here, at this cave, we are being given, in extraordinary detail, the other half of the lives of those people at the sites on the Clyde. In fact we're exceeding the Clyde.' He jabbed his arm towards the clifftop. 'We're finding the people themselves. We've stood looking into the grave of a hugely important man. We've handled his bones, his grave goods! That, I assure you, is not something you'll be granted at every site in your careers. So don't for a minute assume that your remaining here means you've chosen the lesser site. You haven't.'

A hard, flat voice in Annette's head said, *And the rest, please.*

Aled must have seen the same thought in other faces, because he tilted his head, exhaled a long breath. 'Not the last word on the matter, I see.' He looked at them again. 'First, let me say, it won't be the only time you see a major disagreement at a site. I proposed to my wife that we stay together and finish here, then return to Canberra, put in a proposal for new funding — which, let me tell you, would have been granted in a trice on the photos alone! Then at Easter and properly in May, up on the headland, all of us, this same team. She, for whatever reason, chose not to see the logic of that. That a site unseen for millenia can't wait a few months longer.' He opened his hands. 'So there you have it.'

'And, what … you're saying she didn't *give* a reason?' Paul said softly.

'Ahh … no-o. I just don't accept that the reason I was given is the true one.' He turned to find her. 'I could use that drink now, Vick.'

Normally so biddable, Vicky didn't move.

'Fine.' Aled clasped his hands beneath his chin. 'Any archaeologist — if you're worth your salt — you want your name on a big site. My wife would like hers to be the principal name on that site up there. That, of course, is not the reason she gave, and equally "of course" denied it when I put to her that it was.' He lowered his hands. 'Those of you who are new to my methodology would, over the last weeks, have gathered that I don't like to see a site hurried. You can ruin a site picking the eyes out of it. Truly, you're better off not being a part of what my wife intends up there. I certainly wouldn't wish to be.'

Annette instinctively turned her head to find Sue. They'd have rolled their eyes at one another. Aled wanted *badly* to be the one in charge up there. It, too, was only a day from the Clyde. If there were pieces of quarry silcrete down in the Pleistocene levels, *he* wanted to be the one who found them. The evidence that 'his' people had camped and hunted here when North Teapot was not a lake and beach but the rim of a wooded plain. Unbroken occupation from ten, twelve, even twenty thousand years Before Present to a few hundred. How many archaeologists could boast a sequence to match it? But the major name on the papers would not be his. Nor would he be the one to conduct *This Day Tonight* into the cave, explain to camera the site's enormous significance to an understanding of the east coast in the last ice age. His wife would be that person.

'I might get that drink.'

'I'll get it,' Paul said.

Brandy said, 'So ... will we even get to see up there?'

Aled lifted his hand towards Paul moving away towards the soak.

Annette watched the sand sifting over her insteps and didn't look up till she heard the squeak of feet. Paul began to rotate the pannikin to offer him the handle, but Aled seized it by the belly, threw back his head, and poured the water down his throat. He retained the pannikin in his hands, turning it in his palms as if memorising the gaudy flowers decorating its sides.

'I've been asked, Paul, will you all get to see the site up there. I can only say that you should make every effort to. Whether you actually *do*, however, isn't up to me. But, as I say, make the effort.' He pointed with the pannikin handle towards the cave mouth. 'All right — get back to work, shall we?'

'Um ...' Greg said, 'won't they be needing stuff from here?'

Aled spoke at the cliff. 'No equipment, of any description, will be leaving this site. Nor the cabins. Is that clear?' No one spoke. 'Good. Now let's get cracking.'

Annette turned and, with Vicky and Paul, began heading to the sieves.

'Annette. A word?'

He watched past her shoulder until satisfied the others were out of hearing, then met her gaze. 'I don't think it's transgressing common knowledge that you'd have reasons other than archaeology for wanting to go up there —' he gestured towards the headland — 'from time to time.' Annette opened her mouth to protest, and Aled cut her short. 'I'm not testing you, I'm actually suggesting that you go. Apart from the ah, personal reasons, I'm sure you'd like to see the bone that comes out of that hearth. The most obvious spot for a test pit, wouldn't you say?'

He didn't need her opinion. But he waited.

'Yes.'

'I doubt she'll have any objection to your going up there,

in fact I suspect your eye will be very welcome. And there's no objection at this end. Okay?'

Annette woke knowing the soft knocking on the wall behind her head was not Aled's morning knock. She peeled out of her bag and crept to the window. The louvres were fully open. She put her nose above a louvre and peered down and made out, through the crusted flywire, the pale oval of his face. She whispered, 'What do you want?'

Brian Harpur put a finger to his lips, signed with the other hand that she come outside.

The lock was rusted, loud to unlock. She listened towards Vicky's room. Surely the knocking had woken her, too. But after a moment she heard a whimper and the hiss of polished cotton as Vicky turned in her bag, then a sleeping silence. She gripped the key in the fingers of both hands and turned slowly till she won the tongue's metallic clung.

He was standing at the bottom of the steps. Her head fizzed with possibilities. Likely but dull was that he had bone to show her. The wilder hope, and fear, was that he'd decided to make a move, believing he mightn't see her again. She pulled the door to and started down the steps, feeling for each before placing her weight. Would he, when she reached the bottom, reach for her hand? But he took a step back, and moved off, leaving her no choice but to follow.

The night wasn't as dark as she'd first thought, the cabin walls, tussocks, the bush along the fence lit by a milky light falling from the sky. Brian Harpur led her to where wattles and gum saplings made a cave of shadow and turned to face her. Annette held her hands in plain view, within reach, then asked herself why, when he'd already refused, and dropped them.

'I was starting to think you'd moved in with Vick.'

'I do cope on my own.'

'It was a joke. Sorry. Not a jokey time.'

'No.'

'I came to fill you in on what we're doing.'

'Oh yes?'

He picked up on the tone. 'What's that mean?'

'Nothing. Anyhow, I'm free to find out for myself. He doesn't mind me going up there. If she doesn't.'

'How come?'

If you can't work that out, Annette thought, *I'm not 'filling you in'.*

'So what *are* you doing?'

'Done, mate. Heaps.'

They'd been in to the Bay. The Kombi was Marilyn's, not 'theirs'.

'Yes, I know,' Annette interjected, 'I've ridden in it.'

They'd bought pointing trowels, tape measure, paper bags, stringline, timber, and mesh to make sieves. Marilyn had hired a dumpy. He'd made a couple of ranging poles. Annette thought,

You're in archaeology whether you want to be or not, the way the terminology now rolls off your tongue. He'd walked out to a firetrail and slashed a foot track back in, so they had access to the road without needing to come near Teapot. Marilyn wanted the fern flat kept intact, so they'd set up a camp on the other side of the creek. She and Sue had a dog tent, he was sleeping under a tarp. They'd rigged another, bigger, tarp for storage and a workspace. If it didn't bucket they'd be okay. Enough to keep the creek running would be good. He'd made the women a loo. He was using the bush. It was all a bit rough, but no rougher than the Clyde sounded. They were ready to start excavating.

So — the point of his visit — she should ditch the beach and join them.

Anger boiled up in her. She wanted to jab a finger into his chest for every word. *I might have if you hadn't been so quick to stick up your hand, and without so much as a look at me! You wanted to gift me the place, remember. Where did that go? As if I don't know.*

She tried to keep her voice level. 'Did *she* send you?'

He shook his head. 'They wouldn't even know I'm not there.'

'Brian, I hate this. I want to do both. So do the others. But he'd have to give in, and he won't. I don't have a choice, he's my head of department *and* my supervisor!'

'Head of department's not bothering Sue.'

'I'm not Sue.' Annette didn't want to be asked to explain that statement and said quickly, 'So has she decided — Marilyn —

where she's putting a pit?'

'Yeah — on the hearth.'

He was, she noted, no longer calling it a 'fireplace'.

'And she's done what you said, given me naming rights. I came up with "The Ferns". So that's what we're calling it.'

Annette waited to be asked if she liked it.

'So … when do you reckon you might be up?'

'I don't know. I wouldn't think before there's some bone for me to look at.'

'What if there's heaps? And keeps coming?'

'It won't change my answer. Anyway, it's not even certain I'll be welcome.'

'I can ask for you.'

She didn't want another nocturnal visit if it was to be as futile as this.

'I think I can do that myself.'

She waited for him to speak, which turned into just looking at one another. He made a pushing gesture as if she were a gate he was closing, and stepped back, then turned and strode towards the gap in the wattles that marked the steps down the cliff to the beach. Annette followed the grey of his blue shirt until it dipped into shadow. No pale oval looked back at her.

Next day, after knock-off, Paul, Stuart, and Vicky visited what they came back calling 'The Ferns'.

Greg and Brandy went the day after. By dinner they hadn't returned.

Annette was lying on her bed reading in the last of the muddy light filtering through the louvres. She thought it was her memory playing tricks when she heard her name whispered. It was repeated. The voice wasn't Brian Harpur's. She dropped the book on the mattress and went to the window.

'Can we come in?'

She warned Vicky that they had visitors.

They sat at the table. Vicky ghosted in and perched on the arm of the settee. Annette had already guessed their purpose, her guess soon confirmed. They wanted to defect. She knew Aled better, how did she think he would react? Badly, she told them. But they might not learn *how* badly till they were back on campus. The look they exchanged said they'd argued the same question all along the beach.

'What you saw's a test pit. When she gets the funding, there'll be a proper excavation, and you can put your names down. He can't hold that against you, it's a separate dig.'

'What if she doesn't want us?' Greg said. 'We've blown *this* chance then, haven't we.'

Annette heard he didn't want empty reassurance.

'Yes. But she's not stupid. She's seen you're both good on a site. And you heard what she said, she wouldn't take anyone's decision personally.'

Brandy leaned into her gaze. 'So what are the odds they'll sort this out? They'd have to, wouldn't they? At some stage they're going back to the same house.'

You lie and they're gone, she told herself. *They'll decide you're Aled's.*

'She already runs her own sites, like out at the Cotter. He doesn't play any part, or not a visible one. I can't say what happens at home.'

'So, what you *are* saying is — they *won't* sort this out.'

'Not if it means him working under her direction.'

Brandy looked at Greg, who tilted his head, *I told you.*

They stayed at Teapot, but the enthusiasm went out of them. Over the next two days she felt hers, too, ebb away. Stuart and Paul caught the malaise, then Vicky. Soon all of them were little better than robots.

Annette found her state of deadened curiosity baffling. Especially so when Aled's promise was being realised. The pit was down a metre, into a lens of sand grey with charcoal and dense with flakes, bone, and shell. The trench had hit what appeared to be an oven, complete with scorched cooking stones and fragments of charred bracken. There was so much fish bone she was forced into counting only the species markers and weighing the rest. She and Aled extracted from the oven floor the first dateable whale bone he'd ever found.

Yet, despite all this richness, despite an ochred dingo, despite the 'clever fella', the place she and the others wanted to be was up on the headland. Still doing the same tedious jobs — sieving, counting, and weighing bone, sorting flakes — but watched over by those painted walls, and knowing that the flakes and bone were coming from a pit that was almost certainly going down into the Pleistocene. As much material as the beach was yielding, neither pit nor trench would, or even could, go past the mid-Holocene, at best 3000 or 4000 BP. The beach itself would be only a few thousand earlier. The real game was up at The Ferns, 'chasing the oldest'.

Aled suggested it might be time she went 'up there'. From the beginning, he'd refused to give the site its name. Annette thought the ban childish. 'Up there' became a coded joke. Now she was going 'up there'.

She'd told the others the only route beyond the ledge was the creek bed, but, when she reached the ledge, she found an opening hacked in the burrawangs and a track carpeted with slashed fronds. The track emerged at the fern flat. The three were standing at a sieve set up against the blank wall, well beyond the art panels. They heard her and turned. Brian Harpur's hand shot up in a wave, then, as quickly, he lowered it and glanced at the two women, a guilty glance, Annette thought. But Marilyn's smile was a welcoming one.

'You finally got here. Again.'

Sue murmured 'hi', and Annette returned it. She didn't look at Brian Harpur.

'These are from today.' Marilyn lifted from Sue's palm the biggest of three quartzite points and passed it to Annette. She felt the tip, as sharp as when it was flaked.

'We're into a lot of small tools, mostly quartz, nothing from the Clyde. No dates, of course, but I'm guessing occupation here ceased well before our dates for there. Probably when the sea arrived.'

Annette proffered the point back, and Sue reached and took it and returned it to her palm, the proprietorial edge to the gesture a statement to Annette of her status in the tiny team, that she'd made the right choice and Annette the wrong one.

Marilyn appeared not to notice the silent exchange. She inclined her hand towards the cave mouth. 'Come in.'

The pit was against the wall, but, cleverly, pegged a half-metre further in than she'd expected, thus exposing the profiles of both the hearth and the sitting area to its rear, the warmer side. The points had come from the sitting area. Another one was projecting from the base of the pit wall. Annette's eyes went, though, to the mass of charred and compacted bone in the hearth itself. 'Yes,' Marilyn said, 'by the kilo. Mainly roo and wallaby, which I can sort. But I'd love if you could take a look at the smaller stuff. Do you have time?'

'A couple of hours. I'd rather not go down in the dark.'

'We can lend you a torch. Or a blanket.'

'I'd prefer to get back.'

But she was pleased, after the cold parting on the beach, to have found the woman so friendly.

Marilyn asked her over to camp, suggesting to Brian Harpur that while she organised some samples he show Annette his 'handiwork'.

The clearing was a made one, and old. He'd trimmed or grubbed out only the necessary shrubs, defronded but left the burrawangs. He led her first to the firepit. It was big enough for logs, with a boulder surround. A wire chop-griller leaned against a boulder, and a newly blackened billy hung on a hook and chain over embers, from which the smoke of a lunch fire leaked. There was a shower enclosure of tightly compacted tea-tree lashed to a sapling frame beneath a gum with a bucket rope thrown over a low bough and hitched to a fresh nail. A washing-up table of callicoma stems had a burrawang frond for a drainer. Three T-shirts hung on a line propped in the air by a forked pole. He pointed out the loo at the edge of the trees. 'If you need it.'

When they returned to the tarpaulin 'lab', Marilyn took one look at her face and grinned. 'Yes, we could have done with him at the Clyde.' Brian Harpur's neck and face flushed a wild pink.

Marilyn sent him back to help Sue and led her in under the tarpaulin. Annette read her work strategy immediately — dig fast, sieve only samples, bag the rest. Cartons of sealed and labelled plastic bags already occupied half the space beneath the trestle table.

Marilyn caught her look of horrifed disbelief. 'Only if we run out of time, otherwise we'll sieve that, too.' She laughed.

'The poor old Kombi'd never make it up the mountain.' She conducted Annette to where five smaller bags were lined up beside a writing pad with a magnifying glass lying on it. 'They're in vertical order. It's brushed, but not washed. Sorry, why am I telling *you*. Not exactly a lab scope, but the best the Bay had to offer.' She rested her hand on the first in the row of bags. 'Thus far, no fish. From my observation.' She lifted her hand, fingers crossed.

'What about from a river?'

Marilyn turned fully and looked at her. 'What river would that be? Up here?'

Annette shrugged. 'I just thought I should ask.'

'I suppose, yes. Tick every box, even non-existent ones.'

She smiled and went.

Annette's procedure was the same with each bag, a rapid sort into macropod bone and the rest, before setting about identifying as much as she could of the rest. Most was small mammal — bandicoot, potoroo, brushtail and ringtail possum. The small percentage of reptile was goanna and blue tongue. Only two birds, cockatoos. And no fish.

She left the bags as she'd found them and lay the magnifying glass on the pad, now bearing a species list. She visited the loo. It had tea tree walls, frond roof, a plank seat, and a view down a fern gully. They could definitely have used Brian Harpur at the Clyde.

She jumped the creek and walked up through the ferns to

where Sue was working the sieve. Sue stilled the frame. 'So —
any?'

'No.'

'Great.'

'Well, it's what the walls say.' She'd spoken more tersely than
she'd intended, saw Sue bristle.

'You were given the choice.'

'What choice? For me.'

Sue lifted the brush to point at the panel. *Even after you'd
seen that?*

Annette went into the cave and told Marilyn.

'Excellent! And thank you. Still doesn't mean there isn't any,
but less likely to be. So you can tell Aled — if he asks, that is —
that no one here went fishing.'

Outside, the light was dropping. Annette said she'd get going.
Brian Harpur stood up at the creek, the billy's sides shining.
Annette looked slightly past him, shook her head. She asked
Marilyn would she mind if she sat for a moment round the
corner, at the other panel, she wanted another look at the little
white creature.

'Sketch it.'

'I didn't bring anything. It's okay, a look's all I want.'

She nodded to Sue, who answered with a lift of the chin.

The long walk back to the cabins was the loneliest she'd ever
done.

*

Gorman came to the breakfast fire next morning. He had a letter for Vicky. His eyes, though, didn't leave Aled.

'Haven't seen the Kombi or your wife for a few days. Not got crook and gone back, I hope, is she?'

He caught the darting looks. He must also have noted the smaller number around the table. Annette couldn't think what explanation Aled would give.

'I don't think we've *ever* seen your wife, Mr Gorman. Perhaps if you'd lend us your binoculars.'

The blood drained from Gorman's face, then flooded back in. He turned and rocked away up the paddock as fast as his hips allowed, his gammy arm jerking. Annette felt almost sorry for him.

As if to mock the man, Marilyn showed up that evening, in the Kombi. Aled was in his cabin, the rest of them were at the fireplace. Marilyn got out clutching paper bags. Annette had thought — the clatter unmistakeable — Aled would come to the door, but it remained resolutely shut. Marilyn smiled hello and cocked a finger towards the cabin, and they nodded.

They spoke in murmurs, wanting to catch any raised voice. The only sound in half an hour was the muted screech of a chair on the plank floor. She came out alone clutching the bags, closed the door behind her. Paul called did she want a cuppa. Marilyn shook her head.

'Thanks, I'll get back.'

No one spoke until the Kombi clattered into life, moved off.

Greg got in first. 'She looked pleased. Might be time for another visit.'

'I think we wait and see how pleased *he* is,' Brandy muttered.

He'd no sooner spoken than the cabin door was snatched open. 'Annette! Could I see you a minute.'

The Kombi was idling at the sliprails, Marilyn sliding the top rail back into place. Aled's eyes didn't leave Annette. She was almost to the steps when he skipped down them and set off towards the cliff, glancing once to see that she was following. She tried to guess where they might be going. If the beach, they'd need a torch to get back. But at ten paces he stopped and wheeled round. She halted where she was, warned to by his face.

'She says she's already down a metre. Is that true?'

'It was nearly that when I saw it. So by now I'd say so.'

Aled slammed his right fist into his other palm, and she jumped. 'What the fuck is she using, pick and shovel!'

He glanced past her, though, towards the fireplace. He wasn't so angry that he didn't care whether his words carried.

'She's bagging whole spits and just sieving samples.'

Annette sounded to her own ears calm, which made her calmer.

'At least she's doing *that*.' Aled jammed his hands onto his hips and turned his back to her. Had she been dismissed? But on a site they were — his word — colleagues.

'Um ... so what did she bring?'

He said over his shoulder, 'Points and scrapers, all quartz, a hatchet, and what she *claims* to be a pebble chopper, found this morning, but which defies logic, seeing I gather she's still finding small tools.'

Her stomach clenched. She wanted to say, but didn't dare, *Well, a pebble chopper is or it isn't, and I think she'd know.*

'She'd like us to sink a second pit, and I've said no. She said, too, you'd been through the bone and there's no fish. I'd like to know how she arrives at that conclusion, given her methods.'

He'd said 'she', but Annette heard he'd meant her as well. She told him she'd examined sampling from five vertical quarter-spits and had a good look at the hearth profile. There was so much bone it was impossible not to have sampled fish if it was there.

Aled gave a savage flick of the head, but didn't look at her.

'That's one answer. Thank you.'

She lingered, but the lengthening silence made clear she *had* this time been dismissed. She turned and walked to the fireplace. They leaned in around her, hissing questions.

'Wait, just wait!' she hissed back.

At last he spun and strode to his steps, leapt up them, shut the door.

Annette told them. Marilyn had found her first pebble chopper!

Next morning Aled got them started, then set off up the beach. Paul climbed a dune and sat. They continued to work, but watched him. Finally he stood, called that Aled had gone into the gully.

He returned late morning, hunted them out of the cave, and worked for the rest of the day on his own.

The others left at five. Annette was rostered with Vicky for the tent. They cleared the sieve, bagged and labelled for a further half-hour, then fetched their towels. They kept their swim short, wanting to get a fire going and cook before dark.

They were drying themselves when Aled emerged fom the cave. He must have seen them against the green of the water, their skins orange, the pink of her bikini almost fluorescent. She dropped a hand from her towel, ready to return a wave. Aled trudged out into the bay of sand. They watched his shrinking figure, each alone with her thoughts, or so she thought. But when Vicky muttered, 'The fun's sure gone out of this,' she plucked the almost-identical words from Annette's head.

Later, lying in their bags in darkness dense as ink, Vicky said, 'Can I … ask a personal question?'

Annette knew who and what it would be about. 'Depends how personal.'

'You can probably guess. It's how you feel about Brian being — you know — up there.'

She stalled. 'What do you mean?'

'I thought he'd choose to stay here.'

She wasn't prying, Annette knew that. Sue, too, was gone.

She was offering herself as a friend.

'We weren't on together, even though you all believe otherwise. He found the place, he was always going to put his hand up. End of story.'

Vicky persisted — and was as perceptive as Annette had feared. 'What about ... Marilyn?'

'What about her?'

'The others are saying — the boys — that she's, you know, his reason. More his reason.'

Despite what she'd told herself a minute earlier, she felt the coldness that was for her the first stage of anger. 'Based on what?'

'Well ... they've been up there.'

'So have you. Why are you telling me what "they" think?'

'Because I'm not very experienced at these things. But I just thought you might want to talk to someone.'

'No. I don't.'

Deliberately making the cotton of the bag shriek, she rolled over to face the wall of the tent. The canvas was invisible, but the coolness it emanated she felt on her wet cheeks.

The tide was coming in, the shore break dumping. In the hush between two waves, Vicky whispered, 'Sorry.'

Aled worked through lunch. The rest of them sat with their sandwiches in the shade of the ancient coast banksia growing near the soak.

It was Paul who raised the subject of Aled's sullenness. He no longer bothered to hide his dislike of the man. 'Whatever he saw up there yesterday pissed him off mightily. We should go up for a look.'

'What, just go?' Stuart said.

'This arvo! Once we knock off it's free time. Only, we should go as a group.'

The others looked at Annette. 'Not much he can say if it's all of us. I wouldn't mind seeing.'

She wasn't sure, though, of the reception they would get, the six of them turning up uninvited. But the mood at The Ferns was an elation Marilyn and Sue were more than willing to share. Brian Harpur scampered across the creek to awaken the fire.

Two days had passed since Marilyn's visit to the cabins. She and Sue were now down over a metre. The hearth had bottomed out at a band of buff sandy clay. The clay went down another seventeen centimetres, almost sterile, then they'd struck another hearth, far older. From beside it, they'd taken eight more pebble tools, horsehoof cores, end scrapers, more waste flakes than they'd yet had time to sort, and — the prize so far — a quartz oblong the length of Annette's middle finger with a cutting edge of evenly spaced pressure-flaked notches, which Marilyn was calling a 'saw'. She took it back and placed in Annette's hand the thighbone of an eastern grey, clay-orange, and split to extract the marrow — the oldest bone Annette had ever held with the pit dirt still on it.

'The only question now,' Marilyn said, 'is how *far* into the Pleistocene we go!'

Late the following morning, Vicky touched Annette's arm and pointed. A large solitary figure wearing a straw hat and what looked like a safari jacket was plodding through the sand towards the cave. Annette thought at first — impossible — that it was Gorman, then recognised the distinctive pregnant belly. Tom Sieglitz. He saw he'd been spotted and lifted his arm.

She said to Vicky, 'You'd better go in and tell him.'

Aled greeted him and shook his hand, dispatched Stuart to the soak for a pannikin of water, but Annette saw that the man had picked up instantly on the hostility beneath the welcome. He'd never set foot at the Clyde. She wondered what had emboldened him to arrive here uninvited and unannounced, then understood. Of course. Word of the 'clever fella' had travelled even during the break. She saw the man look again towards the cave mouth, knew who he was looking for. The arrival of his water distracted him.

Aled took him inside to the pit. Then brought him out to the trench. He'd heard, too, about the 'matriarch'. Aled pointed out the section where she'd lain, the ochre staining still visible.

'And ... the grave? That ... open to view?' He grinned. *To me, surely. Having come all this way.*

'If you don't mind a climb.' Aled lifted a finger towards the near-vertical face scarred by their feet, the short cut they'd made to avoid the trek across the sand. Sieglitz stared in horror.

'That the only darn way?'

Aled, she saw, might have answered yes, but Vicky piped up, 'Did you come on the National Parks track? You sort of passed it.'

Sieglitz shot Aled a look, then returned his gaze to Vicky. 'No, the beach. But if it's not a cliff, I'll take it.' He knew something was wrong. He turned again to Aled and said airily, 'So — where's the lovely partner-in-grime?'

When they came back from the grave, Annette saw he'd been told. Aled called her over.

'I've informed Tom that you're not quite its discoverer, but close enough. I'm no longer welcome. So if *you*'d conduct him up, please.'

'What? He won't be —'

'If you don't mind.'

Even on the flat of the beach, she had to keep shortening stride. When they reached the gully mouth, his face was red blotches and he had his hanky permanently in hand, mopping his forehead and neck. Seated on the sandshoes log, he caught his breath enough to ask about 'this engineering guy — Brian, is it?', how he'd found the site, and what his background was that he had all these skills Marilyn was drawing on. Annette was short, but not curt, not wanting him to think her manner strange.

She lost count of the stops on the climb up from the gully. His cheeks had gone from red to purple, and he was gasping. It struck her that he could actually die! She made him sit, grabbed the hanky from his fist and did as much of a jog as her own windedness allowed, fearful that the slender pipe of water might have stopped. It was thinner, but still falling — a beautiful silver skein. She soaked the hanky, carried it back in her cupped hands. The few sucks it held got him to the overhang. He flopped onto a mossed rock, letting the water shatter on his head and pour down his face into the neck of his jacket.

To get him up the steps, she had to take a wrist in fireman's grip. On the ledge, he again flopped. She told him she'd go and fetch the others, but if he could make it to the stream, there were hatchet grooves. Keeping him in sight for as long as she could, she backed into the burrawangs, then turned and ran.

They were standing together in a patch of sunlight with pannikins in their hands. They heard her and spun.

Marilyn thrust the pannikin at Sue and advanced to meet her. 'What's happened!'

Annette hadn't thought ahead to how her sudden arrival might be read. 'No! Just a visitor.'

'Who?'

'Tom Sieglitz.' She pointed along the track. 'He's back at the ledge. I thought he was going to have a heart attack.'

'What — Aled rang him?'

'No, he just showed up. He asked where you were. It was a bit hard to lie.'

Marilyn stepped past her and started fast along the track.

They met him coming through the burrawangs. He was carrying his hat, the soaked hanky on his head. He lifted the hat in greeting and halted. His chest was still heaving. He signed to give him a moment, jammed the hat on his head, gripped his thighs, and stared at the ground. Finally he straightened and squeezed out a smile. 'Got here! But God! I trust you've found an easier route in.'

'Not really, no.'

'Well, I hope before my next visit.' He flapped his hand, *lead on.*

Annette began to turn. Marilyn widened her stance and folded her arms. 'Sorry, Tom, but this's as close as you're coming.'

'What?' He attempted a chuckle. 'I've darn-near jiggered both myself *and* Annette getting this far!'

'Which is why I said sorry.'

Sieglitz stared at her. 'You're serious?'

'Completely.'

'I shall be too, then.'

He wasn't taking sides. If Marilyn said the site was hers, she'd get no argument from him. He just wanted a look, be of any assistance he could, offer an opinion on the lithic material. Marilyn had begun to shake her head, did so until Sieglitz petered out. The last thing she wanted, she said, were other opinions. Nor did she want tentative conclusions aired prematurely. He protested that he had no intention whatsoever of shooting off about the place. That, Marilyn said, could be guaranteed by his not setting foot there. Sieglitz turned sarcastic. It must be a model pit she was putting down if the only people permitted to see it were students. Marilyn told him he sounded like Aled.

'Now, I'm sure Annette would prefer not to be listening to this. So let's end it, shall we.'

Fury propelled him downhill, fed him the breath to speak. Marilyn was 'loony', he'd never been denied entry to a site in his life, he was writing papers when she was still plain, un-doctored *Miss* Herr!

He'd cooled to a simmer by the time they emerged from the gully onto the beach. The tide was low. Annette walked him over to the dune that gave the best view of the trap. A big school of mullet was swimming a slow circuit of the walls. She repeated some of Brian Harpur's story of seeing the trap used. Her thanks was a grunt. She couldn't resent the man's ill humour. He'd risked a coronary to stand at a rare east-coast Pleistocene site, and here he was being offered a glorified fish tank. Sieglitz muttered something at the water.

'Sorry?'

'I said, I *so* need a beer!' He blew a massive sigh, exhaustion and frustration. 'Human beings. Hard enough that we have to live with them, without digging them up.'

They ate royally that night from the cartons Sieglitz carried from his car, steak, marinated chicken wings, home-made potato salad, red wine from bottles. He shared Aled's cabin.

He stayed the next day as well, rising at the same time they did and trudging again along the beach. Aled called an early knock-off. At the cabins he informed them that he and Tom wouldn't need dinner, they were going in to the Bay. Sieglitz, it was clear, had gone from intruder to ally.

Aled was up next morning at the usual six, but looking bleary. Sieglitz didn't appear. When they returned to the cabins, he was gone.

The following afternoon Annette worked with Aled for a further half-hour after the others had left. When they emerged from the cave, Aled brought a folded envelope from his pocket and asked if she'd mind taking a note 'up there'. He apologised for asking her to do the climb again so soon, but she heard the apology was a formality, that he thought he was doing her a favour — the excuse to see Brian Harpur.

Annette glanced at the tent. Its flaps were closed. Greg and Brandy were out collecting driftwood. She bit her lip, slid the envelope into the pocket of her shorts.

She started across the beach to walk the hard sand at the shoreline, but the glare, and the stored heat striking up from every grain, changed her mind. She veered to the dunes and into the lengthening shadow of the cliff. From a crest, she looked back towards the cave. Aled had set out for the cabins. Annette took the envelope from her pocket. The single initial, *M*. She turned it over — sealed. She could leave it on the sandshoe log with a rock on it. But Aled would ask. Annette didn't like lying. She refolded the envelope and slid it back into her pocket.

She looked towards the headland. There was no obvious route. The dunes weren't neat parallel lines but a jumble of hummocks, the floors of their hollows a tangle of blackened iron-hard kelp and seagrape. The shoreline would be so much faster. Annette tugged down the brim of her cap and squinted. The shimmer had turned the ocean to green jelly. She set her face towards the headland and started down the dune.

She saw the blue blob of his shirt long before she understood what it was, had to top two more crests before she recognised his figure lying down the back of a dune. Good, she didn't have to do the climb. She cupped her mouth to shout, then closed her mouth, lowered her hands. Why was he there? In such an odd place. And lying down? She took a bearing, descended the dune, and walked a careful zigzag through the hollow — the brittle seaweed could draw blood. She climbed the opposite slope to just below its crest and slowly craned her neck.

Brian Harpur was still there, grown more detailed. Deepening the mystery, the fishing satchel lay at his right hip. He was propped on his elbows, his head level with the lip of the dune and his hands either side of his face. He was watching something.

But why from hiding? The answer was somewhere out on the beach. To see, she needed to be higher. She didn't want to risk standing on the crest of the dune. The only means was back.

An old channel led her up to the shelf of sand below the cliff. She clambered onto its hard, packed surface, the coarse grass pricking her knees, and stood. She saw instantly the dark head bobbing on the green of the gutter to the right of the trap. She instinctively ducked, as she did so realising that she'd seen not a face but hair, the back of a head. Sue never went in past her waist. It could only be Marilyn. Brian Harpur was waiting for her to leave the water and stride naked up the beach to her clothes.

Annette spun, scanned the base of the cliff. Her father had taught her to throw like a boy, flat and hard. On sand she'd be silent, could get so close she couldn't miss. She'd pelt him! She snatched up and discarded rocks till she had five filling the basket of her left hand. She straightened. Brian Harpur hadn't moved, Marilyn was still in the water. Annette walked to the lip of the shelf — and was almost felled by a bolt. Marilyn knew! She couldn't give him herself, but she could give him fantasies. The thought should have been mad. But twice she'd witnessed Marilyn use her beauty on him — the day they first took her to The Ferns, and the evening of his gift of flathead. She spilled the rocks from her hand.

'I hate you both.'

*

Smoke was rising at the tent. She didn't want even to see another male, much less speak to one. She snaked through the dune corridors till she reached the unmuffled roar of the surf and could creep, bent double, along the line of the front dune and out onto the bay of sand. A glance over her shoulder told her she could straighten.

Their daily trek from the cabins and back had created a 'road' through the marram. She joined it, sped up. But the thought had been growing — the hissing thuds of her feet not loud enough to blot it out — that she'd allowed jealousy to swamp both common sense and the sense of Marilyn she'd formed over the last year. It simply wasn't possible for Marilyn to be complicit. Yes, she'd be aware of his infatuation, it was so obvious. But if she knew it had grown into perving, she would confront him, even perhaps order him to leave.

The extension of that thought brought Annette to a halt, turned her to face the sea. She could actually *tell* Marilyn and get him not just barred from The Ferns but thrown off the whole dig, gone from North Teapot. It was what he deserved. And the shame of everyone knowing. But should she? Their time here was almost up. Back in Canberra might be a better place, he no longer a daily presence. Marilyn would be shocked, but they could agree in private that he wouldn't be invited back to The Ferns, nor on any other dig. She'd decide in bed. She set off again, fast, along the road.

She went straight to the cabin and put the envelope under

her pillow. She carried her sloppy joe down the steps and, ostentatiously pulling it over her head, walked to the fireplace. Aled was in his chair, nursing a mug. He looked at her, arched his brows. Annette nodded and turned to find a plate, her face burning.

She stayed at the fire talking with the boys till she saw the glow disappear from Vicky's window, knew the Bible-reading had ended. She stood and said goodnight.

She lit her the lantern at the table and carried it into her room and placed it on the floor, then undressed and slid into her bag to the waist and reached under her pillow and brought out the envelope. Beneath the talk at the fire, her mind had been twisting, turning. It was impossible to arrive at The Ferns without Brian Harpur seeing her. If Marilyn then confronted him, he'd know who'd dobbed. But what if she used the envelope? Didn't deliver it, left it in the gully mouth for one of them to find. Obviously she couldn't write on the outside, she would have to open it, write on the back of the same sheet, or insert her own. *I need to see you, but alone. Annette.* How personal, though, was Aled's message? Marilyn would assume she knew what it was about, had even read it. There was even the wild possibility Marilyn might think the messages were linked, that something had occurred between Annette and Aled! She slapped the envelope softly onto her stomach and closed her eyes. Every answer led to another question. The only definitive answer was that she did *not* want ever again to see Brian Harpur!

'Just leave the bloody thing somewhere visible and be rid of it,' she whispered at the roof. She would avoid The Ferns and him till the dig ended and speak to Marilyn back in Canberra.

At first light, Annette was on the beach. She did a fast walk to the gully. One of the banksias behind the sandshoe log had a cleft in its bark facing the path. She pushed the folded envelope into the cleft, stepped away, and turned to see. It was a little flag, impossible to miss.

The tent's flaps were now open, the boys crouched rekindling their fire. They were surprised and puzzled to see her. Annette told them she'd felt like taking a proper walk along the rock platform. It was always too hot in the afternoons.

Had she had breakfast, Brandy asked.

'If you count a drink of water.'

He gave her his plate and cutlery, made a sandwich of his bacon and eggs.

In the middle of the next morning, Annette was on the sieve when she heard a woman's voice whisper her name. Vicky, who was sitting nearly at her feet labelling a bag, didn't look up. Annette dismissed it as a trick of the surf and resumed rocking the frame. The voice, her name, came again. Vicky, too, heard, looking first at her, then along the line of the cliff where it seemed to come from. Annette dropped the brush on the mesh.

Sue was standing at the bulge in the cliffline. She saw that Annette had seen her and stepped back behind the bulge. Greg had stood up from the trench. He mouthed, *What's going on?* Annette shrugged.

Sue was standing with her back against the stone. She looked scared. And she'd run — for part of the way at least — there were sweat circles at her armpits and a wet vee between her breasts.

'What's happened? Are you okay?'

'Is Marilyn here?'

'Here? No.'

'Did she stay at the cabins?'

'What — last night? No. Why on earth are you asking?'

Sue spoke at the dunes. 'Because she's … missing.'

'Missing?'

'Yes.'

Annette's mouth was suddenly dry. 'Is *he* there?'

Her tone turned Sue's head. 'Brian? Yes, he's searching round the headland. I woke up pretty early, and she wasn't in the tent. I don't know if she even slept there, her bag was cold. The Kombi's out on the firetrail — we looked. We figured the only place she could be was here.' Sue lifted her hands and pressed the heels together, a gesture that was beseeching, almost prayer.

'You need to tell Aled.'

'I can't.'

'You "can't". What's that supposed to mean?'

'She made us agree not to go to him for help of any sort.'

'This's not "help", if she's missing. And they're married!'

Annette saw Sue's lips purse, read the thought, *what would you know about 'married'?*

'When did you both last see her?'

Her voice sounded different even to her. Older — and cold. Sue, too, heard, didn't answer immediately.

'After knock-off, Brian went fishing. We were nearly out of food. She and I ate, then she walked off down the track, I'm guessing down to the beach.'

'Where Brian was.'

'Yes, I just said, he went fishing.'

'And how do you know that?' She could *see* him! Marilyn striding from the water wringing out her hair, and him lying down the dune, peering through the marram.

Sue was looking at her as oddly as the question deserved. 'Because he brought back four bream.'

If she persisted, Sue would guess. 'Look, forget what you agreed, you have to tell Aled.'

She took Sue warily by the elbow, expecting resistance, met none.

Aled remained on his knees in the pit, the trowel in his hand. He asked most of the same questions, but his tone was the one he employed when grilling them about a feature, and his logic the familiar relentless progression from fact to fact until he'd led Sue to the question that seemed already to have its answer. What actual evidence was there that Marilyn was 'missing', the word Sue kept using? None, Sue admitted. But both she and Brian had the feeling something was wrong.

'And on that basis you'd like us to close up shop here and accompany you up there, where we'll probably find her puzzling over why you and he are "missing". Yes?'

Sue refused to be bullied. She said quietly, 'The headland's too big for just two of us.'

He tilted his head and studied the cave's ceiling, then closed his notebook and placed the trowel on its cover. 'How did you come here, along the beach?'

'Through the dunes. I could see along the beach.'

There was no need to call a halt, the others were gathered at the cave mouth.

'I take it you've all heard,' Aled said. 'Another in our litany of interruptions. Never mind. Grab the iron.'

They started along the shore in a group, but within minutes were a ragged line. Brandy, Paul, and Greg were walking just above the tidemark, their feet audibly punching holes in the baked crust. Annette saw that all three were scanning the water but trying to hide that they were. Aled was walking alone. He, too, had chosen to keep his feet dry. Stuart was in the lead, walking in the wash, and she, Vicky, and Sue were following the sloppy craters left by his feet. The surf was loud, and no one had spoken since they reached the shore.

Stuart veered towards a black thing, half-buried and trailing in the retreating water. Annette wondered what he wanted with a piece of rotting kelp. He bent over and stared, then straightened and found them with his eyes and pointed down before turning and scanning the sand ahead. He broke into a hesitant, almost unwilling, jog.

They reached the half-buried thing. It was not kelp. Vicky took hold of the trailing edge and tugged, then had to use both hands. The thing broke from the wet sand. It was a T-shirt, black because sodden, but dark purple, the cotton strong and unrotted. Vicky shook off the clots of sand. Both of them looked at Sue.

She nodded. 'I think so.'

Stuart sent a low whistle. Annette saw him glance over his shoulder to find Aled, then he held up by the waistband a pair of jeans shorts dripping slop. They were unmistakably hers. All of them had watched her one night at the fire cut off the legs just above the split knees, then pink the hems into sharks-teeth that would fray to a fringe. When they reached him, Stuart swivelled and drew breath, but Vicky grabbed his arm. 'No.'

She thrust the cold, heavy shirt at Annette, who, without thinking, took it, then wished she hadn't.

Vicky and Brandy led Aled back. He stepped in a trance of absorption, his head in advance of his feet, eyes seeing nothing but the clothes. Annette and Sue walked up onto the dry sand to meet him. He put out his hands, and Annette draped the shirt over them. Stuart added the shorts.

Aled stared at them, then dropped to his knees. A mewling sound trickled from his mouth, and he began to rock back and forth. The awful sound brought tears to Annette's eyes. She glanced at the others. They, too, were blinking, and smearing their cheeks. He needed comforting. But by whom? He was as remote as a weeping parent.

Annette heard Paul murmur, 'We've found her clothes,' and saw that Brian Harpur had joined their circle. She turned to face the water.

Brandy said, 'Aled?' The mewling didn't stop. 'Aled.' She had to watch. Brandy had a hand on his shoulder. 'We have to get help.' He waited. When still he didn't get an answer, Brandy leaned into Aled's eyeline. 'I need you to stand up, okay.'

Aled stopped rocking and closed his eyes. 'Would you find her sandshoes, please.'

Brandy elected to stay with him. They went a short way, straggled to a halt when Vicky said, 'Would she have been wearing them?' Sue thought so.

But you'd know, Annette said at Brian Harpur. The words were in her mouth. To speak them was impossible. She put a hand in the small of Vicky's back. 'We'll check along the water.'

When they'd walked some fifty paces, Annette looked over her shoulder and saw the others spread out and moving towards the gully.

'Sorry, Vick. Just, I needed to be away from him.'

They walked as far as the first boulders of the headland platform, were starting back when a two-finger whistle stopped them in their tracks. Stuart was holding aloft something white.

Aled was seated on the sand hugging his knees, the shirt and shorts at his feet on a strap of kelp. Stuart lowered the sandshoes into his sight. Aled snatched them and plunged his face into the footholes and sucked in great gulps of air. Stuart, appalled, looked to their faces for what he should do.

Brandy tugged the shoes gently from Aled's grip. He took Aled's elbow, said kindly in his ear, 'Come on, mate,' and stood him up.

It was no easy task to move him along the beach. He refused to turn his head from searching the surf and so stumbled on the ridges and gullies scoured by the waves. Or, without warning, he halted and turned full face to the ocean, slapping his thighs with the backs of his hands and the mewling breaking from his mouth.

For Annette, each time brought tears. At the same time she couldn't believe Marilyn was actually out there, covered by water.

When he judged it enough, Brandy would murmur, 'come on.' Aled would allow himself to be started once more into his old man's totter, and all of them, too, would move, but keeping behind the pair in unspoken agreement not to intrude on his grieving communion with the sea.

Annette kept close to Vicky. Once, when she sensed Brian Harpur drifting towards her, she stepped to Vicky's other side, putting her between them. He didn't try a second time.

At the cabins, Aled became almost calm. He nodded when Brandy told him he was going over to the phone box at the store, and even began to pat his pockets, before Brandy realised what he was doing and said he wouldn't need coins. Aled asked to be given her 'things'. They were put in his hands. He thanked them all, making strange little bows, then turned and walked quite firmly to his cabin. The open louvres clacked shut.

They gathered at the fireplace. With Aled now absent, Stuart voiced what had been in their minds since the finding of her clothes.

'How the hell would she drown? She was out there every second day!'

'Yeah,' Paul blared, 'and not just "out there", fucking halfway to New Zealand!'

The dam broke, everyone wanting to speak. Vicky cut through quietly. 'There's not just drowning. That far out there'd be sharks.'

'Not even far out,' Brian Harpur said.

Yes, Annette's mind retorted, *exactly what you* would *say!* She couldn't trust herself to look at him. A different, calmer, voice, her father's yet not, said, *That's emotion speaking, Annette, not what's in front of your eyes.* And yes, the obvious explanation made far more sense than her inventions. Not that she wanted *them* to be true, either. She wanted *none* of this to be true! She saw the same disbelief in the faces around her.

'What about, she got caught in a rip,' Stuart said, 'a big one? It could've taken her right around the headland, and then she's swum in.' He spun to find Brian Harpur, who shook his head.

'I went all the way round to the next little beach.'

Sue, who'd been sitting quietly, suddenly sucked in a loud, shivery breath that scared everyone. Annette took a step towards her, then stopped, fearing the embarrassment should Sue shrug her off. The gate to the store path squealed.

Brandy had spoken to a detective. They'd be thirty minutes. 'I said we'd meet them out at the road.' He started towards the sliprails and they fell in behind him.

The police arrived in three white Land Cruisers coated with dust. A big, red-haired man got out of the passenger seat of the front cruiser. His chest and shoulders filled a short-sleeved check cotton shirt. The men in the other cruisers wound down the windows. They looked to be in sky-blue overalls. Brandy stepped forward.

'Mr Brandjes?' the man said.

'Yes.'

'I'm Detective-Sergeant Isles.' He didn't offer his hand. He pointed along the wheel ruts. 'You're in the cabins, that right?'

'Yes.'

'Artie about?'

It was only then Annette realised they'd not seen Gorman at his gate, stickybeaking.

'Ah … not that we've seen,' Brandy said.

Annette saw the man pick up instantly on the careful neutrality. His lips smiled. 'We'll find him. So, where is it you think this person might have drowned?'

Think, might? Annette glanced at Sue. An anarchist poster in her bedroom at Masson Street was a boar in blue uniform with a bullet hole in the forehead.

Brandy answered, began to add that they'd have to —

'I know the beach,' Isles cut in. 'I fish here. You're in the cave, I take it.'

And at a site up on the headland. That was where —

Isles again cut him off, this time with a lift of the hand. He called to 'Mick' in the second cruiser to take his and the third cruiser back to the Parks track and walk the gear down. He turned again to Brandy. 'Better meet the husband, eh.'

They followed him along the ruts back towards the cabins, he addressing questions over his shoulder to whoever chose to answer. How long they'd been digging? What they were looking for? What they'd found so far? He seemed genuinely interested in the answers, slowing to look at Paul — 'You're kidding me, a dingo?' — and at Stuart when he gave the cave's probable occupation age — 'That old, eh!'

Annette began to revise her first impression of the man, but warned herself that it was his job to extract information, and he was probably good at it. The 'clever fella' would have stopped him in his tracks. But she sensed the others, too, had picked up on the intelligence beneath the seeming affability. The Land Cruiser growled along behind them.

He halted at the fireplace and flicked his eyes over their domestic mess, then studied the cabins. 'Where do I find him?'

Brandy pointed. 'The end one.'

'You got pen and paper?' He asked would they all please put their full names, addresses, and a contact number on a sheet. He started towards the cabin, and Brandy fell in beside him. Isles stayed him with a hand. 'I'll manage.'

After forty minutes, Vicky keeping time, the door opened, and Isles came down the steps carrying the clothes in one hand and the sandshoes in the other. The driver jumped from the cruiser with plastic bags. He and Isles bagged, sealed, and tagged on the table, shirt and shorts in separate bags, the sandshoes together. The driver carried the bags to the cruiser. Brandy gave Isles the list. He skimmed it, did a swift silent head count. The driver had returned carrying a manila folder. Isles gave him the sheet.

'Ah … Professor Wray would prefer to stay here. He's suggested I ask for Annette and Sue?'

The tone was polite, but contained no hint of choice. Annette raised her hand, Sue a finger.

'And you are …' Annette gave her name. He grinned, nodded at Sue. 'So my powers of deduction tell me Sue is you.'

Sue stared at him. Isles dipped his head.

'I'm not, I assure you, making light of the situation.' He clicked finger and thumb, and the driver placed the folder in his hand. He consulted the list, looked into Annette's eyes. 'Miss Cooley.' He gave Sue the same direct look. 'And Miss Klima. How's my pronunciation?'

'Close enough.'

'Czech.'

Annette saw Sue's surprise. The man had reasserted his authority.

'What I want, if you would, is for you to come with me and talk me through what you've been doing. At both sites. And show me where the clothes were. You both okay with that?'

Annette nodded, didn't look at Sue, not wanting any exchange of glances misconstrued. He pointed them towards the Land Cruiser. Annette saw the faces in the back seat and realised there was nowhere to sit but on laps. Isles saw her falter.

'Sorry, the cage — round the back. It's only a short ride.'

The driver ushered them inside. Annette's eyes went straight to the spy grille. She looked at Sue, pointed with her chin.

'I'm not stupid, thanks,' Sue murmured.

The driver ran the cruiser in under trees beside the other two. Isles got out wearing a scrub hat. Shouldering packs, the two men from the back seat went first, he next, Annette and Sue behind him. The driver followed. Annette had walked the full track from road to beach only once before. Poorly maintained, it was more a watercourse than a path. Its silted hollows were studded with fresh bootprints.

She and Sue exchanged glances when they recognised they

were nearing the turn-off to the grave. Isles passed by without slowing. Annette saw when she, too, reached the opening that the marks of their coming and going had been grown over, then erased completely by the storm. She began getting glimpses of the water.

Isles cleared his throat, a self-conscious prelude, she heard, not a necessity. He spoke over his shoulder. 'Professor Wray said his wife didn't bother with a cozzie. That tally with your observation?'

'Yes.'

'Miss Klima?'

Sue didn't answer. The man, wisely, didn't press.

They arrived on the clifftop just as a single-engine plane flying on the point of one wing came along the line of the breakers. It clattered past and, on reaching the end of the beach, didn't bank but followed the broken water along the rock platform to the headland and disappeared round its sheer face. They were halfway down the first of the two sets of plank steps when the plane reappeared and flew back along the beach, but further out. Annette watched it become a speck, was waiting to see what it would do, when she saw two figures jog round the cliff and out onto the bay of sand. Isles, too, had seen them. The detectives in the lead had halted.

Isles called, 'I'll see what they want.'

When Annette reached the sand, the two were close enough to recognise, Stuart and Greg. They blurted out that Aled —

Professor Wray — had sent them to be at the tent. They were too breathless to explain, and she took over.

Isles nodded. 'Well, there won't be any lack of security today. But I've no objection.'

They all turned at the thin drone of the plane. It was out past where the swell began building. A radio crackled, then they heard the roar in the cabin. The driver had taken a handset from his belt. The pilot asked did they want another run? Isles flicked a thumb across his throat. The driver spoke into the handset and, a moment later, the wings waggled and the plane did a steep banking climb that took it to a safer height, before it again turned south.

Nine men in blue overalls were standing some ten metres apart along the foot of the dunes. A black labrador on a leash sat eagerly patient. Two of the men carried spades, and all held metre-long skewers.

Isles lifted his arm and waved *go*. The shock must have shown in Annette's face, because he said, 'We have to consider every possibility, Miss Cooley. Same reason we need to take a look at your trenches, if we may. Just give me a minute.' He beckoned Stuart over. 'And you are Mr …?'

'Webster. Stuart.'

'Were you one of the party this morning that found the clothes?'

'Yes.'

Isles pointed to the two men wearing packs. 'Could you go

with the detectives, please, and show them exactly where.'

Sue came with them to the cave, but made no move to help. It was no longer her site. Annette and Greg removed the sheets of iron from the trench. Isles's eyes went immediately to the red staining.

'That's ochre,' Annette said. 'Where our dingo was.'

'And that's … the customary thing, is it?'

'No. It's usually only human burials.'

'Go on.' Again, his amazement seemed genuine. 'How old? Your dingo.'

'We don't know yet.'

'She unearthed it,' Greg said quietly. 'Dr Herr.'

'So this's before the headland.' He caught the flick of their eyes to one another. 'No need to panic, Professor Wray's told me there was a bit of a falling-out.'

Greg looked at Annette, *you're senior here*.

'Um …you mean over this, or …?'

'Why, was there a falling-out over this as well?'

'He insisted on doing the removal. Which was his right, it's his site.'

'But, right or not, she didn't like it.'

'No. But they resolved it.'

Isles stared at her. She felt the skin of her throat tingle.

'Okay. I'll just take a look.'

He did a slow walk the length of one side of the trench, leaning to peer at the floor and walls, then walked round the working face and came back along the other side.

'And you've both worked in here?'

'Yes.'

'And it's ... as you remember it? No disturbances?'

She said *yes* to Greg's *no*. Isles looked quickly at him. Redness was flowing up into his face from his beard.

'I mean, no disturbance.'

Isles told them they could lay the iron back.

The questions were the same inside at the pit, but put without conviction. Even he could see the smooth, hard walls bore nothing but trowel marks. They came outside.

'So ...' Greg said, 'you want us to wait here?'

'If you would.' Sue had gone to stand in the shade of the cliff. Isles lifted a hand towards the sieves. 'I use one of those for top-dressing my lawn. Not quite so elaborate. So — Miss Klima — we'll take a walk up to the other site.'

Without consulting him, Sue started towards the shore. The police were in the dunes.

Annette and Greg climbed the nearest dune and sat on its crest. The appearings and disappearings of the blue figures were random, their details blurred by the salt haze now blowing in. They spoke little. In her case, because she was afraid that if she started she wouldn't be able to stop. She kept seeing the metal skewers. She knew the exact dune Brian Harpur had been lying down. Greg was intelligent and calm, and Annette liked him. He would, she believed, respect anything told him in confidence. But she couldn't ask him what she should do. It was fairer to him, then, to say nothing. Neither decision would stay fixed, though — the voices in her head kept on at one another. They stopped only when Greg touched her arm and pointed. Stuart was jogging back along the wash, deliberately kicking up spray.

He climbed the dune and flopped full-length beside them. He was soaked from the hips down. When his breathing slowed, he sat up. The cops had taped a corridor between where the clothes were and the gully and were walking bent over, combing the sand with their fingers. 'Like bloody chooks.' He barked a laugh, then as quickly fell silent. 'Dunno what they'd be looking for.'

Annette knew what he wanted one of them to say, that it was just what police do.

'For anything that says she didn't drown,' Greg said.

Annette stood before they saw her face and strode down the dune towards the soak.

The interviewing began at one. Isles had set himself up in the farthest cabin, empty since Brian Harpur left and Stuart moved in with the others. The fireplace was shadeless, and they carried the camp chairs into the lean-to of shade thrown by the girls' cabin. Annette waited till Brian Harpur had placed his chair, then placed hers with her back to him and signed to Vicky to join her.

A constable stood, arms folded, against the chimney end of the boys' cabin. They were not under guard, Isles had assured them, he was just the runner. They decided, though, that the man had probably been instructed to make sure no one went for a wander. The door of the interview cabin opened, and Isles looked out. The constable came to loose attention. Isles pointed — the professor.

The door opened so quickly after the knock that Annette thought Aled must have been watching. He spoke to the constable, and the man nodded. 'If you could make it short, though, sir, please.'

Aled came over to them. He'd shaved, and changed into a buttoned shirt and jeans and leather sandals like half-shoes. He had a pen clipped in his shirt pocket and had strapped on his watch. His eyes, though, spoiled the brave effect. They were red and puffy. 'You're all here! Did you not explain, about the tent!'

'There's cops at both sites, Aled,' Brandy said.

'Ah. Yes. Of course.'

Vicky informed them when he'd been inside for an hour. Annette found herself thinking that, for a man in shock, he had a lot to say. The cabin's louvres were closed, but the busy clacking of a typewriter carried. Stuart stood and asked the constable could he fetch cordial and mugs, and the man nodded.

'You want one?' Stuart asked.

'No, sir, thank you.' The formality was unexpected, and a little chilling.

The typewriter stopped, but the door refused to open. They had to wait a further ten minutes. Annette had naively imagined Aled would come back and join them. But with not even a glance in their direction, he walked towards the sliprails. A man, not Isles, appeared in the doorway. Annette sat straight in her chair, they all did. The man pointed up the paddock. The constable stepped out into the glare.

Paul voiced everyone's thought. 'What's he want with *him*?'

Brian Harpur had been silent the whole time. Now Annette waited for him to speak. A minute passed. Should she turn and stare him into it? Or announce into the air that they should ask Brian? Neither, she decided. This wasn't about Gorman.

He came rocking down the paddock in his holed green T-shirt and football shorts, staying ahead of the constable in a refusal to be escorted.

Again, Vicky was timekeeper. At thirty-two minutes the typewriter stopped. But instead of a delay the door was snatched open, and Gorman appeared, hot-faced and angry. He lurched down the steps and started up the paddock, wanting to get away faster than his hips could carry him, his gammy arm out and rowing the air. The others couldn't know the suggestions he'd had put to him, but weren't stupid.

'He's been in the shit before,' Greg said.

Isles cut short speculation. 'Miss Klima, please.'

Brian Harpur was next.

Neither returned to the circle.

Then it was her turn.

When the door closed, she was hit by a soup of body smells. A glance told her why — all the louvres were shut. The only ventilation was the usual missing ones, and the gap at the eaves. The cabin was furnished similarly to her own, but with its own unique mismatches. The pink dresser holding crockery and canisters belonged in a bedroom.

Isles ushered her to a straight-backed chair placed at the side of the lino-topped table and took the one at the head, his back to the glare striking the windows, their louvres golden with dust. Annette studied the chair a second before she sat.

'It hasn't broken so far,' Isles said.

'No, just ours pinch.'

'What, chairs belonging to the fastidious Artie?'

The other man smiled. Isles introduced him, Detective-Constable Hite. He sat behind a black portable Corona, to his left a slit ream of paper and an open box of carbons, and on the green lino to his right ballpoints and pencils, stapler, ruler. Four manila folders lay piled within reach of Isles's left hand. Annette read the top one upside down, *Harpur, Brian Charles* in blue block letters.

'We ready?' Isles was looking only at her. She swallowed and nodded. He missed little. He pointed to the jug and glasses on a folded tea towel. 'Water there whenever you want.'

Isles explained that no one was being investigated, he just wanted to take her through the events and put some questions.

170

The assurance didn't quell the churning in her belly.

'For starters, would you give us your details, beginning with full name.'

He asked then what she was studying, how long she'd been a student of Professor Wray's and Dr Herr's. Annette corrected him, only of Professor Wray's. She'd been with Dr Herr before on digs, that was all. Isles picked up a ballpoint and made a note. He asked then why there'd been no towel on the beach. The abruptness of the jump flustered her. Isles watched impassively while she found words. Marilyn — Dr Herr — never bothered with one, if she dried herself at all she did so with her shirt. Isles grunted and looked down at the sheet in front of him. Annette took the opportunity to glance at Hite. The typewriter had stopped an instant after she'd finished speaking. She couldn't believe he'd taken down every word. But he was poised and waiting.

'Something the matter, Miss Cooley?' Isles said.

'No.'

'Okay, I'm going to ask you a policeman's question. I'd like you to try to answer it. What's your opinion of the suggestion that she swam out as far as she could then stopped swimming?'

Annette was watching Hite's fingers from the corner of her eye. He finished a second after Isles stopped speaking. Only then did she hear the words.

'Is that what someone's said?'

Isles tilted his hand. 'Just after your opinion.'

Annette felt heat — raw anger — swell in her belly and surge into her chest. She didn't care that it might also be showing in her face. The fear she had of the man was gone, even if only in the moment.

'That site up there's only the most important yet found on the whole South Coast. Does that answer your question?'

Isles was not, she saw, ruffled by sarcasm. 'It's a similar answer to what I've been given. If with less passion. We'll move on.'

'My *passion* comes from —'

Hite's fingers had sprung into action as soon as she began to speak. The sound was not of individual keys being struck, but continuous, like speech itself. She had never been in the presence of typing like it. Isles asked again was something the matter. A concern she had with Detective Hite? She couldn't admit the truth, which was the spooky feeling that the man knew what she was about to say before she said it. Annette told him she couldn't believe how fast Detective Hite typed.

'Leo,' Isles said.

Hite explained that he'd been a court stenographer before joining the police.

'You get to read what he's taking down,' Isles said. 'At the end. And you're free to make changes.'

Annette nodded and felt sweat trickle down her forehead. She ducked her head and wiped her face with her T-shirt. She wanted to ask could they have a window open. What stopped her was the thought that the heat was deliberate.

Isles took her through the events leading up to 'the split'. The discovery of The Ferns. Going up there with Mr Harpur. The decision to tell Dr Herr in the absence of Professor Wray. Would she agree that Dr Herr was 'professionally ambitious'? Annette didn't need to ask, agree with whom. Yes, she said. Professor Wray had admitted, Isles said, that the split had angered him, but that he'd understood Dr Herr's motives for wanting to begin work immediately at the new site. Had Aled called her 'Dr Herr', she wondered. She'd observed Dr Herr that first day, Isles was saying. What did *she* understand those motives to be?

He'd given the main one, Annette told him. She wondered if Aled had mentioned getting out from under the weight of his name. If he'd left that unsaid, so would she. It was calming to discover that she could be calculating.

Isles asked why they'd told Dr Herr — she and Mr Harpur — and not waited and told both. Annette gave him the truth, that she'd believed the new site so important it didn't matter who they told, because work at the beach would be suspended, and they would all move up there. But, she added, knowing what Professor Wray thought of colleagues 'chasing the oldest', she maybe shouldn't have been so sure. Isles cocked his head, asked her to explain. Hite, too, listened before hitting the keys.

How clever, Annette thought at the end of her explanation, *to throw in some jargon.* She'd led them neatly past Brian Harpur.

The self-congratulation was premature. Isles looped back. Why had Mr Harpur come to her with his discovery and not directly to Professor Wray or Dr Herr? She gave a non-answer while her head raced, he'd come to her first with the trap so he did again. Isles wasn't distracted, he repeated the why. Annette chose to gamble that Brian Harpur wouldn't have answered with the truth. 'Mr Harpur' had probably told them he wasn't in archaeology. Isles nodded. Well, even to them who were, the two could be intimidating. Mr Harpur had preferred to approach another student, knowing that, as an honours student, she was sort of third in line. She must have sounded calmer, more matter-of-fact, than she felt, because Isles didn't, as she'd feared, reach over and tap the top folder and say, *Mr Harpur believed there was a bit more going on between you than that.*

Isles glanced down at the sheet on the table, returned his gaze to her. Okay, would she tell him, please, about the note, the one she'd carried on — he glanced again — the twenty-ninth, Tuesday afternoon. Aled, too, she realised, had been calculating. Not to have mentioned the note would have been dangerous. Did she know its contents? Wasn't it found up there, Annette wanted to ask. She answered the question she'd been asked. No. Professor Wray hadn't hinted perhaps, when he gave it to her? No. Isles continued to hold her gaze. She knew then it hadn't been found. All right, what about his manner, did she gain some idea from that? She gave her third unadorned *no*. She was rattled, though. Why was she being asked to speculate on a note Aled should have been able to quote, and must have been asked to? Isles sat back and lightly folded his arms. She'd been his go-between on at least one other occasion, too, hadn't she. So why her? And she was back again on the dangerous ground of Brian Harpur. All she could do was again gamble on his natural reticence. She told Isles that, Professor Wray being her supervisor, she was sort of 'on call' whenever he needed something done. It was the same reason she was obliged to remain at the beach when, like everyone else, she wanted to be up at The Ferns.

Isles smiled. 'Even in the police we know a little about professional suicide, Miss Cooley.'

Hite quietly chuckled. His fingers resting on the keys didn't move.

Isles stretched his arms, waggled his shoulders. He picked up the ballpoint and skimmed its tip down the sheet in front of him. Okay, would she take him, please, through the events of the morning. From when Miss Klima arrived at the cave to when Mr Brandjes rang the station. Annette was already beginning to be anxious about how long she'd been inside. She said her account wouldn't differ from Sue's — Miss Klima's — or whoever came next, they'd all been together.

Isles studied her. Her chest prickled. Had he trained himself not to blink? He shifted his gaze to Hite and lifted a finger towards the jug. Hite turned a glass upright, filled it, handed it to her.

Isles read, or pretended to, while she drank. Annette made to hand the glass back to Hite to place again on the tea towel and Isles, instantly alert, motioned that she set it on the lino. When she'd done so, had laid her hands back in her lap, he said softly, 'So what is it you do want to talk about?'

The prickling rose up her throat and into her face.

'When you're ready. No hurry.'

'Could I have some more water?'

Isles let several seconds pass before he nodded to Hite. Annette studied her hands, the calluses from the sieve, but could feel Isles's eyes on the crown of her head. Water gurgled into the glass. When it stopped, she looked up. Hite held the glass, waiting.

Still she couldn't begin. Isles gave her a smile. Of encouragement, he must have thought, but he couldn't see his own eyes.

This isn't playground tattle you're about to tell here, said the calculating voice. *Yes, it's necessary that you tell it, and he deserves for it to be told. But you won't be able to take it back. And one day he may find out. That it was you.*

'If she's drowned, then this — what I'm about to say — it's irrelevant. So I don't want it taken down.'

'Is it true?'

'Yes.'

'Then what are you worried about?'

'It can ... damage someone.'

'How about you let me be the judge of that.'

'No. I don't want it taken down.'

Isles stared at her. She looked away in the direction of the low, fluctuating moan she'd been aware of since first sitting, but which had grown louder. A set of louvres not quite closed. She heard the rasp of afternoon bristle as Isles rubbed his chin, and had a flash. She would ring her father! His court days were erratic, but he was mostly in the office. She didn't think, though, that Isles would allow her to leave. Anyway, it was too late, she'd made her decision. They were just waiting for his.

She turned her head enough to see him. Avoiding her eyes, he faced along the table and nodded. To be sure, Annette looked. Hite exaggerated the lifting of his fingers from the keys.

Isles listened without interruption. She described only what she'd seen, said nothing about her now dangerous thought of Marilyn's complicity. When she said she was finished, he thanked her, said that he understood why it had been difficult for her to speak. He asked then would she mind just a few questions, just to clarify a couple of things. The cold fist again gripped her bowels, he'd sensed something of her and Brian Harpur's tentative connection. But no, both questions were as he'd said, clarification. Could she remember the position of Mr Harpur's hands? The carefully neutral tone told her he was asking what she thought he was. She told him Mr Harpur's hands were beside his face, he was using them to part the grass at the top of the dune. And the note. Annette hadn't put it in Dr Herr's hand. What made her think she'd got it? Because of where she'd left it, she said. No one else used the gully.

'Didn't he say? Or Sue?'

Isles gave a small shake of the head. 'Neither of them saw it.' He opened his hands, *you have another question, or …?*

Annette, too, shook her head.

'We're finished, then.'

Hite had silently assembled three thin piles of paper. He now stapled the top left corner of each. He handed her the typed copy and placed a ballpoint on the lino in front of her. 'Make any change you wish, but initial it, please. And each page, please, at the bottom.'

The seven pages lacked even a typo, at least that she found in a single reading. He asked her to sign the top copy, then the first carbon, slid the second carbon across the lino to her. 'That's your copy.'

Isles had stood and was tugging with both hands at his shirt, stuck to his lower back. He conducted her to the door, rested his hand on the knob before turning it. 'The same advice I've given the others, go for a longish walk.'

When she reached the foot of the steps, Isles called above her head to the constable, 'Give me ten, then I want Mr Brandjes.'

Annette started abruptly towards the sliprails, the direction Aled had taken. She had no idea where he, Sue, or Brian Harpur were, but was sure she wouldn't meet any of them on the faint track she'd seen from the car on their first day. She didn't herself know where it went.

The track snaked along a rainforest gully and up into a forest of spotted gum, then down to one of the fingers of the lake. She'd hoped for distraction, but everything was simply a backdrop to the scenes playing in her mind. She played over and over, sometimes aloud, her account to Isles. What could she have phrased differently to sound less incriminating? Should she have admitted that Brian Harpur wasn't just 'anybody'? It didn't change what she'd seen, so how was it relevant? Her father said, *It's relevant, my girl, to the issue of motivation.* She hadn't, she retorted, been motivated by spite. A woman — a friend almost — had vanished! The obvious explanation wasn't necessarily the only or the true one. The police were told someone had drowned, but hadn't they turned up with a dog and metal skewers? Even if her body washed up tomorrow, who could say it had been an accident? She'd been right to speak. Isles had thanked her. But words weren't just air, they were facts, they had consequences.

She was moving up a gully towards a break in the trees she hoped was the camping ground. She slowed to a halt, sucked in a breath, blew it out. *All you're thinking's, you, you, you! The reason for all the bloody questions is, Marilyn's not coming back!* The track blurred. She sank to her haunches, then sat, sobbing into her hands.

She couldn't have said for how long. When finally she raised her face and looked about her, the light was dropping. She shouldn't have stayed away this long. She scrambled up and broke into a jog.

It wasn't as late as she'd feared, the tiny store still open.

Annette jogged past and onto the path to the cabins. When their roofs came in sight, she slowed to a stroll she hoped wouldn't appear staged. Her acting evaporated when she saw the white Land Cruiser still there. She began to look for a place in the tea tree to watch from, but she'd been seen. Brandy gave her a wave in which she detected relief. Annette waved back and unchained the gate.

Smoke was rising from the fireplace, but no cooking was happening. Her eyes flicked to the closed cabin door.

'Brian,' Brandy said. 'He wanted him again.'

Her impulse was to grab bread and cheese and go to her bedroom. She quelled it, as much from cold curiosity as the fear of being the only one missing when he rejoined them. Sue was standing at the woodpile staring at the ground, her arms folded. Annette sat beside Vicky.

'You were gone *ages*,' Vicky whispered. 'We were discussing should we go find you.'

Before Annette could begin to describe the track, there came the squeal of hinges, and Brian Harpur appeared in the doorway of what had been his cabin.

He almost fell in getting down the steps. When he reached the ground, he jerked forward and dry-retched. He retched again, and spat, then swayed round and looked at them, not accusing, Annette saw, more in disbelief and shock. She was shocked herself, she'd always thought 'sick with fear' just an expression.

You did this.

No, the calculating voice said, he *did.*

Brian Harpur's mouth worked, then he covered his face with his hands and, sobbing, stumbled away towards the sliprails. They heard him even after his shirt was swallowed by the tea tree.

'Jesus,' one of the boys breathed.

'You able to tell us what the hell that's about?'

Annette froze, then dared to turn her head. Greg had spoken — but to Sue. Sue didn't look at them.

'No.'

Annette glanced at faces and saw she wasn't the only one who'd heard *yes.*

Isles stepped out of the cabin carrying the folders, Hite the cased typewriter and a briefcase. Isles locked the door, displayed the key, hung it from the knob. Sue spun and strode away towards the steps to the beach.

'Should you … you know, follow her?' Vicky murmured.

'I don't think so.'

They lapsed into silence, but a silence loud with the unspoken, and the ocean's reminder, every eight seconds — Annette counted — that it was there. She thought someone would crack, have to speak. She resolved it wasn't going to be her. She saw in the quick averting of faces when eyes accidentally met that others had made the same decision, even Vicky.

Paul stood. Without looking left or right, he walked to the table, slid the cutting board towards him, selected three tomatoes from the vegetable carton, and picked up the serrated knife they used for slicing. The others stirred, found jobs, setting out mugs and adding cordial and water, buttering bread, feeding the fire. Speech, too, returned, but only to do with tasks.

The meal was basic fare — sausages, tomato, and limp lettuce between slices of fork-toasted white bread. When the sausages were nearly done, Stuart volunteered to tell Aled.

He opened the door to the knock, lifted his face to the sky as if amazed that it was night. He disappeared, then reappeared pulling on his khaki jumper. Stuart had waited. Aled followed him to the fire. He said hello, then stood looking bewildered. Brandy spoke his name and pointed to his chair, unfolded and waiting in its customary place. Greg brought him a sandwich and a mug of cordial.

Annette had the conventional belief about what grief did to the appetite. All of them did, she saw from their startled faces, as he quickly emptied his plate. There were more sausages, Paul told him. He ate another sandwich, followed it with a second mug of cordial. He stood and nodded thank-you, placed plate and mug on the table, and began walking towards his cabin. Halfway there he exclaimed, and turned.

'How are we for perishables?'

Brandy was the first to understand. 'We need eggs and milk. And probably bread.'

'Come over to the cabin and get some money.'

With nothing else to watch, they watched them go.

Greg got to his feet. 'This's bullshit. Eggs and milk. It's not just another bloody *night*!' His quiet voice cracked. He blundered into a chair, didn't stop, marched off towards the boys' cabin. It was the trigger for them all to bolt.

Only when she was at the cabin steps did Annette remember the fire. A silhouette wreathed in steam was already dippering water onto the coals.

Vicky stood her torch on the table pointed at the roof, and each fetched her lantern. Annette lit both wicks, but let Vicky trim her own. Vicky lowered the flame, then dropped her hands to her side.

'Annette ... in school ... did you do that poem called "Beach Burial"? About drowned sailors? We did it for eisteddfod. There's this line, "At night they sway and wander in the waters far under." Like seaweed.' She shivered, crossed her arms on her chest. 'I don't want to think about her like that! Like a piece of *weed*!'

She burst into tears. Annette had picked up her lantern. She stood it back on the table and took Vicky in a hesitant embrace, but, at first touch, Vicky wrapped her arms around her and buried her face in Annette's shoulder. Her distress was contagious, and Annette cried with her, but not as she had on the track. After two or three minutes, she stopped, lifted her right arm, and wiped her eyes on her wrist. Vicky was still releasing pent-up breath in small shuddery sobs. Annette stepped back. Vicky didn't want to relinquish touch, groping for and seizing her hand. She opened her mouth to speak, but all that came was a sob like a hiccup.

'It's all right,' Annette said. 'Whatever it is, say it.'

Vicky shook her head. Annette waited. Vicky coughed and cleared her throat. 'I'm not going anywhere near the beach.'

'You won't be the only one.' Annette prised Vicky's hand from hers and picked up her lantern. 'You think you'll be okay to sleep?'

Vicky tried to smile. 'If I can stop reciting.'

'We're leaving the door unlocked.'

'Won't she go up to the empty one?' Vicky heard the ambiguity and her face contorted. 'Sue.'

'I don't know. But if she doesn't want to be on her own.' Annette took a step towards her doorway. 'Okay, goodnight.'

She stood the lantern on the floor and sat on her bed, and looked at the depression in the mattress on the other bed. Over the dividing wall came the start of that night's prayer. Since Sue's departure, the words had again become audible. Sue had been brutally direct. On their first night in the cabin, she had interrupted Vicky mid-prayer and told her that they next door didn't want to share her conversation with the Lord thanks, and to lower her voice or take Him outside. Even as a child, Annette had been unable to reconcile dinosaurs with the Creation, and at thirteen had quietly, but definitively, stopped going to church. She respected, though, that Vicky hadn't allowed herself to be bullied into total silence. Now, on nights when the words were fervently audible, Annette simply distracted herself for ten minutes, humming a song, or reading aloud. Tonight, she listened.

Vicky did not doubt where Marilyn was, and what she needed. The Lord was asked repeatedly to welcome her into the Kingdom of Heaven. Annette pressed her palms to her ears, closed her eyes. But had to fight herself to begin, even in a whisper.

'Marilyn ... I don't know where you are ... but I hope it's the ocean ... and I hope that you're found. Amen.'

When Annette unblocked her ears, the words from the next room had stopped, the lantern's glow no longer furred the top of the wall. She lifted her own lantern, thumbed the lever and blew out the flame, placed the lantern back on the floor. Then found it again with her hand and slid it to beside the bed leg, out of the way of a foot entering in the dark.

She lay on the unzipped bag. The polished cotton was uncomfortably cool against her bare legs. She slithered out of her shorts and got into the bag and zipped it as silently as she could, not wishing Vicky to hear that she was still awake. She *did* want to talk, very much. But not to Vicky, to her father. He'd still be up, reading. She didn't, though, have sufficient coins for longer than two or three minutes. Whatever hurried assurances she gave, all he would hear was *my little girl needs me*. It wasn't beyond him to throw clothes in a bag and grab his wallet and drive the five hours down here. She couldn't put him to that risk. And how would his arrival strike Isles? That she'd summoned a solicitor, no matter that he was also her father.

She lay on her back, ears tuned to the night outside. The sound she did *not* want to hear was footsteps come to stand under her window. She shouldn't have allowed in the thought. But now that she had, where would he be? The Ferns? That was the obvious place. His swag was there, with the tent and everything he'd built for her. But the police were supposedly camped at both sites. Would Isles have told him not to leave Teapot? Probably. But if not, it was possible, even likely, that he'd walked out to the highway and hitched a ride. She hoped so. She wanted never to see him again.

She continued to lie on her back, knowing she couldn't fall asleep while she did. She began to count waves, stopped at twenty. Sue would come, or she wouldn't. Annette rolled onto her sleeping side and closed her eyes.

A Land Cruiser arrived at the sliprails while they were eating breakfast. Hite ducked through the rails and walked to the fire. Isles wanted Miss Klima. Brandy was explaining that the last they'd seen of her was last night, heading down to the beach, when the door of the interview cabin opened.

Sue came to the fire, gave them a cold smile, took an apple from the fruit carton, and turned and walked towards the waiting Land Cruiser. Hite farewelled them with a lift of the eyebrows.

The sun drove them into the shade of the wattles by the cabins, their lower branches trimmed by Gorman's cows. The rhythmic thump of waves carried to where they sat. The sound was almost sinister. Vicky suggested a walk, pick one off the National Parks map in the store. It was better than sitting all day. They were stirring themselves when they heard a car.

Isles had warned them that the press would show up, but they needed Gorman's permission to set foot inside the fence. The arrival — Laurie, from the *Examiner* — must have been refused. He stood at the sliprails calling. They remembered him ay, they must, he just wanted a couple of minutes. When none of them responded, he switched to calling to 'Professor Wray'. They had a deal, remember. Wasn't the dig over? His voice, half demand, half plaint, went on and on.

Finally Paul erupted from his chair. 'This prick needs telling!'

He came back carrying a slip of paper. He posted it under the door of Aled's cabin, then turned to the man and signed that it was delivered as promised and clamped a hand over his mouth. The man retreated to his car.

The reason for his desperation arrived half an hour later, a second car. A man in a brown suit got out, spoke to Laurie, then came on to the sliprails. He climbed onto the lower rail.

'Hey! *Canberra Times*! Can I talk to one of you! It'll be worth your while!'

'Fuck off!' Paul yelled.

The man returned to his car and backed out. He must almost

have collided with a white van. A man and a woman got out and walked to the sliprails, the man with a camera on his shoulder. The woman pointed to what she wanted — Gorman's house, the cabins, them. She then turned her back and did a piece to camera. The two returned to the van and reversed out. It had all been so cold-blooded no one joked about being television stars. Then Laurie left, in such a rush he crunched the gears.

Ten minutes later, another car pulled up at the sliprails. Tom Sieglitz got out and began wrestling with the crooked top rail.

He'd been sent by the vice-chancellor. The university understood the god-awful situation they'd been pitched into, and he was here with full power to deal. Essentials first, how were they fixed for food? Enough for a few days, Brandy told him. Aled was still functioning, had given them money.

'He in his cabin?'

Brandy shrugged. 'Far as we know. He didn't eat, but we haven't seen him leave.'

Sieglitz was inside for an hour, came out alone.

'Okay, folks, work to do.' He'd spoken, he told them now, with a Sergeant Isles on the way in about protecting the sites. Isles had granted permission to backfill. Aled had given his approval. He understood Sue Klima was already at The Ferns. So they'd go to the beach. All but Annette and Greg. He looked at her. 'He's asked that you two help with packing up.'

The bewildered Aled was gone. He was all purpose. There was no chat. The only words spoken were his instructions, and their questions about how he wanted something wrapped, or which box to use. Annette understood why he'd asked for two. If her alone, silence on Marilyn would have been impossible.

The fish skeletons were displayed at Annette's workspace. She'd hardened them with polyvinyl acetate. Padded and boxed, they would travel. And for as long as they lasted, they would transport her back here. She cleared the tabletop all around them, unable to decide. Soon, though, Aled would ask. He went into the bedroom, Greg was bent over a box. She swept the skeletons into a paper bag and took the bag outside to the rubbish drum.

They were nearly finished, the trestle tables bare, the last boxes being filled and taped, when the familiar clatter of the Kombi came through the open louvres. Aled was crushing newspaper into springy balls and lining the base of a box. He straightened and spun towards the windows. The blood had left his face, he closed his eyes, began to pant. Annette thought he was having an attack of some sort and started towards him. Greg signalled *wait, leave him a sec*. Aled's breathing slowed, and he opened his eyes.

'Could I have a glass of water, please.'

Greg fetched it. Aled clutched the glass in both hands. The Kombi pulled up near the fireplace, and the clatter died.

Aled said in a high, breathy voice, 'Annette, would you find out please what that's doing here.'

As she descended the steps, a young policeman in sky-blue overalls swung from the Kombi's cab. Sue was walking over from closing the sliprails. The policeman called when she got close, 'Keys are in it,' and set off towards the steps down to the beach. Sue reached out and slapped the door shut. Its duco now sported a long, vivid scratch.

Annette pointed. 'What's that from?'

'A tree. He inside?'

'Yes. We're packing. He sent me to ask why the Kombi's here.'

'Where else is it supposed to go?'

Annette stepped aside and waved her towards the cabin, *I'm only the messenger.*

Sue took a couple of steps, lifted her arms, let them fall. 'Sorry. I've just come from dumping all the bagged spits back in the pit.'

Annette couldn't bring herself to unbend. She nodded towards the Kombi. 'So what's in there?'

'Our gear. And her stone. Some of the bone.' She hooked her head towards the other cabins. 'Is Brian here? I've got his swag.'

'No.'

'What — he hasn't been back?'

'Why would he?'

Sue stared at her. 'What's that supposed to mean?'

Annette shrugged. 'You'd know better than I do what was going on up there.'

'There wasn't anything "going on"! What the fuck's wrong with you!' She spun towards the fireplace, spat over her shoulder, 'They're *all* of her keys, tell him.'

*

Sieglitz came to the fire that night breathing whisky and announced that he'd just carried Aled to bed, and he'd be remaining with him until Aled chose to give up waiting. 'How ever long that is, our friend the ocean not reputed for being hurried.'

They, on the other hand, were free to leave in the morning, as early as they chose. They should take both the Kombi and the Land Rover. He brought the keys to both vehicles from his pocket, handed the Land Rover's to Greg. 'I'm informed you and he've had the conversation about the peculiarities of this beast, and where to unload.' He looked towards Sue, dangled the Kombi's key.

She walked to him and closed it into her palm.

'Park it at the Research School and leave the key with security.'

She nodded and, ignoring them all, walked towards the cabin she'd made hers — the interview cabin.

'Don't wait to be waved off, okay,' Sieglitz said. 'I think someone might have a sore head.'

Annette didn't watch him go, she watched Sue. Sue closed the door hard, locked it.

With Brian Harpur gone, Brandy had taken over the lighting and feeding of the fire. It needed feeding now. Annette waited for him to notice and followed him to the scattered remnants of the branches and blocks that had, on their arrival, looked like a small smashed hill.

'Can I ask you something?' She saw his face cloud, quickly added, 'Nothing dangerous. Greg's taking the Land Rover. So I'm wondering … can I get a lift with you?'

'Ah … yeah, I suppose. But he'll need Stu to help unload. And Paul's with me. So unless Brian shows up, Sue and Vick are each on their own.'

'I think you've seen already that'll suit Sue. And Vick's done the road once, she can do it again.'

'You've spoken to her.'

'No. I'm telling you what I prefer, which is get a lift with you.'

He looked past her towards the fire, returned his gaze to hers. 'Okay. You bring much?'

'Rucksack and sleeping bag, that's it.'

They were out of the cabins just after six. They didn't bother with a fire. No one took a 'last look' at the beach. Paul wanted to leave the keys for Gorman on the nearest fresh cowpat. Brandy poked them under Aled's door. Avoiding Vicky's eyes, Annette carried her rucksack and sleeping bag to the warpainted FJ and stowed them in the boot. Brandy insisted they be first to leave, not wanting to be stuck behind the smoking Kombi or Vicky crawling along in the Anglia.

First the jolt and rattle of the track, then — when they were finally on the highway and could wind down the windows —

the rush of air made talking close to impossible, a state that suited all three.

But coasting down the long hill into Queanbeyan, Annette leaned forward and said what she'd been rehearsing for the last hour.

'Hey … do either of you know of a house with a room going? I think Sue and me are finished at Masson Street.'

She saw the two exchange glances, Brandy nod. Paul swivelled to look at her.

'We got a junk room. Wouldn't take much to clear. You can stay there if you want. While you're looking.'

'That'd be great. Thanks. I'd prefer that right now to strangers.'

'How soon do you need it?' Brandy said at the windscreen.

'Is … today possible?'

Again, they exchanged glances.

'You want we pick up your stuff? Or you want a look first?'

'I don't need a look. Where are you?'

'Not far from you — O'Connor, Tate Street.' He caught her eye in the mirror. 'The Kombi'll be hours. We'll drop you, then dump our stuff and get the roof rack.'

The letterbox was choked with fliers. Annette separated them from the envelopes, dropped them in the bin. The hallway smelled of trapped air endlessly reheated. She strode through to the back double doors and threw them open. After the cabin, walking through a house felt almost luxurious. A ceiling was strange.

She packed fast, clothes in her suitcase and overnight bag, books and journals in cartons, bedding and towels in a knotted sheet. She would have to leave the bedbase, take only the mattress. It would fit on a roof rack. The desk could be tied upside down on the mattress, her chair go on the back seat. She carried everything but desk and mattress to the hallway. She would be abandoning all claim to the lounge room and kitchen.

Even as she told herself Brandy was right, the Kombi would be hours, she was nervous, her ears tuned to the street. She went to the kitchen and boiled the jug, then — the last time she'd sit with a tea at this old friend, the table — got the shopping pad and pencil and sat, pulled the small stack of envelopes towards her, laid the two for Sue in the empty fruit bowl, and opened the bills. She fetched her wallet, counted out three tens, and left notes and bills beneath the sugar bowl. Then she placed her door key beside the bowl and went out to the front steps to wait.

The Tate Street house was a red-brick bungalow behind a bottlebrush hedge. A huge eucalypt — a *mannifera*, Brandy warned her, brittle gum, don't stand under it in wind — roofed the entire front yard. Their feet crackled up the driveway.

The third person in the house was Paul's younger brother, Warwick, starting his second year of science. He knocked shyly at her open door while she was taking books from the cartons. It was a fair bit further to campus than from Masson Street.

They all used bikes. He'd got a new one for Christmas. Annette could use his old one. Did she want a look? She dropped the books onto the mattress and walked with him out to the garage.

They learned from the television that night that North Teapot, 'the suspected drowning of ANU academic Dr Marilyn Herr', was already old news. The segment was a spoken update, without footage. Police were questioning local fishermen about currents. A watch would be kept on beaches to the north and south for the remainder of the week. The reader began a recapitulation. Paul stood and strode to the kitchen.

'You?' Brandy said quietly.

Annette shook her head. He walked to the box and jabbed the power button.

She rang home and got her father, heard the relief in his voice. They'd rung the university, but no one there had been able to tell them anything. Annette assured him she was all right, just shaken. Her mother spoke over him, did she want them to come down! No, she said, she was with friends, from the dig. But at a different address.

'Give it to me, please,' her father said. 'And the number.'

She'd decided before dialling that she couldn't talk to him about Isles, the interview, she needed to be watching his face. But with his calm, competent voice in her ear she almost blurted out that she had to talk to him about something important, and would he ring her back. What stopped her was the phone itself, in the open hallway.

Afterwards, sitting at the table in their bare kitchen, Paul asked what she thought would happen with the sites. They'd just about finished at the beach, but The Ferns was hardly started. She didn't know, Annette said. They could maybe ask Sieglitz. What the protocol was. But she supposed both sites remained ANU 'property'.

'Well, I won't be going back there,' Brandy said.

Paul looked at her.

She shook her head. 'I honestly don't know. I'm not being evasive. Just too soon to be able to say.'

'Not for me,' Brandy said. He didn't look up. 'The place, how the cops were, Brian taking off ... whole thing's bloody weird.'

'And it ain't over,' Paul said. 'And it's not just down there we got to worry about.' He laid his hand briefly on Annette's wrist, withdrew it as he spoke. 'Sorry to be blunt, mate, but right now I wouldn't give you much for your honours. Can't say I'm thrilled, either, by the idea of being back on campus. I don't have the choice, but. I walk, I'm straight into the army. So's Greg. Brandy's okay, he was balloted out.'

'Doesn't mean I'm not thinking about it.' Brandy looked at her. 'At least you're up on us two, you've *got* your piece of paper. You can do your honours somewhere else.'

'But *here* is where I want to do it, Canberra. This's home.'

He shrugged. 'You're in the same boat, then.'

The night was hotter than nights at the coast. The sash was as high as it could go, but the air in the room was an immovable block. She lay on her back on the top sheet. There'd been tension at the cabins, but a fixed routine. She'd lain down each night knowing what she'd be doing next day. Now her head held nothing but questions.

She needed money but didn't want to ring the Maelevis at the patisserie, explain that she was back early and could she come in. They read the papers, watched the news. And her honours, yes. Paul had only stated what she already knew. If Aled took indefinite leave, or resigned even, she didn't have a supervisor. But as she'd said, Canberra was now home. After three years, the only friends she had were here. So what — or, more precisely, who — were her options? She didn't much like Sieglitz. Worse, didn't trust him. She hadn't said so to Paul and Brandy, but was sure in the coming days he would ingratiate himself with Isles to get the look at The Ferns denied him by Marilyn. Patricia Meylor wasn't particularly likeable, either. But if there was to be a conversation about her academic future, it should probably be with her ex-tutor. 'Seeing you're pretty low on choices,' she said at the ceiling.

Start of term wasn't far off, just over a month. She needed to go in to the department. Aled had given her four hours a week tutoring first-years. Annette hadn't begun preparing in more than a general way. Before going down the coast, she'd glanced at her lecture notes of three years ago, had stood for a few minutes in the broom closet of a room she'd been allocated as an office. She didn't, though, have a copy of the new handbook.

She needed one soon, this week. And running under all these questions was the question she didn't yet want to face. Had North Teapot killed the passion?

When she woke, she told herself she was going in that day. But it was an effort just to get dressed and walk to the kitchen and pour and eat a bowl of cereal. Brandy and Paul, too, seemed dazed, unable to do more than sit at the kitchen table stripped to shorts and sucking on cans of VB until the back yard was cool enough for them to flop on the lawn. Annette sat with them in her bikini, sucking on ice cubes.

Next day was the same.

But on the third morning, before the others emerged from their rooms, she had a shower and washed her hair, put on a clean T-shirt, jeans, and sandals, and wheeled her borrowed bike from the garage.

The department corridor was empty, all its doors closed except that of the secretary, Jan. Annette stepped along the wall, hoping to use the corridor's width to pass by unseen. Impossible if Jan was sitting at her desk — she was a hawk. Annette halted and listened. No sounds came from the room. She advanced another step and peeped in. A mug sat on the desk, wisps of steam rising from it. A tap squealed and water ran into a steel sink. Annette skimmed along the wall to her room, silently let herself in, as silently closed the door.

The room was exactly as she'd seen it last, even to the fluff on the carpet. There was a dustpan and broom on the bookshelf, themselves furred with dust. Annette flicked her rucksack from her shoulders and lowered it by its straps to the floor.

She had taken two steps when there was a gentle knock. She froze. But she couldn't pretend she wasn't here, clearly Jan had glimpsed or heard her. She prepared an apologetic face and went to the door. Standing in the corridor was Brian Harpur.

Her reaction was purely instinctual — as he opened his mouth, she blurted 'No!' and slapped the door shut.

He knocked and called her name. Annette retreated to the desk. The lock, she saw now, was unsnibbed. But her heart was slowing. If he knew, he wouldn't be gently knocking, he'd be hammering, demanding that she speak to him. Or he'd barge in. He knocked again. Annette opened her mouth to call *what do you want*, and stopped herself. If she started a conversation through the door, eventually she'd have to open it.

In the last weeks she'd lost the habit of strapping on her watch. She looked at the wall clock. The sweep hand didn't move. The silence, though, had begun to grow. She leaned towards the door, straining to hear. The lino of the corridor was thick, soundless. Annette counted to thirty, the voice beneath the counting telling her *this is ridiculous, you're not a child, open the door, if he's still there talk to him*. She couldn't. She was seeing him lying down the back of the dune.

She picked up the dusty receiver, praying that Jan was back

at her desk. The woman answered after two rings, alarm in her 'hello?'

'Hello, Jan. It's Annette Cooley. I'm in the casual tutors' room. I'll come and see you in a minute, but could you look in the corridor, please, and tell me if there's anyone outside my door.'

There was the clatter of the receiver being put down on the desk. Annette waited for it to be snatched up. Instead, there came a fierce double-rap and the woman barking her name. Annette scurried to the door. Jan waved both ways along the empty corridor.

'What's this about, Annette? I've had reporters here. Is one of them harassing you?'

'No, no. One of the boys from the dig. He's interested in me, but I'm not interested in him.'

Appalled by the lie, Annette felt heat infuse her face. Jan, though, she knew, was concerned more with the fact that her corridor had been breached — and not once, but twice.

'And you've told him that?'

'He knows, yes.' Annette saw her flicking through possible names. 'He's not in Prehistory, he joined us for the dig.'

'Ah.' The woman's face relaxed. 'And is he likely to be back?'

'I don't think so. I hope not.'

'Well if he's so brash as to return, you call me immediately. He has little right to be in the department, and none at all without seeing me first.'

Jan was her mother's age. Annette fought down the impulse to fling her arms around her and tell her. Who Brian Harpur really was, and what she'd told Isles about him.

'So … how are you?' The woman's voice was softer. 'I didn't know you were in.'

'Sorry. I looked in at the office. We're all sort of … in a daze. The whole thing's just …' Brandy's word came, 'weird.' Sieglitz would have spoken to her. 'You'd know about the second site.' Jan nodded. 'So have you had any word from Aled?' The woman's nostrils flared. Annette began to correct herself, then didn't care. 'About when they might be back?'

'I spoke on the phone yesterday to Dr Sieglitz. He and Professor Wray are still down there. As to expecting him back, I think that's not a question anyone, including the university, should be putting. Certainly not at this stage. I quite understand, however, why you'd be asking, and you're not alone. I'm being pestered from all points.' Jan looked through the doorway, pursed her lips. 'This room needs cleaning. I'll speak to them.'

Annette asked if she had a copy of the new handbook. She did.

Four mornings later, Annette rode from the gateless driveway at Tate Street and Brian Harpur stepped from behind the grevillea growing on the verge. She braked hard and the weight of books in her rucksack almost pitched her over the handlebars. He grabbed the bike and her arm and prevented her falling, then quickly let go.

She swore from fright, not of him so much as from how close she'd come to a spill.

'Sorry, sorry! I just need to talk to you!'

She was still shocked by the unexpectedness. How had he found her! 'How are you ... here?'

He motioned behind him. Annette saw a much better bike than the one she was riding propped in the gutter.

'No — *here*! Did you follow me!'

He waved the demand away. 'Please. I'm in hell!'

The truth of that was in his face. The rims of his eyes were red-raw, his hair was matted, he hadn't shaved since knocking at her door, when he'd been clean-shaven, one of the few details she remembered of that blurred encounter.

'I know why you're avoiding me, whoever told the cops told you, too.'

Her stomach flipped. But Brian Harpur didn't pause to observe the effect of what he'd said, he gabbled on.

'It was only the once, I swear it was! I can't even begin to say how ashamed I am, that it was even once. But it was *all* I did! Please believe me, you have to! I never touched her. The fucking cops —' His hands fluttered like birds in her face, 'Sorry, sorry, I'm sorry. I'm only swearing because I'm ...' He wiped his eyes and blew a gout of air, brought his breathing under control. 'Isles — you know, in charge — he asked me to my face did

I rape her then get frightened and kill her. He asked me *that*!'
Brian Harpur began to cry.

Her mind, as he'd spoken, had grown cold. She needed him
gone before Brandy or Paul saw him. They weren't stupid, they
would ask what he'd wanted with her. She'd need a good answer.
He couldn't go home, Brian Harpur was saying — Isles would
have told the cops in Cooma to keep tabs on him.

'The news'll get around why. They only let me go, he said
— Isles — because they didn't have the evidence to arrest me.
But soon as they did they'd be on my doorstep like a shot.' He
smeared his palms across his eyes. Annette heard a click as he
swallowed. When he spoke again, his voice had lost its shivery
quality. He boarded with his cousin out at Woden. She and
her husband would have a fit if the cops turned up. The bike
wasn't his, his was at their house. He'd nicked this one, but was
taking it back. He'd slept the last three nights in his swag behind
Engineering. He wasn't asking to stay, he added quickly, he was
just telling her why he looked the way he did. Tears welled again
in his eyes. 'I just wish she'd wash up so they find her!'

I bet you do, she thought. She looked past him at the grevillea
to prevent disgust triggering her tongue.

Still evading his eyes, she told him she didn't know who'd
spoken to the police, that the stuff she knew about him, that
he was referring to, had come from Isles. Isles had come over
to the fire before he and the other detective had left that day.
'He was telling us, he said, only because we'd all seen you leave

203

the cabin in a "distressed state" and he didn't want us jumping to worse conclusions. That when you came back the boys shouldn't think they needed to do something, it was a police matter.' She glanced at his face. He wasn't scrutinising her, he was looking up, unseeing, into the brittle gum. Her elaborate lie had confirmed for him, Annette saw, the explanation he'd arrived with.

She asked would he allow her past, please. She appreciated all he'd done for her down there, she was sorry for the situation he was in, but there was nothing she could do to change it. He might see her as a friend, but she thought she'd made plain before they left North Teapot that she no longer saw him that way, so would he please accept that and leave her alone. As she finished the speech Annette stood on the raised pedal and the bike coasted down onto the road.

She didn't look back, but listened intently until she reached the turn into Westgarth Street for the ticking of another hub.

Annette saw him once more, at the memorial gathering.

It was a secular affair, beneath the giant casuarinas on the bank of the Cotter, a week before term began. She drove out with Brandy and Paul. Sue, already there, looked through her. Annette stood with Vicky. Prehistory staff were there, and people she guessed were from the Research School. Tom Sieglitz gave the eulogy. Annette found that odd, even if no one else did. That he would even have offered. A cousin spoke of Marilyn's early life, a girl growing up on a lonely farm who always dreamed of going to university. Vicky leaned in and whispered, 'Is he it for family?' Annette whispered back that she didn't know. She remembered Aled once cancelling a joint seminar on the Clyde because Marilyn was in Armidale, her mother sick. 'Lonely' carried the suggestion of an only child.

Aled stood surrounded by colleagues, but seemed only tenuously present. He didn't speak. Annette found herself watching him more than she did the speakers. He didn't watch the speakers at all, held himself very still, alternating between bowing his head and looking up into the gently heaving brooms of the casuarinas. When he'd arrived, he'd shaken hands and permitted himself to be embraced, but woodenly, as if he'd forgotten that these were the rituals. Annette had held back, not wanting to 'perform'. So had most of them from North Teapot. The only one she saw go and shake his hand was Greg, and his face as he walked away was hurt and baffled.

The vice-chancellor spoke of the university's loss, and of the loss to Australian prehistory, most famously of course, to that of the Clyde River, but also to the prehistory of the Murrumbidgee River, beside which they were standing today, and lately — her time there cut tragically short — that of the New South Wales South Coast. He looked up from his notes to flick a worried glance at Aled, aware that what he'd said were the right words, but of little comfort to a husband robotic with grief. Annette felt sorry for the man, having to feign knowledge of staff he might rarely, if ever, have met.

Vicky nudged her elbow. When Annette turned, Vicky nodded away to their right. Brian Harpur was standing against the trunk of a casuarina, too far away for him to be hearing what was being said, or for her to make out his expression. She wondered how he'd travelled out there. He was fit enough to have done it on a bike. They hadn't, though, passed him on the road.

When the tributes were over, Annette looked quickly again along her shoulder, hoping he hadn't come closer and she'd find herself looking into his face. But he was gone.

She'd half-expected the suggestion to be made of crossing the stream and walking up, those who wished, to Marilyn's site on the sand ridge, which had been the backdrop to the speeches. Few people there, she supposed, knew of its significance. But someone did, apart from Aled, to have chosen the Cotter.

Aled wasn't capable of suggestions. Sieglitz was escorting him up the grass slope to the car park, a hand hovering at his back like a father with an unsteady toddler. A woman Annette didn't know, possibly from the Research School, walked shyly, almost surreptitiously, to the crossing stones, stepped out onto the first, and bent and launched a hand bouquet of wattle into the current, bobbed her head, retreated to the bank. She was emblematic, Annette thought, of the whole ceremony — no one, herself included, quite knowing what to say or do. Nothing had been announced about a wake. People milled about for a bit longer, then drifted over to their cars and drove away.

The decision, when it came, came fully formed.

Annette was sitting in the casual tutors' room with *Prehistoric Societies* and her old lecture notes open on the desk. A voice so clear she sat straight in the chair and almost looked over her shoulder said, *You don't believe any more in any of this.*

'No,' she said at the splayed book. 'You don't.'

She nodded three, four times, then stood and picked up her rucksack, opened the door and inserted the key in the external lock, pulled the door closed, and walked along the corridor as if merely going to lunch.

At five o'clock, Brandy drove her to the station.

Part Two
January 2005 – May 2006

Annette was drenched. She stood on the hallway runner and stripped to bra and underpants, then grabbed the old towel Brent used for wiping down his bike — too angry to care what state it was in — and gave her hair a drubbing. Her wheat-straw linen trousers were speckled from the knees down with what looked like rust. She draped them over the handlebars, hung her shirt from the mirror. On her way to the kitchen, she glanced into the phone alcove. Blinking, three.

She put on her downstairs dressing gown and made and poured a tea, and stood at the kitchen windows warming her fingers on the mug. The courtyard table was awash. Bruised grape leaves were plastered to its planks, the citronella candles she'd meant to bring inside days ago sat drowned in their bowls. The pond was a lake, a creek running into it. From where? Annette leaned her forehead to the glass — and let out a moan of protest. A waterfall pouring over the blocked laundry gutter had torn half the hardenbergia from its trellis! She took an involuntary step towards the door. There was no point, the damage was done.

Another bloody job! *And* unclog the downpipe! She knew
what Brent would say, *don't you get up there, get 'rambling boy'*
on the ladder. She lifted her wrist before remembering her watch
was folded into a tea towel. She swivelled and looked at the
clock. Brent wouldn't be in yet from the field. But would be if
it was bucketing there, too. He might be one of the messages.
Annette topped up the mug and carried it, cradled in both
hands, into the alcove.

Her father-in-law's deaf bellow boomed from the speaker.
She stabbed the skip button. Chris, their accountant, couldn't
find travel receipts for November in Brent's BAS folder. The
third message was silent. Then a woman croaked 'hello,' gave a
strangled cough, and cleared her throat.

'Try again. Hello, Annette, it's Susan Klima. Yes, a very long
time, but I thought you'd want to know. It hasn't yet hit the
news. Marilyn's been found.'

The spastic jerk of her hand threw tea over her wrist. Annette
set the mug on the phone table and clamped a hand to her
mouth. The red and green lozenges of the glass panels down
the sides of the front door blurred. She groped her way to the
bottom of the stairs and sat.

'So you were there. God. All this time.' But 'found'. What
did that mean? She smeared her palms up her cheeks. 'What it
means is, you were bloody right!'

She stood and replayed the message. Sue's voice had deepened
and darkened. She'd delayed hanging up, either debating with

herself whether to say more, or if she should leave a number. Annette had, over the intervening years, done sporadic trawls of the literature looking for names from North Teapot. The only one she'd ever found — apart from Aled Wray's — was Sue's. In her last trawl, some six or seven years back, Sue was at La Trobe. She must have returned to ANU. Nowhere else would Marilyn's name still carry instant recognition. The call had come at ten-fourteen. By now the story would be well and truly in the media's maw. Annette strode back into the kitchen and looked at the clock. She'd missed the first ten minutes of *SBS News*. The ABC then, at seven.

In the shower, their young faces came crowding in. Annette made them stand in line, spoke each name, looked at the face. Sue's was as clear as a photograph. And Brandy's. He'd left a deep mark. The others were fuzzier. But the face she didn't want to see was as sharp as Sue's. Brian Harpur was looking up at her from the creek at The Ferns, the just-dipped billy in his hand. It was possibly the last time Annette had liked him. She knew what would come next, and it did, the image locked in her brain — the dune, his back, the dark head out beyond the breakers. Annette hadn't had a visitation in years, not even in a dream. The squares of the tiles came back into focus. The bathroom was a cloud of steam! She lunged for the taps.

She filled a glass from the opened riesling in the fridge and carried it into the lounge room. The screen was still giving tasters of the evening's fare. Normally she'd have paid attention, but now growled, 'Yes, enough — hurry up!'

The Boxing Day tsunami was finally receding from the headlines, the rocks of domestic politics resurfacing. The Labor Party's 'new' leader, elected that day, was Kim Beazley, his second attempt at the job. Of more potential damage to the government was the first Australian casualty of the Iraq War. A photograph filled the screen of the flight lieutenant and his widow on their wedding day, followed — for 'balance', Annette supposed — by smiling lines of people outside a polling station. She was too impatient for anger, muttered, 'Come *on*,' and, in answer, the newsreader returned. He glanced at his running sheets, then looked into the camera, at her. Annette took a gulp of wine.

'On the South Coast of New South Wales, a mystery spanning thirty-four years almost to the day is close, perhaps, to being solved. Police believe human remains washed from a gully at North Teapot beach may be those of Dr Marilyn Herr, whose disappearance in nineteen seventy-one, while carrying out archaeological excavations, sparked an intensive search.'

A gully? The track gully?

But Marilyn was on screen. Annette's initial reaction was confusion, at the mismatch with memory. Then tears filled her throat. Even in grainy black-and-white, the woman was beautiful. An elbow intruded. The portrait was blown up from a group photograph! The trunk in the background was a spotted gum. Was it the Clyde? If so, she, Annette, was almost certainly in the same photograph. She could be the elbow! She leaned to peer, and Marilyn vanished, the gully mouth filled the screen. A long, fluttering curve of crime-scene tape was tied at each end to a banksia trunk and half-hitched about clean new tomato stakes.

'Evidence was given at the inquest into the disappearance of the thirty-six-year-old Canberra academic that she was a strong swimmer who frequently surfed alone, including at night. Items of clothing found on the beach initially led police to believe that on the night she disappeared she may have got into difficulties and drowned.'

The sight of the lomandra in the gully mouth sent a hot prickling down Annette's legs. Wading through the blades were two men in white overalls, each carrying flat, and almost reverently, a heavily taped cardboard dress box.

'However, after evidence was given of tension at the sites, and the admission by a team member to having been a peeping Tom, the coroner declined to hand down a finding of probable death by misadventure, and returned instead an open finding.'

Keeping the boxes level, the men ducked beneath the crime tape and strode towards a trio of white Land Cruisers parked on the harder sand between dunes and sea.

'The verdict gave rise at the time to controversy, but appears to have been vindicated in the light of this morning's grim discovery.'

The camera cut back to the gully mouth. A man in a white open-necked shirt and jeans stood flanked by banksia trunks.

Annette took a startled step towards the screen, the trunk on the right had a deep fissure. Was it where she'd jammed the envelope? She didn't get the chance to see, the camera closed on the man. *Det-Serg* something, read a caption across his stomach, gone too quickly, while Annette was still studying his face. But she couldn't possibly know him, he'd have been a child.

Who'd made the discovery, a young woman's voice asked. A local resident, the man said into the lens. The resident had recognised the remains as human and contacted police. No, until a forensic examination had been carried out police weren't in a position to state whether the remains were, in fact, those of Dr Herr, but the location, yes, made it a strong possibility. And did he have an opinion on whether, if the remains turned out to be Dr Herr's, she had drowned or was murdered? Annette snorted in disbelief. Who was this fool! Did she think the dead climbed into their own graves! The detective, too, did a double take, before answering smoothly that neither precluded the other, but, as with identification, cause of death would also need to be established. He was one of the new breed of policeman that had arrived on television, comfortable before a camera, vocabulary and syntax educated. Annette swore at herself for not getting his name and magically the caption appeared again, *Det-Serg Wayne Townshend, Batemans Bay*. She hushed her mind for the next question. Instead, the screen cut to a long shot of the beach, sunlit, a lazy swell running, the shore break blinding white. Consider, the camera saying, the beautiful places death inhabits.

The newsreader reappeared behind his desk. 'That report from our South Coast correspondent, Jemma Campbell.'

Annette strode to the set and hit the power button. 'What idiot sent a baby! She wasn't even born!'

Annette lifted the glass and only then saw it was empty. When had she drunk it? And she'd forgotten the cop's name, too angry at the baby. Then pictured again the caption, *Townshend*. She walked out to the phone table and scribbled the name on the pad.

The rain had eased to drizzle. She stood staring into the yard, but seeing the gully. The only possible place was where she'd never set foot, beyond the boulder. The police had supposedly done a thorough search. Little would have shown on the track as far as the boulder, it was trodden hard as concrete. But beyond there, any disturbance would have been visible, certainly footprints or dragmarks. Highly visible after only a day. The burrawangs themselves retained a faint wake from any passage through them. Was it, then, another gully? But there *was* no other.

She'd been staring out as she stared inward. She was looking at the answer. Water from the blocked downpipe was still flowing across the path. The creek itself! He'd carried Marilyn up the creek bed. Not in his arms, he couldn't, the banks were too choked. No, down his back. Her arms over his shoulders and clutching her by the elbows. But, God, her dead breasts pressing into his shoulderblades. Annette could *see* him. He and his burden were just out past the window.

217

But this was dusk, not night. At night, it would be feeling with your feet to stay in the flow. Meeting a rock with your big toe, working round it. Moving crouched because a stumble, any sign imprinted on the bank, would make all this terrified carefulness for nothing. And he must have been terrified. Whatever he'd imagined himself doing would not have included killing her. That much Annette would grant him.

He'd been a year older than she, so he was fifty-five. Barring accident or disease he was alive. He might already be in custody. Gorman, too, had been named, but him they could now discount — his hips had barely carried *him*.

'Anyway, you'd be dead.'

The yard was still light, but in the kitchen night had fallen. Annette walked to the side wall and flicked on the spots, then to the counter and pulled out a stool. This time there'd be a trial. She'd never been inside a courtroom. Brent would have to overcome his antipathy to courts and the legal system — 'the tool of the enemy' — and go with her. The person she really wanted, though, who would have *insisted* on being present, was her father.

Annette had told him in her first week back from Canberra — just the two of them sitting on her bed, the door closed — about Brian Harpur. How he'd come to be on the dig, and the feelings she'd developed for him, and his 'betrayal' of what she'd thought existed between them.

Her father had, since childhood, been the one she'd gone

to for advice. But never about her emotional life. That, she'd kept strictly to herself. He displayed no open unease at this crossing of boundaries, but she saw his lawyer's antennae bristle, his mind already sifting the possibilities of where this might be going. Which she then gave him. What she'd seen in the dunes two days before Marilyn disappeared, the interview with Isles, and the statement she'd made on condition it not be taken down. She was quietly proud, thinking he would be, too, that, in a stressful situation, she'd had the wit and coolness to extract the condition. He'd quickly deflated her, telling her bluntly that her 'condition' was worthless — that her 'interlocutor' would have made notes as soon as she left the cabin and got the other detective to witness. She still remembered his exact words. 'The reason being, my darling, not duplicity, but because your obliging sergeant was conducting what might well turn out to be a murder investigation.'

By the time the inquest had come on, she was in London. Her father had dealt with the coroner's office. But, as he'd predicted, a copy of her 'verbal' statement had arrived in the mail requiring a statutory declaration.

'So today makes you twice right, Dad.'

That would have pleased him.

She closed her eyes and pressed fingers to her forehead. The incredible typist was Hite. The sergeant's wouldn't come. Annette had his face. Still it wouldn't come. It was upstairs, a minute away. 'No! Hite and ...' She opened her eyes, clapped her hands in front of her face, 'This is ridiculous!' She stood and snatched up the magnifiers she kept on the counter for cooking in.

Sixteen years ago, she and Brent had rationalised their two studies into one so Gaby could have her own room. This room had been Brent's, but had always been too big, a third of it filled with suitcases, superfluous chairs, a mini pool table. He'd welcomed her in, was used, like Annette, to working in the presence of others. He'd kept the window overlooking the park, having call still sometimes, despite computers, to pore over maps. He usually lowered the matchstick blind to protect the cedar of his desk and his leather chair from the morning sun, but had neglected to. The light over the park was a dense, eerie purple, the city's reflection on the underside of the storm clouds. Annette didn't pull the switch cord, instead walking to the back of his chair to look out at the light. The smell of him drifting up from the leather returned her to the room.

He kept a tidy desk, even his keyboard perfectly centred. They could sit at their respective computers for an hour without exchanging a word, but it was a companionable silence. Annette liked having the familiar shape of his head in the corner of her eye. She liked also that, in the pattern of the huge Moroccan rug that covered most of the floor, there was a winding path that joined the runners of her chair to the runners of his. Annette had never pointed it out, Brent would have given her his 'spare me' look. She moved round to the side of his desk and released and lowered the blind, realising as it hit the sill that she should have first turned on a light. But she could see. She walked to her desk and switched on the lamp.

The binder was on the top shelf, hard against the end. Its neighbours were the only archaeological volumes she still owned — the three *Mankind* that contained the Clyde papers and Aled's 'preliminary', and only, paper on North Teapot, and the *Archaeology in Oceania* that contained Tom Sieglitz's and Sue's excavation of The Ferns. The last time Annette had touched them was sixteen years ago when she'd placed them here. She'd not opened any of them since 1972, when she'd read The Ferns.

She reached up and hooked her finger in the binder, to start it from the row. It came easily, being virtually empty, a half-dozen sheets of carbon paper. The cardboard creaked when she raised the cover.

ISLES — yes! It had even a whimsical sound, but only now. He, too, if he was alive, now had his answer. The other names on the page were also in capitals — her own, Marilyn's, Aled's, North Teapot. Annette took the magnifiers off, but continued to stare at the page, taken by its strangeness. It was years since she'd laid eyes on a carbon. It looked so primitive, the minute crinkling left by the roller, the watery blue of the type.

Annette shut the binder and inserted it into its narrow slot, tapped it home. As her fingertips left the spine, the phone rang, making her jump. She spun her chair and sat and snatched up the receiver. 'Hello, darling.'

'That was quick. I thought you'd be watching telly.'

'No, I'm upstairs — nothing worth watching. Your father rang. I didn't play it. Do you want me to?'

'No, I'll just give him a call.'

'And Chris, about missing receipts.'

'Oh hell. Okay.'

He would have come in too late to have caught the news. The only name that might have chimed was North Teapot. Brent had spent time on the South Coast, both before they'd met and on fishing trips with Lucas. They'd almost never spoken of her abandoned profession.

'So how were the coal trains after a few days away?'

'Didn't hear them. I must be getting used to the place.'

'You said you might have some idea this week how much longer the job'll run.'

'It's only Tuesday, love. Hopefully by Friday. Why?'

He would ask if she wanted him to come home, and she would say yes. Annette dipped her head and wiped each eye quickly on a sleeve and lifted the receiver again to her mouth.

'Oh … just, empty-house blues.'

She hadn't got the tone right, too self-consciously cheery. Beneath it, the choke of tears. There was a silence while he replayed her in his head.

'You sure?'

'Yes.'

'I take it, then, that rambling boy hasn't put in an appearance.'

'Not tonight, no. So far.' Annette waited to see whether it was just their old argument. 'Why — did you want him?'

'Only if he was there.'

'Don't be mysterious.'

'There's a Fender fretless bass, pretty good nick, in the window of the hockshop here. It's a steal, hundred and forty bucks, which I'll knock down.'

'No, Brent! You can hardly get into his room for instruments now. And it'll become one *more* distraction!' She was acting more vehemence than she felt, glad to have found her own distraction in this low-level domestic.

'Agreed. Finito. So, did we get any rain? It's pissing down here.'

'I got very pissed on.'

He laughed, quickly stifled it. 'Sorry. Not a lot else at this end, mate. I better go — haven't had dinner, and I still have to download.'

Annette didn't tell him she'd not eaten either, that would have set a bell ringing. She said goodnight, waited till he hung up.

She took the bottle from the fridge and put it back and made a camomile. She fried tomato halves and two eggs, which she ate with left-over rice. She rinsed plate and pan and turned off the spots, deadlocked the back door. The hallway light she left on.

She set the alarm for six and got into bed. She didn't want to read, but couldn't bring herself to switch off the lamp, not wanting, either, what the dark might bring. She forced her mind to go to the library. The rest of the shelving was due to arrive in the morning. Who knew, though, whether capital works would turn up. It was a lottery at the moment, renovation going on all over campus. At least the painters would be out by mid-morning. That was the promise, anyway. Annette hoped for Oliver's sake they kept it. He'd reached his limit. She wouldn't be up to a major dummy-spit. She wasn't sure she was up even to going in.

She did a short pranayama and turned off the lamp. So, at last, an answer. Painful stuff to come, yes, plenty. But an answer! For them all, wherever they were.

She was woken by the *clung* of the front-door deadlock. She was still on her back. She held her breath and listened. He was alone — or the girl had been worded up. But Annette's ears picked up only one pair of feet. And not going to the kitchen, but climbing the stairs. His bedroom door sighed open, closed with the faintest of clicks.

Annette heard the soft bump of the viola case being stood in its corner and arched her neck to hear what he picked up. Her boy could never go straight to bed, there was always some riff he had to transfer from his head to an instrument. There came a run of notes on guitar, then the same run, but slower, finishing with a chorded seventh. He began again. Annette released her neck and turned onto her sleeping side.

*

224

In summer, the corner shop opened at six. Annette bought the top *Herald* from the just-cut bundle. She made herself fold it and tuck it under her arm.

But once inside the front door, she kicked off her thongs and strode to the kitchen and slapped the paper open on the table. More on the Labor Party's woes, the dead lieutenant and his bride, the tennis player Lleyton Hewitt to marry. Not front-page news, then. Page five, said the 'Inside' column, *Beach skeleton identified*. While she'd slept, others, it seemed, had been busy.

The photograph of Marilyn was the same grainy enlargement. Annette's gaze jumped to the other, that of a man standing at the tape fencing off the gully. If it was Aled, he was changed beyond recognition. But no, the man was Lionel Flett, a retired science teacher and the finder of the 'remains'. She moved down the page to the two break-out boxes. The smaller was a biography, the familiar jumping out, *doctorate University of Sydney, married to fellow archaeologist Dr Aled Wray, Clyde River 'village'*. Unfamiliar was Guyra. A memory stirred, of Marilyn mentioning she was off a farm, the cousin at the memorial gathering. The bigger box was a description of The Ferns and a statement by an archaeologist Annette didn't know of the importance of the site to Australian prehistory. It wasn't a fact she wanted waved in her face, nor the names of the excavators. She returned to the main article and Mr Flett.

The storm that drenched her had come up the coast. When the seas abated, Mr Flett had walked up the beach to check on the 'Aboriginal fish trap'. Its walls had endured, then, for a further three decades. And they had a guardian, his shirt buttoned to the top, the part in his thinning hair as straight as a stringline. How strange that Marilyn should be found by this man, her apparent antithesis in every respect but his passion.

After satisfying himself that the walls were intact, Mr Flett had seen a wombat at the back of the beach. It was skittering about on the sand, making sudden short dashes towards the gully mouth, then circling. After watching the animal for several minutes, he became convinced it was distressed. Since moving to North Teapot, he had taken an interest in wombats. Contrary to popular belief, they were not good engineers, often dug burrows in silly places. Perhaps a tree had come down, trapping her young, or the burrow had flooded. The animal finally noticed him and bolted into the gully. He gave her a safe start and followed.

At the head of the gully he came to an earth bench riddled with wombat runs. No trees were down, but a lot of soil was. There was no sign of the mother, apart from clawmarks in the collapsed soil. At the edge of the slip, though, the opposite had occurred, an old burrow had been exposed. Projecting from the mouth was a bone of what at first Mr Flett took to be a long-dead wombat, but which, on closer inspection, he knew, having taught anatomy, to be a human shinbone. He'd read and heard the stories attached to North Teapot.

'So I had a pretty strong inkling of who I was looking at, poor woman.'

The sandstone paving at the library's entrance was carpeted with the drop sheets that, for the last fortnight, had shrouded the shelves.

The oldest of the painters was coming through the demobilised doors with a fistful of caulking guns. He flipped one into his hand and bailed her up. 'See! And yous didn't believe us, did yous!'

Annette placed a hand on her heart. 'I never doubted for a second.'

The man feigned to choke on the lie, then, with his wheezy smoker's laugh, pointed her to the door with the barrel.

Inside, it was a library again. Figures in white overalls were drawing the drop sheets from the serials. Those on the floor remained, but were bare, ready to be folded when all risk of spills was over. Oliver was standing before the circulation desk, arms folded, his face dark.

Annette halted beside him. 'Morning. Why the face?'

'I'm just informed they need to come *back* and do the windows and frames. It seems our allotted time is up. So there's to be another invasion later this year.'

'It won't be an "invasion", surely, for just a few windows.'

Annette had worked there as long as he had, and longer than any of the others. It fell to her to avert his glooms.

'You'd like to think not.' Oliver heaved another sigh. 'The bright side, I suppose, is that they're out when they said.'

At nine-thirty, weaving a dance around the departing painters, the men from capital works began assembling the new shelves in the annexe from which the old, indeed nineteenth-century, wooden shelving had been removed. It was now, Annette mused, a 'modern' library, almost entirely devoid of the warmth of timber, the sole survivor being the long table of English oak in the reference room. The men were clearly under orders to work fast and get to more important jobs, for there was none of the byplay and wandering around she'd come to expect of university workmen.

By eleven there were two walls of brown anodised steel waiting for books. Annette stood looking through the arched doorways that linked the three rooms. The transformation that had begun with a single row of computers was now complete, the place wholly a creature of moulded plastic, vinyl, and steel. Strangely, Oliver — whom she'd always assumed to be even more of a romantic than she — loved the bright, hard surfaces. He'd been all for getting rid of the oak table with its century and a half of graffiti.

Though the doors were open, the library was closed. She and the other staff began wheeling the trolleys of books out of the dead aisle where they'd stood like trucks in a railway siding. Annette was glad of the physical work of pushing and lifting, knocking spines into line. And the solitude. The steel shelving clanged and echoed, drowning any attempt at chat, and they were working apart so as not to get in each others' way. Nonetheless, after an hour, Julie, the closest of her work friends, stopped her emptied trolley beside the one Annette was emptying and asked if she was okay.

'Me? Fine.'

'Just, you seem a bit … absent. Not having to play referee again, are you?'

It was an intimate workplace. They celebrated birthdays, buying a house, once, a modest Lotto win. They knew the names of spouses or partners, children, and discussed them freely. So it should have been no surprise that Julie remembered the fights.

'No. He seems actually to be doing some work. At last. And Brent's still up in the Hunter.'

'Aah.'

'Not *that*, either.'

But Julie stayed, watching her face.

It was still too raw, it wasn't the place. But the biggest barrier was age. Julie was forty-one, seven when Marilyn disappeared. Even Brent would require too much explanation. Sure, Annette intended to tell him, tonight. But she craved a listener for whom the names Clyde I and Clyde II, North Teapot, The Ferns were enough, contained their histories. The others, too, would have noticed that something was wrong, they just hadn't yet got around to asking. They would over lunch.

Annette shrugged, attempted a smile. 'I didn't sleep very well

— not for any particular reason. But apart from that I'm fine.'

Julie studied her a moment longer, then cocked her head, *okay, but the offer's open.* She kicked the trolley's brake bar and started the heavy treads rolling.

Just before one, the others still shelving, Annette ducked into the office and grabbed her bag.

She ate her sandwich sitting on the low sandstone wall opposite the ground-floor entrance to the new Arts building. There was no reason for the man to be in over the break. But if he had school-age children it was possible he was escaping home to prepare lectures or get a paper written. The quad was a good place for a lunchtime stroll to clear the head.

She sat for twenty minutes, then shouldered her bag and walked to the nearby Student Information Office, showed her ID, and asked to use the internal phone. The departmental secretary answered. Annette identified herself again and asked if Dr Myrne had been coming in at all, there was a book for him.

'He's in today,' the woman said brightly. 'I'll put you through.'

'Thanks, no, I was just wondering if he's picking up his mail. I'll send him a notification.'

Annette had not until today set foot in the new building. Archaeology was on the third level. The lift was stainless steel and plastic, every colour a primary. The corridor she was disgorged into was as long and featureless as a large hotel's, its ceiling sky-blue, doors egg-yolk yellow. Annette was conscious of how she must appear, a nervous mature-age searching for the door behind which lay salvation.

She reminded herself that the man was actually more nervous of her. Both times he'd come to the library when she was on the desk, Annette had steered him from the book he asked for to the book he needed. Not archaeology, which were in the main library, but animal anatomy — the first time Australian rodents, the second freshwater fishes. He'd sent her an email asking whether the library held anything specifically on the fauna of the Snowy Mountains and Monaro. It did, Annette had replied, but the best book, no, it was long out of print, he'd have to go online for a copy. She gave him author and title, but hadn't let on, and he hadn't yet asked, how it was that she knew better than he what he needed.

She passed the door with his name, realised, backtracked, again conscious of how she must appear. But she'd encountered only one other person since leaving the lift, a young woman with jagged blonde hair and mauve-tinted glasses, who'd ignored her. Annette knocked, in a part of her mind half-hoping he wouldn't answer. But her finger had barely lifted from the door when he called, 'Come in!'

Expecting a student, the man had remained in his chair, which he'd wheeled to the window, in his left hand a triangle of wholemeal sandwich with a corner bitten off, in his right a journal, its pages curled for grip. He gulped down what he was chewing at the same time as he tipped forward and jumped to his feet, ponytail whipping, the olive skin beneath what Annette had dubbed his 'pruned stubble' darkening further.

'I'm terribly sorry, I thought you were a student.'

He didn't know which to put down first, sandwich or journal.

'Not for quite a while. Do you have a few minutes?'

His boyish confusion had set flight to her nervousness. His clothes today were a long-sleeved pink cotton shirt, buttoned to the throat yet billowy as a blouse, and faded but ironed jeans with a purple belt. Annette couldn't help the same sour inward smile as the first time they'd met, at an image of him suddenly dropped among the shaggy beards and duffel coats of Prehistory circa '68.

'Of course! Please!'

He slapped the journal facedown on the desk, deposited the bitten sandwich on the upturned lid of his lunchbox, and almost ran to fetch the straight-backed chair wedged between a bookcase and a stack of cartons. He placed it and retreated to standing at the corner of the desk.

'Steven. As you know.'

'Annette.'

'Yes.' He touched a finger to his own left breast, where, on duty, she wore her name tag.

She sat and dropped her bag to the floor.

'I can't offer you a coffee or anything, we're not allowed anything as subversive as a kettle.'

'I've just had lunch.'

He skipped to his chair, wheeled it to the desk and sat, then had to jump up again, the screen of his laptop a wall between them. He didn't lower it, but lifted the laptop entire to one side. Annette took advantage of his flurry to glance around the office. Given the size of the building and the vanishing-point length of the corridor, the room was pinched, cramped. It had accreted few personal touches. A photograph on the desk of which she could see only the backing, a squash racquet in a zip cover standing in one corner, on the bare side wall a map of south-eastern Australia with delineations in red texta of the drainage basins straddling the New South Wales–Victoria border. She spiralled her hand to suggest larger surrounds. 'I take it you have lab space elsewhere.'

He aimed a finger at the floor. 'Down in the bowels.' He fisted his hand at his mouth, coughed lightly. 'I've been meaning to ask. You've … worked in archaeology? Or a related field?'

'The Clyde, and North Teapot. Aled Wray was my honours supervisor.'

'My God. Really? Shit!' He was so stunned he didn't apologise. 'I've read all those papers, of course. So … I've seen your name!'

'Only in the acknowledgements. I did faunal IDs.'

'And kept up, it seems.'

'With the biology, not archaeology.'

An avid curiosity was now awake in his eyes. 'And … North Teapot's … suddenly and dramatically topical again.'

'Yes.'

'So, were you …?'

'I was there, yes, when she disappeared.'

'It looks to have been somewhat more than that.'

'Yes.'

'The news mentioned a peeping Tom.'

'Not from Prehistory. If you don't mind, that's not why I came. I'm wondering ... how well you know Aled? His whereabouts and so on. I could google him, but the entries tend towards the edited and bland. I preferred to ask. I'm assuming he'd be retired.'

The only sign of self-control being exerted was his fingertips lightly pressing together, parting. But he would, Annette foresaw, angle a way back. 'Only from academia, not from work.'

'He's in Canberra still?'

'Never left, to the best of my knowledge. I ... know him from conferences. Nothing like your association.'

'Which ended thirty-four years ago.'

'Nonetheless, those papers are seminal.' His brown eyes were so serious. *Oh dear,* Annette thought. *A good lecturer maybe, but don't kid yourself you're an actor.*

'They weren't mine. Did he ever re-marry? I know you have to wait if there's no body. Seven years, is it?'

'I've no idea, sorry. But to answer your first question, he did, yes. His daughter's followed in his footsteps. She's at Monash.'

'To another Marilyn?'

Myrne's eyes narrowed. 'I'm not sure I'm with you.'

'Another archaeologist.'

'Oh! No. I ... *believe* she's a linguist. I'm not sure where I heard that. I can enquire for you.'

Annette shook her head. But clearly Aled had wanted no more competing. 'What's he "retired" to?'

'Well, actually, Dr Wray spotted what's probably our only growth area. Some fifteen years back — before my time — he set up a company to do contract fieldwork. Local councils, water boards, and the like. Mining's the big one, of course, pays rather better than universities. I'm told he doesn't do much of the actual fieldwork any more, and nor would he need to, he seems to snap up the cream of our graduates from here every year. Jobs in academia aren't exactly booming, as I'm sure you're aware.'

'I'm not sure how making money earns him an Order of Australia.'

The remark was sharper than Annette had intended. She saw him slightly cock his head, wondering, perhaps, how to phrase a question that explored her tone. But he said, 'You're not entirely ignorant of his recent history, then.'

'I saw it in the paper. Just his name.'

'Yes, well, we're all after one now.' He gave her a stage grin. 'I've got about thirty years to go.'

These outbursts of self-deprecation, almost abasement, she began now to find annoying, even slightly patronising. She was hardly a prehistory superstar. Something of the annoyance must have shown in her face, because the grin wilted.

'Actually, Dr Wray has continued to lecture, and he's still writing. And he did return to fieldwork. There's a big gap, certainly, after North Teapot. But then he followed up on your Clyde work. More north of where you were, and shading into anthropology — where, I believe, he started?'

Annette nodded.

'I gather he was already pretty much the ethnoarchaeology guru, but by the time I graduated he was definitely wearing the mantle. Or the possum-skin cloak, should I say?' The smile this time was cautious, genuine. 'So the track record's pretty long. Others have scored AOs for less.' He tilted forward on his chair, hands hovering above the desk. 'I, ah, actually think I have a card for him here somewhere. If you'd like.'

Annette shook her head. 'I was just curious.'

'If I might return to North Teapot for a moment? Not to pry, I'm wondering if you ever saw the papers. It's just I have them here, if you'd like to borrow them.'

She didn't need to admit that she owned them. 'Thanks, I've read them.' *He's being kind,* she told herself, *at least give him something.* 'A long time ago, admittedly. But I think, like a few other people, I'm going to be revisiting all those places and events whether I like it or not.'

'I'd say so, yes.'

She saw him struggling with his stricture on prying. 'I ... gather, after North Teapot, you ... left archaeology?'

'You wouldn't have?'

'Please, I'm not judging you. It's just that others didn't. Susan Klima, for instance.'

'If you've met her, you know why.'

He acknowledged the barb, and perhaps its accuracy, with a dip of the head. 'Did you know we lost Tom Sieglitz a few years back?'

'I didn't, no.' Annette had a flash of the appalling afternoon she'd dragged him, half-dead, up to The Ferns, only for Marilyn to bar him entry. 'I'm guessing heart attack.'

'That's what most of us would have expected. But bowel cancer.'

'Oh Christ. Awful. Poor man.'

She found her bag with her hand and stood. 'I'd better let you get back to your lunch.'

Myrne shot to his feet. 'It was a very welcome interruption.'

Annette was, she knew, leaving on the wrong note. She lifted a finger towards the map on the wall. 'They look like drainage systems. Is that where you're working?'

'Yes. The Towamba and Genoa rivers.'

'What are you chasing?'

'Oh, all the usuals. But specifically trade and ceremonial routes up into the high country. Hence the books. No shelters so far, but I've got eight open sites and a couple of routes firming up.'

'Anything published?'

He pushed the thought away with his hands. 'Too early. Probably halfway.'

'Let me know when you do. And to let *you* know, we'll be open again by the end of the week.'

'Ah … nothing I need at the moment. But I might drop in — if I may? If things … develop?'

Annette felt herself bristle, she'd not invited this. She should not cut him dead, though. He was a link.

'If by that you mean if someone's charged, I'm unlikely to want to talk about it. But we'll see. Thank you for filling me in on Aled.'

In the morning the stacking had been a distraction, but not now. She would come to with books in her hands and no idea where she was putting them.

The image that kept recurring was imaginary — the shinbone. Shorn of the foot, the bulbs would have been smooth and earth-brown. If Mr Flett hadn't known the beach's history, he might have believed the bone far older, Aboriginal. It would have the same strength markers. In her teens Marilyn had been a hurdler. Her skeleton would be distinctive, the height and proportions, the fitness the bones were testament to. Presumably she'd been intact. They couldn't pull her out, they'd have had to dig down onto her. But the boxes were brought out late morning. A careful excavation couldn't have been done that quickly. Perhaps the burrow wasn't collapsed, just the entrance — all that was needed was to widen the opening, take the positional shots, reach in.

A sharp pain in her right wrist brought her back. How long had she stood in the gully clutching three books on tree farming? She glanced both ways along the aisle and shoved the books into the gap awaiting them.

When she returned to her desk, the others were closing down computers, zipping bags. The goodbyes she got were friendly, but muted. Annette sat and, with a few taps, brought up the national phone directory. She had thought to start with Gorman, just to confirm her belief that he'd be dead. Easy to find if he wasn't, he wouldn't have had the imagination to leave North Teapot. She typed *Gor*, and lifted her fingers. She didn't want his face in her mind. She deleted the letters and typed *H*, then again her fingers stopped. What would she do with knowing where he was? 'Same question,' she murmured at the screen, 'whether you're alive.' She typed the rest of the surname, but hesitated at the initial. The surname was common, but the spelling not — or so he'd told them. A touch on the return key would tell her. Instead, she swivelled the chair. Both volumes of the Sydney White Pages were on Julie's desk.

There were five entries for *Harpur*, none a *B*. Five in a population the size of Sydney's made the name statistically uncommon. There was probably only that number again, or fewer, in the rest of the state. Assuming he was in the state. Even

the country. Even alive. She'd come full circle. She strode back
to her desk and exited the directory, shut down the screen.

As soon as Annette heard his voice, she choked up. He asked
was she still there.

'Yes. Brent ... did you hear any news today — or see this
morning's paper?'

'Glanced at the headlines. Why?'

'It wasn't on the front. There's a story about a woman's bones
being found at a beach down the South Coast, North Teapot.
I knew her. She disappeared while I was there. As a student.
There's a cave halfway along the beach that we were excavating.
She was the wife of the man in charge of the dig, the same ones
I was with at the Clyde. It's definitely her, she's been identified.'

She heard the creak of mattress springs.

'The paper's here. Give me a minute.'

'Page five.'

There was a muffled thud in her ear as he dropped the receiver
on the bed. Annette heard the rustle of newsprint, then the
mattress springs again. Brent cleared his throat before he picked
up the receiver.

'I don't think she "disappeared", love.'

'No.'

'I have a vague memory of you talking about it one time. I
thought you said she drowned.'

'Well, we found her clothes — a group of us. At the edge of the water. But ... you know ... The police weren't convinced.'

'Nor the coroner, by the sound of it. Were you called?'

'Yes, but I was in London. Dad handled it. They had my statement. We all gave them.'

Her throat resented the half-truth, dried the last words to a croak.

'You want to get a drink?'

'No. Brent, can I ask you about courts? If there's a trial ... can you choose whether to give evidence — or it isn't up to you?'

'You're saying you'd prefer not to.'

'It's just ... I said some things to a detective I sort of wished later I hadn't. About one of the boys, another student. I caught him perving on — well, I didn't *catch* him, I saw him, from back in the dunes — perving on her in the surf. This was a couple of days before.'

'She's ... bare-arse, I take it.'

'Yes.'

'So why'd you wish you hadn't? Said what you did.'

'Well, at that stage she was just missing. But I was saying — or implying, anyway — that it was something more.'

'And your instinct was spot on.'

'But not necessarily about the person. Even though it's looking now I was right. Anyway, thanks to me he was questioned again. He couldn't have known who, but he knew it was one of us. He came out of the cabin they were using in tears. He was actually dry-retching. He gave us this look — not accusing, more he couldn't believe it. "I thought you were my friends. I'm an inch away from being charged." On the day I just thought, Serves you bloody right. What I'm saying to you now came later.'

'He wasn't just a good actor?'

Brian Harpur an actor? The possibility had never occurred to her. 'I don't *think* he was acting. But I suppose you'd react like that, too, if you were scared you'd been caught.'

'And he wasn't ever charged?'

'No. How? Without a body.'

'It's happened. What about at the inquest? Was he named as a person of interest?'

'Yes. And the man who owned the cabins.'

'And the husband wasn't?'

'He may've been. I don't remember.'

'They're usually the first.'

She needed to say this next thing before she could change her mind. 'Brent, I know it's looking now like I was right to speak … but my motives back then were always a bit suspect — for singling him out. Suspect to *me*. We were all guilty of our share of perving, even us women. That photo you've got there doesn't go even near doing her justice.'

'His sounds to have been somewhat more organised. You told what you saw.'

'Darling, are you supposed to be meeting Charlie and the others?'

'When I get there. So, who was he?'

'His name's Brian Harpur. He was from a sheep farm near Cooma. We travelled down to the coast in the same car. He wasn't in prehistory, he was in engineering, so he didn't know anyone — so he sort of latched on to me. Because it was over the break, anyone could put their name down. But he turned out to be great. And he'd been there before, as a kid, so he knew the place. He showed me how to stamp for bloodworms, and catch whiting. He got me some beautiful fish skeletons. I actually know more about fishing than I've ever let on. Anyway, it grew from there. If ... what happened hadn't, he might have been the first man I went to bed with. I don't mean there, I mean after, back in Canberra.'

Annette could almost hear his mind working. Brent knew she'd left something out. But he said obliquely, 'I'm not sure I'm following. If this Brian knew you were attracted to him ...'

'Well, he got a bit more interested in Marilyn.'

'I thought the husband was there. You saying she played around?'

'No. But she went off to another site Brian discovered, with him and another woman, a friend of mine.'

He didn't bother to disguise his exasperation. 'I think you'd better give me the rest of this over a bottle. You want me to come home?'

'No, I can wait. Talking's helped. The other thing I wanted to say — I hope all those times I wouldn't go south for holidays now make sense. It had nothing to do with the water being too cold.'

'I never thought it did. Look, I better shoot, Charlie's probably trying to ring the room. Don't be Protestant about taking a sleeping tab if you need.'

Annette poured a wine and walked to the kitchen windows and stood replaying the important parts of what she'd said. She hadn't corrected the impression she knew she'd left that Brian Harpur had 'betrayed' her. In five weeks they hadn't gone so far as to hold hands. And there she'd been declaring that he might have become her first lover.

'He would've,' she said to her reflection. 'You'd decided.'

She drank another two glasses, didn't need a tablet.

Marilyn came, but the dream was not macabre. The two of them were standing at the long table in the Prehistory lab sorting the washed and dried shell from a midden profile into species. They were working companionably, stopping to examine it when a piece of bone or a flake turned up among the shell, apologising when they bumped hands. The only weirdness — not weird in the dream, only when Annette woke — was when, after dropping a *mytilus* on its pile, Marilyn beckoned to her and leaned across the table and, with an un-Marilyn-like giggle, said, 'Don't tell Aled, will you. I'm supposed to be in China.'

At six, Annette went again to the corner shop.

She searched the whole newspaper. Marilyn, North Teapot,

had vanished. She would have to ring this Townshend and ask pointblank why Brian Harpur hadn't been arrested.

She rang the library's number and left the message that she wouldn't be in. Then she went up to the study and took down the binder. The record of interview was seven typed pages, single-spaced, the beginning of her answer immediately after each question, not on a new line. Annette hadn't flattered herself then, and didn't now, that Isles had devised questions for her alone. He must have had a standard line, varied only when an answer was vague or in some way pricked his suspicion. *Were you present at North Teapot on the night of January thirtieth? Can you recall for me, in as much detail as you can, your movements on that night? Did you accompany Professor Wray and others to the northern end of the beach the following morning? Would you describe what was discovered there?*

Annette was not transported as she read. She didn't believe that words could 'transport' in that literal sense. But the cabin, the afternoon, came back in specific details. The baking heat with the door and louvres shut. The smell of old dust that rose each time she shuffled her feet. The cobwebs festooning the roof beams. Her initial confusion over 'the following morning' to mean that morning. The clatter of the keys and the feeling she'd got that each word was being snatched from her lips, so that after ten minutes she'd been constructing answers so carefully in her head before opening her mouth that Isles had called a break to ask what was wrong. 'The typewriter,' she'd said, not looking in its direction.

Isles had assured her she'd be given the statement to read, and alter if she wanted. After that the answers had flowed more freely. So freely, Annette was disturbed to find that she didn't much like the person who emerged from the latter half of the questioning, who was opinionated rather than factual, when factual simplistic, at all times judgemental. The same person who had allowed Isles to 'guess' that she knew something she believed more important than what he was asking her, but which she would impart only on condition that it was not taken down. Annette closed the binder and stared at it. Then opened it again, rang directory assistance, and wrote the number on the inside cover.

A young man's light, cheerful voice identified the station and himself. It was years since she'd had call to speak to a police station. A stolen pushbike, Gaby's. She'd been brushed off. This friendliness flustered her. She asked for 'Mr' Townshend, forgot to give her name.

'And who am I speaking to, please?'

'Sorry — Annette Cooley. I'm ringing from Sydney.'

'And this is in relation to what, Ms Cooley?'

'North Teapot beach, the remains you've found. I knew her.'

The voice changed, suddenly all efficiency. 'Would you stay on the line, please, I'll see if Detective-Sergeant Townshend's in.'

The second movement of *Eine kleine Nachtmusik*, synthesised, tinkled in her ear. Then there was a click, and she was listening to voices in a room and a man's distant laughter, sliced off by Townshend announcing himself, so close Annette started.

'Ms Cooley. Good to put a voice to the name.'

'It's familiar, then.'

'Most definitely. What can I do for you?'

'I just thought that now there's finally … she's been found …
I was wondering if you needed to re-interview people.'

'Are you saying there's information you omitted at the time
that you'd like to give now?'

'No. I would imagine you'd have my interview … that I did
with Jeffrey Isles?' She reached to pull the binder towards her.
'Sorry, I've forgotten his title.'

'Detective-Sergeant also. Yes, I do. Sergeant Isles is some years
retired, but he lives locally. I've spoken with him — soon after
the remains were found, in fact. He retains a keen interest in the
case. As clearly you do, yourself.'

'I think my perspective's a bit different.'

Annette heard a light clack, something being moved on a
desk.

'I get the sense, Ms Cooley, you've rung to ask *me* something.'

'Yes. Related to the evidence I asked Sergeant Isles not to
take down.'

'Okay.'

'I'm wondering, has he been arrested … the man I spoke
about. It's obvious now she didn't drown.'

'If I may just pull you up there. That's not a statement we can
make yet with certainty.'

'What?'

He'd caught the edge to her voice, said quickly, 'We — by "we" I mean the police — we can't permit ourselves to assume, Ms Cooley. I'm sure, with your own forensic background, you can appreciate that.'

If she'd been less agitated, she might have been more startled to hear that he knew her 'background'. But she was already speaking, her voice mockingly flat. 'Just because she was put in a grave doesn't necessarily mean she was murdered.' Annette wouldn't, before today, have believed herself capable of using this tone to a policeman.

'I couldn't have put it better.'

'All the same, I'd imagine you've attempted to find him. Have you?'

Again, Annette heard something moved, the same soft clack.

'Ms Cooley, I fully appreciate that you'll have a strong personal interest in how this investigation proceeds. But I hope that you, in turn, will appreciate that I'm not in a position to disclose what lines of investigation we might or might not be following, or what person or persons we may be interested in. I apologise if that sounds like police-speak for "it's none of your business", because that's certainly not the message I'm wishing to convey to you. I welcome your ringing. Very much. In fact I'd like to pick your brain a little, if I may. Would you like to hang up, and I'll ring you back?'

'Um … no, it's okay.'

'Thank you. Sergeant Isles was a thorough man — he liked to

do his homework. The papers from all the sites you participated in are here on file. I don't claim to understand everything in them, but I've read them. You're mentioned in each. I take it, then, your association with Professor Wray and Dr Herr spanned a number of years.'

'Nineteen sixty-eight to early seventy-one. More him than her, as I made clear in my interview. May I ask where this is going?'

'Going? Just towards giving me a clearer understanding of how archaeologists work, particularly how they work together.'

'Well, I can only give you a snapshot of back then. It's a long time since I was *in* archaeology.'

'A snapshot's fine. So … your impressions of Professor Wray and Dr Herr … you would have seen them together reasonably often. So how would you characterise their relationship — both personal and … professional, working together?'

A small bell went off in her head, Brent's remark about husbands.

'I wasn't a friend. For most of that time I was a student. I don't think I'm qualified to speak of how they were in private.'

'Nor am I asking you to. But you observed them together. For weeks at a time. Sorry, all right, let me be a bit more explicit. Would you characterise their relationship as an equal one?'

'Their working relationship?'

'If you wish. Characterise that for me.'

'Well, they didn't, as a habit, work together. Before the Clyde took over, Marilyn had her own project mapping camp sites along the Murrumbidgee River. The Clyde was very much Aled's — Professor Wray's — site. Why his name's first on the papers.'

'And in the press. From the clippings. Even so, I gather she did quite a bit of the work there.'

'It was his site.'

'I see. Could we go to North Teapot. You don't, but several of the other interviewees mention a disputation over a dingo. Did you, ah, witness that?'

'Yes.'

'Well, can you, would you, enlighten me a little further?'

'It was pretty minor. She uncovered the bones of a dingo in the trench outside the cave. Aled wanted to be the one to remove them.'

'And she … took exception?'

'Yes. And later they resolved it.'

'How?'

'I don't know. Not in our presence. Next day she was back working in the trench.'

'Then a week or so later there was the actual "split".'

'More like a fortnight.'

'Which you described as being about "ownership".'

'*I* did?'

'Not in your interview. You were quoted.'

Annette saw them, Marilyn striding back along the beach towards the cave, Aled trudging in her wake. *What do you reckon that's about*, Sue had said.

'By Susan Klima.'

'Yes.'

'Has she rung you as well?'

'She has.'

Annette didn't want her memory being measured against Sue's.

'Well, she'd be a better informant for what you're wanting to know. Marilyn probably confided in her a bit up at The Ferns. And she'd have seen them together the times Aled went up there.'

'She *has* given me some of that. I'm interested, though, in the view from all points.'

'You're still better off talking to her.'

The man waited. She'd used the tactic herself, let a silence grow until the other person couldn't help but fill it. Again came the clack of whatever it was he fiddled with on his desk.

'Okay. Thank you, I won't impose any longer on your time and patience. I *will* get your contact details, though, if I may. And I'll give you my direct number, if you have pen and paper.'

After hanging up, she went on staring at the phone. What had she expected? That he would treat her as special? Yes, Annette made herself admit, she *had* expected that. She'd given important evidence, difficult evidence. Now finally, after thirty-four years, it could be acted on, should already have been. So why hadn't it! Wasn't she, of all people, deserving of an answer? He didn't appear to think so. What if she rang Isles? She had his full name, he still lived locally. But, an ex-cop, he was probably unlisted. And he didn't owe her anything. Annette stood. She needed a strong coffee.

The garden drew her outside. She sat on the sandstone block beside the pond and balanced the plunger on the mossed bricks at her feet. Its cells in direct sunlight, the pump in its cave was emitting a low whirr, audible below the run of water. Annette had wanted an electric pump, to have the sound of water when they sat at the courtyard table in the evening. Brent had wanted, and installed, a pump that died with the light. It was fanciful perhaps, but she wondered now how much her wish was fed by the nights she'd spent camped by moving water, firstly the Clyde, then North Teapot. She'd loved the nights of guard duty — before they were fouled by Gorman — sleeping with Sue or Vicky in the tent pitched on the beach. Being woken by the different note of the waves when the tide changed, some nights sounding so close Annette had half-waited for the wash to sweep into the tent, surge around them in their bags.

How different things might have been if one night she'd had the courage to ask Brian Harpur to share the tent with her.

In the mood to be ruthless, she fetched secateurs and pruned and retied the torn hardenbergia, then worked from one end to the other of her herb bed with bucket and trowel, digging out oxalis and sheep's sorrel till just before midday and the news.

Marilyn was the lead story. A preliminary forensic report, just released, had identified sand grains found lodged in the teeth as beach not ocean sand, indicating that the likely cause of death was asphyxiation, not drowning. A police spokesman had confirmed that a person was assisting in their enquiries.

The bastard! All the time Townshend was speaking to her, he'd known. She strode to the phone alcove. Then just stood. Her heart was thudding. She pulled out the stool and leaned her back against the banister post.

'He's not a bastard. He told you.'

She began to cry.

By five, he'd been named and charged with murder. Annette turned off the radio, and the phone rang.

The throaty clatter of compression brakes filled her ear, she snatched the receiver away, listened for the clatter to fade.

'Where on earth are you!'

'Sorry — didn't see him coming. Just outside Pokolbin. Have you listened to any news today?'

'Yes. Just now.'

'Right. So ... you okay?'

'I don't know. I'd sort of guessed —' she couldn't tell him about Townshend, not yet — 'but it's different having it confirmed.'

'You disappointed?' Brent had always possessed this ability to put the question she least wanted to answer.

'No. Why would I be?'

He laughed softly, but was not mocking her. 'For one, because it'd be perfectly natural, darling.'

'I stopped liking him, Brent, but I never hated him. I'm not glad, either, it's Aled.'

'They could still have the wrong bloke, prove you right. But it sounds unlikely. I'd say he's put his hand up.'

'But he'll still plead "not guilty", won't he?'

'I'm just reading between the lines, love. That he has.'

'But it'll involve calling witnesses, testifying and so on.'

Annette heard the thought behind the hesitation, *Come on, you're not that naive.* 'A trial — yes.'

'So I should ring the police and let them know where I am.'

If they'd been talking across the dining table, she'd have seen Brent's eyes narrow. It was probably happening as he sat in the car. 'It'll take them all of thirty seconds if and when they want you, mate. I might get moving, it's hot sitting here. I'll watch the news and ring you, okay.'

'Yes, please.'

Annette poured a wine and walked to her habitual spot at the kitchen windows. She wouldn't mention Townshend. Brent would believe they'd simply traced her.

Annette knew his past, but hadn't known *how* deep his contempt ran until the Subaru was stolen. He'd refused to report the theft. Instead, he'd got on his motorbike and cruised laneways, old factory sites, the railway yards, until he found it, four nights later, stripped and up on bricks, in a dead-end behind the cement works in Erskineville.

He rang the insurance company, but it was she who had to go to the police. The two on the desk said nothing, but Annette saw in their faces when Brent's name came up that so had his history. At twenty, he had spent fifteen months being moved from safe house to safe house, twice having to jump from a window, once lying for an entire winter's night up a stormwater drain, before he and others who'd refused to register for conscription were quietly taken off the 'wanted' lists. Brent had never forgiven the police their willingness to be co-opted. Nor their brutality at anti-war demonstrations. He could still name individual detectives who'd hunted him. It was better he didn't know a detective already had their number.

Annette reheated a fish soup, ate in front of the television. There was the same photograph of Marilyn, a repeat of the footage of the two policemen leaving the gully with the boxes. None of Aled leaving or entering a paddywagon. She'd been torn between hoping and dreading there would be. Instead, a solicitor addressed a scrum of journalists and television cameras from the courthouse steps.

'My client has instructed me to inform you that we have advised the police and the DPP that if the charge of murder is reduced to manslaughter, my client will plead "guilty". Thank you.'

Annette barely heard the words, she was staring at the man. He was a giant baby in a suit, the resemblance heightened by his being red-faced with suppressed anger. She couldn't believe that this was a man the Aled she remembered would engage. The solicitor started down the steps, irritably sweeping his briefcase before him.

A journalist called, 'At your suggestion was that, Mr Cowper?'

The baiting tone stung the man into again facing the bristle of microphones. 'My advice was otherwise. Now, if you'll let me through, please!'

The moment the item ended, the phone rang. Annette hit the power button and walked out into the hallway.

'You saw that, I take it,' Brent said without preamble.

'Yes. I'm not exactly sure what it means, though.'

'To you, or in legal terms?'

'Well … to me. Both.'

'To you it means that if they buy it — and I'd reckon that's a pretty big "if" — but if they do, you won't have to testify, no one will. He'll plead, the beak'll hear submissions, and he'll be sentenced.'

'So … none of what happened will even come out?'

'I wouldn't say "none". But probably not the complete story. Not if he's still putting his hand up.'

'But how is that fair? It's not fair at all! Everyone there — especially Brian Harpur, but even me — we've all lived under this cloud for thirty-four years, Brent! I'm not the only one who *quit* archaeology over North Teapot! And what about Marilyn? Doesn't he even have to explain *why* he killed her? Or even *how*?'

'Slow down, will you, please, and listen. It's a game, love. You dangle the easier option. But the cops won't be interested if they reckon they can nail him for murder.'

'That solicitor didn't look like he was playing a game.'

Brent chuckled. 'No, he looked like he'd had his nuts wrung. I don't think he takes well to being "instructed".'

Suddenly she'd had enough, the legalese, the fat man on the courthouse steps. 'Tomorrow, what's the earliest you can get home?'

Annette sensed immediately his mind shift. She'd always loved this about him, that he would drop a conversation containing more to say if she didn't want to have it. Not just with her, she'd seen him do it with others, even the kids. She'd never asked where he'd learned this forbearance. Perhaps as far back as his fugitive days, the need to be a smooth pebble in whichever household he temporarily lodged.

'I'll try to get away about four, be there around seven. I'll talk to Charlie.'

The phone rang as the alarm went off. She was already awake. She hit the button, then reached over the clock for the phone.

'Good morning. I've got the paper here, thought I'd save you the walk. You sleep all right?'

'Not great. Are you already out?'

'Nearly. Five minutes. Got to earn my early mark.'

Neither laughed. In the distance — his distance — Annette heard a kookaburra.

'It's only short, couple of paras. It'll tell you more than it tells me. But yeah, it sounds like he has an argument, at least, for manslaughter. His story is they met on the beach just on dark, things got heated, he did his block and hit her and stormed off. When he came back, she was dead, face-down in the sand. He panicked, made it look like she'd drowned.'

'What — that's the whole *thing*?'

'I warned you it was short. It's just a statement through his solicitor, love, not an interview.'

Annette's eyes blurred. She tugged the sheet to her face. After all these years, she knew, finally, what the envelope had held.

'I set that up, Brent. The meeting.'

'*You*? In what way?'

'I told you. The afternoon I saw Brian Harpur. I was carrying a note to her from Aled.'

'Please don't start telling yourself shit like that, Annette.'

'I'm *not*, that's what it was. Aled lied. Not about there being a note, he couldn't — but he said it was about when we'd be finishing and going back to Canberra.'

'Look, I have to get moving. Don't go in today. Ring Julie and tell her enough so they get it.'

Annette laid the phone on the bed, slid her arms back under the covers.

There'd been times she wanted to hit Brent. One time when

he'd certainly come within an ace of hitting her, after the
party where she'd got drunk and gone for a harmless walk —
what turned out to be a harmless walk — with a man she'd
been flirting with. The argument would have started over the
methods Marilyn was employing at The Ferns. 'Ruining' it for
future work. Where it had gone to from there, only Aled knew.

Annette was at the sink, breaking a mignonette under the tap
and lobbing the leaves into the spinner, when she heard the
front door. There came the thud of a dropped boot, then its
mate. She was unsure which of her males it was until she heard
the approaching clink of bottles. She flicked off the tap and
grabbed up a tea towel.

Brent dumped his bag on the floor and, scarcely less roughly,
the six-pack of wine on the table, enfolded her in his arms,
kissed her hair, her forehead, and, finally, her mouth. Annette
held her damp hands away from his shirt, then got a whiff of
the sweat in it and returned his embrace.

'I am so glad you're home!'

'That makes two of us. Will it *be* just the two of us, or is
"rambling boy" expected?'

'Shh.'

Brent drew slightly away, but kept his arms around her.
Annette leaned back to look at him. His cheeks and temples
were even more burnished, the crow's-feet standing out as if

pipeclayed. His chin was stubbled with silver, each blunt hair distinct against the dark skin.

'You want to have a shower? Dinner'll be another twenty minutes.'

'Yep. Open a bottle first, though.'

He gave her nose a peck and broke his embrace.

The bottle he opened, a red, bore only a white office label, hand-lettered with a marking pen.

He saw her frown. 'You wait.' He fetched down a glass and poured a finger, sniffed at the rim, offered her the stem.

Annette didn't bother with sniffing, she raised the glass to her lips, swilled the wine round her mouth, and swallowed. 'My God,' she breathed. 'And they want to put a coal mine through this?'

'Hey — no "rambling boy"; no coal mines.'

'Sorry. It's gorgeous.'

Despite the truce, Brent said softly, 'There won't be any coal under where that came from, I can assure you.'

He went upstairs. Annette basted the lamb for the last time. She thought of ringing Lucas to ask whether he *was* considering showing up for dinner, and actually started towards the hallway, before checking herself. Friday night, unlikely he'd be home at all.

She set two places. When they had full plates and glasses, Brent lifted his glass and they clinked rims. 'Thank you. Beats any restaurant.' He watched her sip, didn't himself. 'So, you up to answering a few questions?'

'I'm going to answer a lot of questions.'

He looked alarmed, set down his glass.

'I don't mean court,' Annette said quickly. 'If that even happens. I decided this afternoon, I need to write it. You only know the bits I could talk about. There's a lot I couldn't — as you've found out this week. And the kids know bugger-all about me back then. Other than I quit being something that sounded interesting to become a librarian.'

'I wouldn't have met you if you hadn't.'

Annette smiled. That, too, feeling like something she'd almost forgotten how to do. 'Anyway, so that's my plan. It's so long since I've done any writing it'll be interesting to see if I still can.'

Brent nodded down at the table. 'How about you find out if you can still chew.'

Annette awoke to his hoarse snoring in her ear. He'd collapsed across her, his left arm and leg pinning her to the mattress. She lifted his arm and slid from under, did the same with his leg.

She knew exactly where to begin, the first few sentences were in her head, had come with her out of sleep. She looked at the green numbers. It was only ten forty-seven. Footpath voices were still rising to the open balcony doors, cars passing, the pleasantly distant hum of Friday-night King Street in full cry. She walked to the armchair and found T-shirt and sarong.

She had filled a page — the walk with her Ancient History

class to Vincent Megaw's site at Curracurrang — when she heard the front door. She'd so convinced herself that he wouldn't be home, she half-rose from the desk and capped the pen. But it could be no one else. A minute later, the clink of the cutlery drawer reached her. The lamb was on the benchtop covered with a tea towel. He'd be hacking rough wedges from the fatty end. The light from the lamp didn't reach down the stairs. Annette debated whether to close the door. But she wanted to touch and smell her baby.

She swivelled the chair. Lucas would watch some rubbish to slow his head. But she hadn't uncapped the pen when she heard the creak of the bottom step, then the hollow knock of the viola case against the banister. He halted, he'd seen the glow. He completed the climb, left the viola at the door of his room, and came on to her doorway. Annette pretended she hadn't heard, her entire world the pool of lamplight. Lucas knocked softly on the jamb. She jerked her head round, but each knew it was the little play they performed for one another.

'I wasn't expecting you, I thought we had a burglar.'

Lucas was in his usual gunslinger-black, shirt open. He gave her his grin and slipped along the wall to the brocade armchair and straddled its padded arm. He'd been with a girl.

'Where's Dad?'

'Asleep.'

'I thought he'd be watching the cricket. Late finish, Perth.' He craned his neck to see onto the desktop. 'What's that?'

Annette knew what he was asking, but took him literally, her reminder that laziness too often rendered him cryptic.

'A beautiful old foolscap ledger of your father's I found in his bottom drawer with not a mark in it.'

'So what are you "ledgering"?'

'A slice of autobiography. From about the age of seventeen to twenty-one.'

Lucas frowned, made a mouth. 'What for?'

'For you. Among others.'

Annette watched him do a double take, then, thrown by her weirdness, retreat. 'Why aren't you using the computer?'

'Because it's not something I can do on a computer. Would you believe I did my whole degree this way?'

'Pretty backward place, the twentieth century.' He leaned slightly to look past her. 'That a fountain pen?'

'I hope you're joking.'

'It yours? I've never seen it.'

'Probably not. It's been in my drawer for longer than you've been around.'

'How do you get the ink in?'

Annette studied his face for even the glimmer of a smile. He was serious. She pulled open the drawer and lifted out the bottle of Quink blue-black she'd bought after finding the ledger. 'Come here.'

She emptied and refilled the pen, then passed it to him. He emptied and refilled it twice, the second time holding the shaft to the lamp to read the level in the small window. 'Huh.'

'I'll get you one for your birthday.'

'I think another Red Eye voucher.' Lucas placed the pen back in her fingers, let her cap it. 'I'm gonna crash.' His hug was one-armed and brief, but she contrived to press her face fleetingly to his belly.

Annette waited to hear his door close, then uncapped the pen, her eyes already skimming the last sentence. But as she brought the nib to the page, her eye shifted from the line to it. She sat back and looked at this object, which, despite its long neglect, felt so comfortable in her fingers.

What does that say, that I've had to teach a nineteen-year-old how to fill a fountain pen? Not much. Of any great profundity, anyway. More to the point, what does it say about you — that one of your icons of civilisation is the fountain pen! No wonder you went into prehistory. She laughed low in her throat, abruptly stopped, thinking she'd heard footfalls, and glanced over her shoulder. Her returning gaze snagged on the four journals together on the top shelf. If Marilyn were alive, she, like Steven Myrne, would be writing papers about stone tools on a laptop. Not a very profound observation, either.

The nib had been exposed to the air for too long. Annette knew from bitter experience not to dart her wrist to start the ink flowing. She moved her hand to the blank left-hand page and dabbed the nib till dots formed, then wrote *Pretty backward place, the twentieth century.*

Brent carried the ledger, a plate of cheese and Vitaweat, and a thermos of coffee upstairs to the study and closed the door. It was how he read the field reports he was paid to appraise.

Annette couldn't settle to anything. She wanted to be invisibly in the study watching his face. The ledger was thick, and she'd filled all but the last six of its right-hand pages. She lifted her hand into the sunlight streaming through the kitchen windows. Two days and two showers, and the faint blue stain, the dented callus were still there on the side of her finger.

She was planting out broccoli when the screen door squealed. She dropped the seedling into its hole and firmed the collar of soil, drew a new hole. She heard the click of his knee as he sat, then the clink of a stubby set down on the paving bricks. She said as she popped the seedling from its cell, 'Are you … just taking a break, or …?'

'No, I've finished. Still working through it in my head, though. It's a bit strange reading something that's … a story, but you're the "I".'

'And not a particularly likeable "I", I'm guessing.' Annette dropped the seedling in its hole and firmed around it.

'I don't think anyone comes out of it all that well. About the only one I warmed to was Vicky. What became of her?'

She'd asked for honesty when she gave him the ledger. An honest judgement had been delivered and Annette found herself stung, couldn't resist stinging back. 'I think she'd have been a bit Christian for your taste.'

'The best of them are often decent people. She sounds like she was.'

'Yes, I shouldn't demean her. She was.'

'They're all very real. And the places. And parts are quite suspenseful.'

Anyone else listening would have heard the praise as modest. Coming from Brent it was almost effusive.

'Thank you.'

The sense remained to her, though, that the important things were yet to be said. She spoke down at her fingers as she drew another hole. 'The first time I mentioned Brian Harpur to you, you said something like, "That's what you saw, and you told it." Do you … still think like that?'

'Yes. I do.'

'I didn't tell them about Aled.'

'Tell them what — that he was angry? You weren't Robinson Crusoe in knowing that.' He lifted the stubby and took a swig, then proffered it. Annette shook her head.

'You've beaten yourself up a bit over him. Wray. You need to remember you were being played along by a very intelligent man. With detective training.'

She reared, swivelling to face him. 'What?'

Brent was unruffled. 'You had it, too. Gathering evidence, interpreting it, coming up with a story. Just a matter of reversing the process. The hard part's staying cold enough to carry it off, not make mistakes. Wray comes across as that. Even down to the tears. I'm not suggesting he staged it all — part of the grief must have been genuine. And what he's quoted in the paper as saying is probably true, that he didn't mean to kill her.'

'Brent, he shoved her in a wombat hole! That he must've already known existed! He gets us to look for her sandshoes so we trample all over the place where she died. He performs this ... *opera* of grief all along the beach. And *you're* saying, too, now, the charge should be manslaughter!'

Annette saw him glance towards the side fence and heard how loud, and how ferocious, she'd just been.

'I don't recall coming down on one side or the other, love,' he said softly. 'So long as the cops reckon they can make it stick — yes, the sort of things you're saying — the charge'll stay murder.'

'But I should be prepared for that to change, you're saying.'

'In the light of what he's admitted to. It'll be a wait, though, before we find out.'

'Yes. So I'm not — not waiting.' Annette sat cross-legged on her weeding mat. 'There are two "B Harpurs" — the correct spelling — in the national directory, one in WA and the other in Tasmania. Both far enough away to be him, but neither is — the one in WA's Bronwyn, the other's Barry. So I need to start around Cooma. There's three Harpurs still listed. I'm assuming they're related.'

'You haven't rung them.'

'No.'

'But you rang the other two.'

'I had the feeling they weren't him. I don't want to ring the Cooma ones, I'd prefer to go down there.'

'It's a fair drive to be told he lives in Timbuktu. Or he's dead.'

'Still better than them having some strange woman ring out of the blue from Sydney and so they say they've never heard of him.'

'How about if he's living round the corner from them, he's just unlisted?'

'I'll go there. It came to me halfway through that I was writing it for him, too. So I photocopied it at work. If he'll accept it, it's his. He probably already knows it was me. But I need to say sorry. Not for telling Isles, he bloody deserved the grilling he got. Sorry for not telling *him*, letting him believe it was one of the others. How could it have been *me*, who he caught fish for, who he showed the trap to! Who he wanted to give The Ferns to!'

Brent tapped her hand with his folded hanky. Annette wiped her eyes, blew her nose.

'Frankly, I'm not anticipating him being anywhere near Cooma. I just want an address.'

'So when are you thinking?'

'Next week. The following one if that's too soon. I'll work it out with Oliver. He owes me three days, the rest I'll swap with Julie.'

'Cooma's only five hours, you know.'

'I don't want to hurry. All right?'

'I'm not quibbling, I was just thinking … would you like company?'

Annette stared at him. His dense schedule of field trips was on the house calendar.

'If it gets tight, I can fly back.'

To have him in bed at night to talk to, his good sense. But it was *her* good sense she needed to force herself to use. Annette laid her hand on his thigh, the old denim softer than skin. 'Can I have a think about it?'

'Sure.' The flatness said, *simple offer, what's there to think about?*

'It might be something I need to do completely on my own.'

'The *doing* is. I'm talking about the rest of the time.'

'That can influence the doing, Brent. You know that.'

He gave a dismissive flick of the hand and raised the stubby. 'This's getting too subtle for me.'

'That's bullshit, darling. You say similar things.'

'And *that's* bullshit, I don't.'

'Why are we starting a fight?'

'We're not.' Brent drained the stubby and stood. 'You had lunch?'

'I had that cold pizza. There's a slice left.'

Annette remained sitting on the weed mat. The faded red of his shirt came and went behind the kitchen windows. Where had the man gone who dropped conversations she didn't want to have? Well, she was snappier, too. At work, for instance. She'd seen students veer away when they saw she was on the desk. Steven Myrne had left three messages about the funeral, even offering a lift, two by internal phone, the last a slightly cross handwritten note. She'd argued with her mother over two borrowed Patricia Highsmiths, one still unread, which, for no reason other than that they were hers, her mother wanted returned. At another time, to keep the peace, Annette would simply have complied. This new her had been born on the day Marilyn came out of the wombat hole.

In bed that night Annette told him she'd go to Cooma by herself. He'd already decided that would be her answer.

'What about "rambling boy"?'

'I doubt my not being here will make a difference to his coming and going.'

'No, I meant, what've you told him?'

'Well, he came into the study the night I started and asked what it was. I told him it was a piece of autobiography, intended in part for him.'

Brent rolled onto his side to look at her. 'What — you're not seriously expecting him to read it.'

'Why not? I read all his stuff.'

'This's hardly comparable. Would you have read something like this at his age, that your mother gave you? Said what it was about? I don't think so. Ten years on, maybe. But not at nineteen. Even if he did, there's a fair chance he wouldn't get it. What's behind the writing, and your wanting to go down there.'

'He understands regret, Brent, he's not a child.'

'None of his'd go anywhere near this deep, darling. A girl or two, dumping Joe from the band.' He moved his hand, cupped her shoulder. 'There's a good chance he'd see your needing to go down there as a bit mum-being-quaint, or even plain weird, rather than poignant. Wanting to say sorry to someone so long after the event.'

The word had startled her. She'd never heard him use it before. 'There's nothing "weird" or "quaint" about wanting to apologise to someone I caused to be labelled a pervert — and worse — and I never owned up to it.'

'No. There isn't. In our eyes. But where Lucas still is, love, we're parents not people, we're money and food. I'm not putting him down, I'm just being realistic.'

'I think you *are* putting him down.'

Brent lifted his hand and rolled onto his back. 'I'm happy to be proved wrong.'

*

It was dark when Brent left the bed. He woke her again at seven with a kiss, then thumped down the stairs at the bip-bip of his taxi.

Oliver grumbled, but gave her the following week off.

Annette was more than surprised, it was a shock, when she got home and, from the front door, heard the muscular voice of the viola. She halted and listened. Lucas was playing scales, but not resembling any she'd ever heard him play before. These had as many semitones as tones, even what sounded like quarter-tones. Annette eased the door closed and crept to the kitchen. The note she'd left on the table had been read. She took the ledger from her bag and placed it beside the note.

The viola fell silent while she was waiting for her pot to draw. He might just be resting his fingers. Then she heard the creak of a board. He was pacing, he was on his mobile. A moment later there came the thud of his feet down the stairs. Annette saw his fingers first as they locked onto the jamb, then, hair flying, her beautiful son swung into sight, his other hand locked to his ear. He gave a start, then flashed her a grin and pointed unnecessarily to the phone. 'Yeah, yeah — hey, I gotta go — ciao.' He folded the mobile and slipped it into his pocket in one fluid movement almost balletic in its precision.

'What were those scales you were playing?'

'Old Persian. Iraqi. Girl I know's into the oud — the Arab lute?' He motioned towards the pot. 'That ordinary?'

272

'Well, Earl Grey.' *And I do actually know what an oud is.* She held her tongue.

'Might make myself a herbal.'

Annette carried the pot and her mug over to the table, sat at the end away from the ledger. When Lucas placed the dimpled glass on a coaster, she saw it contained not one bag, but two. The brew was already dark orange with a black stain seething at the bottom.

'I gather you saw my note. What it's about is, I'm heading down to Cooma next week — for three or four days.'

'Cooma? What's down there?'

'I'm hoping the family of a man I'd like to find.' Annette lifted her chin towards the other end of the table. 'I want to send him a copy of that.'

'So ... you switched to the computer.'

She shook her head. 'I don't follow.'

'You made a copy.'

'I photocopied that.'

'Oh. Yeah.'

Annette waited. Lucas glanced past her, she thought to see the sky. 'Are you heading out?'

'She wants me to go through those scales with her.'

Again she waited. He didn't ask. 'What the writing's about is, do you remember a news story earlier this year about a woman's remains being found in a wombat hole? Down the South Coast?'

He made his thinking pout, shook his head. 'No.'

'I was there when she disappeared. Her husband — husband then — has been charged with her murder. They were both archaeologists. What I started out to be — which I think you know.' He nodded. 'Well, in an interview back then with the police I said something, which … implicated the man I'm talking about. I owe him an apology. It's mostly about that, but also how I started in archaeology.'

'This's before Dad.'

'Three years.'

'So, the man … he was a boyfriend?'

She felt heat rise up her throat, his sexual radar unerring. 'Not of the sleeping-with variety. But we were working towards it.'

'What was with this other woman, then? The dead one.'

'You'd need to read it.'

He was watching her. She could feel the skin of her cheeks. He knew. He dropped his head, embarrassed, slid his gaze to the ledger, back to the glass between his hands.

'Um … do you mind if I don't? Sorry.'

'No, that's fine. It'll be here if ever you want.'

His nod was instant and grateful. He pushed back his chair, snatched up the glass to take to the sink.

Her eyes were prickling, she needed him gone from the room. 'Leave that, don't keep her waiting.'

Starting at the *C5* marker, Annette watched for the turn-off. She began to think she'd somehow missed it — she was passing car yards, service stations, the first houses — then saw the sign, *Numeralla 23*, pointing down a side road that fell steeply to a railway crossing. She pulled over, her heart thumping against the belt strap. She was threatening to break the logic of her plan.

The Numeralla listing for *Harpur* was *JH* and *P*. If they were alive, they'd probably be, like her mother, in their eighties. Annette couldn't just turn up asking for Brian. Anyway, there and back would add another fifty to the hundreds she'd already driven. She let a truck pass, then pulled onto the bitumen and followed it into the centre of Cooma, noting the motels she passed. Two looked all right. She had a coffee and drove back to the Motor Lodge.

She parted the curtains of her room — and felt conned to find herself looking down on the railway line! Its proximity hadn't been mentioned at reception. But looking more carefully, she saw that any train would be a ghost train, the rails as weathered as the ballast and sleepers.

She fetched her notebook and sat on the bed and dialled the Numeralla number. A young man's voice told her she'd rung Moon and Saffie and to please leave a message rather than hang up. *Moon and Saffie.* So much for her vision of elderly parents. Annette gave her name and the motel's and asked if they might be related to Brian Harpur, who she believed had once lived at their address, and who she was trying to locate. Whether or not they could help, she would very much appreciate their ringing back.

She remained seated on the bed. There were two more Harpurs in her notebook, in Cooma and in Wambrook. She'd decided before leaving home she wouldn't adopt a shotgun approach. But what if the pair had gone away? No, the beep had been short, no bank of messages.

She stood and took the kettle into the bathroom, ran in enough for a teabag. As she came out, the phone rang. It could only be them or reception, no one else knew she was here.

Nerves made her speak her name in her clipped library voice. There was a wary silence, then the young man of the machine introduced himself and apologised — they'd only been out in the garden, but hadn't heard the ring. Quickly, Annette thanked him for returning the call. They weren't related to the Harpurs, he said, but the property belonged to a woman named Cheryl Harpur. They rented from her. Did she have a pen? Yes, she said, and he recited the number for the *C Harpur* she was looking at in her notebook. Annette thanked him again, asked if he knew whether Cheryl Harpur had a brother. Again, there was a silence she heard as wary. Ah, no, he didn't, but if she'd hold a minute he would ask Saffie. He allowed her to overhear the question and the thoughtful pause before a girlish voice answered. No, sorry, he said into the phone, Saffie didn't know either. Annette found the performed transparency odd, but perhaps it wasn't performed, they were young, and, from the names, a bit hippy. They weren't really locals, he added, they were from Canberra. Well, she asked, could he tell her anything about the place's history, had it ever been a sheep farm? It still was, he said, he and Saffie rented only the house. The paddocks were rented out to the neighbours. And the people whose initials were in the phonebook — did he know, were they Cheryl's parents? Had they moved into Cooma? Ah, no — she'd have to ask Cheryl any questions like that. Sorry, before she went, could she spell her surname? Annette did so, again faintly puzzled, and waited while it was, she assumed, jotted on a pad. He came back on and apologised again for not being able to tell her more. Cheryl was the person she needed.

Annette sat again on the bed and opened out the NRMA map of the Snowy Mountains and flipped it to the boxed map on its back. The street in which Cheryl Harpur lived was a long one, running from the main drag to the town's western edge. 'The city's,' she corrected herself. But she'd been to its centre, it was a town. She clasped her hands in her lap and closed her eyes and breathed pranayama until her stomach stopped fluttering. Then she lifted the receiver and dialled *9* as per the typed instruction, got dial tone, and tapped in the numbers.

After four rings a woman said, 'Hello, Cheryl speaking.'

'Ah yes, hello, my name's Annette Cooley. I'm from Sydney, but I'm in Cooma. I spoke to your tenants at Numeralla, and they've directed me to you. They couldn't tell me, but what I'm wondering is, whether you might be related to *Brian* Harpur, the same spelling.'

She was gabbling! She left the receiver at her ear and breathed into her cupped hand.

'Are you another journalist?'

'What? No. A ... friend. From a long time ago.'

'A very long time, that must be.'

The woman's calmness was infectious. Annette's breathing slowed. 'Yes.'

Annette began to say how long, but the woman spoke over her. 'Well, you do have the right number. Brian was my brother. He passed away a year ago.'

'He's dead?' As soon as she spoke, she wanted to snatch the words back. But for the last three months he'd been a living presence.

'That's correct.' A thin blade of sarcasm had been inserted.

'I'm sorry, I did hear you. It's just ... He was only a year older than me.'

'Fifty-five. Yes.' The woman cleared her throat. 'When you say a long time ...'

'North Teapot. If that means anything.'

'It does indeed.'

'I take it you've heard.'

'Not from the people who should have told me. But yes, I have.'

'The ... people?'

'The police. And are you still in archaeology?'

'North Teapot ended archaeology for me. I'm a librarian.'

'Sydney, you said.'

'Yes.'

'So why have you come all this way ... Annette, isn't it?'

'Yes. I've written ... an account. He told me he was from down this way. I was hoping to get an address, or contact, for him.'

'To send to him.'

'If possible.'

'But it's not. So how about we leave the conversation there. I have to go anyway, I'm due at work in half an hour. So, if you don't mind ...'

Work? Annette nearly blurted. What work started at five? Surely she was well past waitressing.

'Wait — please. I *have* come a long way. Could I ring again? Tomorrow, if that's convenient? Or, would it be asking too much to come round and see you?'

279

'It's not asking too much, I just don't know why you need to.'

'Then that's what we can talk about. Please.' Don't say any more, Annette warned herself.

'How long are you here?'

The dreadful cliché flew into her mind and she batted it away. 'I've ... given myself a few days.'

'Well, there's not a lot to do here. So how about we say tomorrow morning. Ten o'clock?'

'If that suits you. I have the address.'

'Do you want directions, or you have a map, too?'

'No, I've got a map.'

'I'll see you at ten, then.'

The line went dead before she could say thank you.

Annette placed the beeping receiver facedown on the bedspread. There was little risk of its ringing, but she wanted none — not before she'd had time to sort out her feelings. Grief, she was only mildly surprised to learn, was not among them, or not the chief among them. He'd come back to her in the writing, but more as a 'character' she'd observed and was now recording, rather than as a person who, for an intense six weeks, she'd wanted to be with more than anyone else she'd known to that point in her life. 'It's the suddenness,' she said into the room. Hopes raised, then, splat. Because her dominant feeling was, she realised, a mix of frustration and anger. Which surely was stupid. No — it wasn't! She'd come all this way to be told, sorry, you've just missed him, like he'd just popped out to the shops. She was allowed to be angry! It was just not very useful. But why, oh *why*, after thirty-four years, could he not have hung on for one more!

The receiver was still obediently beeping. She snatched it up and dropped it in the cradle.

She drove into the town centre and had five-thirty dinner at a small Italian restaurant — an inoffensive veal scaloppine and a half carafe of the house red. So early, and a Monday, she was the only table.

The room, when she returned, was stifling. She shed her jacket and went to the panel and adjusted the setting, then sat on the bed with her notebook and punched in the digits, thinking as she listened to the distant burring how ridiculous it was that they shared a house and a bed and here they were talking from motels at opposite ends of the state. The desk put her through.

He knew it was her. 'Evening. Good trip?'

'Long, and tiring.' Was it too soon to tell him? It was why she'd rung, wasn't it? 'And disappointing. He's dead, Brent.'

'Ah. Well, thirty-odd years, there was always that chance, love.' He paused, waiting.

'I'm still trying to work out how I feel. Anger keeps getting in the way.'

'That's fair enough. So who'd you find?'

'His sister. She's here in Cooma. I'm going round in the morning.'

'What'd he die of? He'd only have been your age.'

'I don't know, but it was only last year.'

'Hence the anger.'

'Yes.'

'What did you tell the sister?'

Annette knew what he meant. About her role. 'Nothing yet. Only that I'd written an account. She was on her way out the door.'

'How'd she come across?'

'Pretty cautious. Her first question was, are you another journalist. I imagine she's copped a bit of attention over the years just being related.'

'I wouldn't have thought so. Unless he was living there. Cooma. Your phonebook in the room'd be last year's.'

Annette glanced towards the dresser and saw the directory set neatly in the left-hand corner. 'Well, the tenants out in the Numeralla house had never heard of him.'

'So what's next, after you've seen the sister?'

'I don't know. I've paid for two nights. Be a tourist I suppose.'

'Did you stop in Canberra?'

'I did like I said I would. I went round — Majura to the airport and out.'

'And like *I* said, love, you should give it a look. You'll find it a very different place.'

'I've still got an archaeological mind, Brent, it won't have changed enough. And physically being there will *not* bring a change of heart, all right. Which is what you're angling at. There's nothing to "revive". I'm actually thinking of avoiding Canberra completely on the way back and going through Kiandra, Tumut, that way.'

'Pretty long detour.'

'Yes, well, about time I saw some country I've never seen.'

He heard it for the dismissal it was and veered seamlessly into describing Cobar, a town and landscape he was seeing for the first time. Beneath the words, though, her mind had remained on Sue. He picked up on her distractedness.

'I might head off, mate. Hope it goes well tomorrow. I'll ring you, okay — about the same time.'

She thumbed the button and laid the receiver on the pillow, stayed seated on the bed.

Sue always made you come to her. She'd done it back when they were friends, and she was still doing it. It was why, Annette had decided, she hadn't appended a number to her message, and not Annette's first explanation — that after so long a gap she was not wanting to seem to presume. She hadn't said all this to Brent. Even his abandonment of friendships appeared to be uncomplicated. He'd have thought her small-minded. The resentment had been so well buried she hadn't known it was still there till the night they sat in the kitchen discussing her trip. His breezy assumption that she'd want to reconnect with Sue on her way through had brought the old feeling welling up. She'd capped it without revealing its source, instead arguing that if they'd made no attempt to reconnect in thirty-four years, there was — as she'd said again on the phone just now — nothing to 'revive'. His counter-argument was that *events* had given them a reason, a huge one. He would even do the research, if Annette couldn't bring herself to do it. Without waiting for yes or no, he'd picked up his phone and begun tapping. 'Brent, stop it!' she'd been forced to say. 'This *pushing* me!' He'd obeyed, but grudgingly — witness the veiled suggestion he'd made again just now.

Since he'd mentioned the directory, Annette had been conscious of it in the corner of her gaze. She stood and walked to the dresser. He knew motels, the directory was last year's.

The listings for *Harpur* were the same as she had. On an impulse, she turned to the Yellow Pages and looked up *Engineers/Engineering*, skimmed the column, clapped the book shut.

When Annette opened the heavy curtains, sunlight flooded the room. She stood in the shadow of the left-hand curtain and looked past the railway line to what, from the troughs, might have been empty horse paddocks and, beyond them, a low swell of bare hills. That way, east, was Numeralla. Was that where he was buried? Or here, Cooma? Or far from either?

She stretched breakfast. Even so, when she'd eaten the last of her toast it was still only five past eight. She could drive to the street and find the house. Then at ten she could go straight there. But she hated this old, boring need to *plan*!

'Go for a walk, then.'

A road beside the motel, little more than a lane, led down to the railway track. The road crossed on a bed of disintegrating sleepers. Annette halted and looked both ways, vaguely nervous, but enjoying the optical illusion of the rails rushing both towards and away from her. She followed one rail to her feet and saw a shard of ballast that on a site might have passed for a tool, except that its faces had been produced by crushing not flaking. Nonetheless, drawn by its shape, she picked it up and did the fit test. About to drop it, she crouched instead and scratched her initials in the rust on the rail — and was shocked when she straightened to see how the letters jumped at her. She flicked the shard into a drain.

The horse paddocks made her itch for a shovel and sack. But in a month she'd be pulling out their weeds. The first house was a kit, nothing planted, toys scattered over grass already killed by frost. The second house, half-hidden by old pines, was the lane's original reason. The roof was slate, the walls were stone and brick, the mortar eaten out. Though losing their leaves, half a dozen netted trees still bore apples and pears. The windows had the blank look of no one home. Brent would have been over the low stone fence in a flash.

Back in the motel room, she took from her travelling bag the unread Patricia Highsmith. But halfway to the window armchair she turned and lobbed the book onto the bed and extracted from her bag the envelope containing the bound photocopy. She flipped through until she found Brian Harpur crossing the oval with his swag on his back. He read differently now that Annette knew he was dead.

She was behind the wheel at twenty to ten, the map open on the passenger seat. She took the more interesting-looking route, past the gaol and museum and twice over the same winding creek. As she turned into the street, her eye for the solid and well-proportioned was caught by the house on the high side corner. 'That's an oldie,' she murmured at the same time as she searched for the number. It was set into the retaining wall, a glazed earthenware tile — and it was *the* house! Not ready, she drove on for a hundred metres before doing a U-turn.

A cold wind she hadn't felt at the motel blew the open door back hard against her hip. Head down, shoulder bag to her chest, she scooted round the front of the car and into the lee of the retaining wall. The irregular stones were the same colour and grain as the gaol's. She still had ten minutes. She would walk to the corner, see how deep these old blocks were.

She halted short, warned to by the thrashing of a row of poplars. Each gust flung a smoke of leaves across the roof and yard of a brick bungalow on the street's low side. Beyond the poplars was a paddock cropped bare by the dozen or so sheep huddled behind a shed bulldozed into a heap. Sheets of iron were strewn over the paddock — by winds like this, probably. A line of willows marked the upper reaches of the creek she'd crossed. Crouched hills were sparsely clothed in a species of mallee with tufts of leaves on spindly white trunks. A treeless gully with chopped sides might have been the source of the wall beside her, and the gaol's. She heard her father's verdict, *You'd have to be born here.* She lowered her head and walked out into the wind. A paling fence ran for sixty or seventy metres uphill to a farm gate. Cheryl Harpur was not short of yard. Annette retreated to the shelter of the wall and looked at her watch. Time to make herself known.

The woman who opened the door bore no resemblance to her brother. Annette reminded herself that, after thirty-four years, she might not have recognised *him*.

'Annette? I'm Cheryl. Come in.' The woman's hand was as slippery-cool as hers probably was. Cheryl Harpur ushered her past and pushed the door closed. Annette was beginning now to see Brian Harpur. The coarse-pored, red skin, the curly, dark-blonde hair, now streaked with grey, the same pale-blue eyes, hers uncomplicated by the brown flecks she remembered in his. 'Come through — it's warmer out the back.'

'Yes, it's not blowing anything like this over where I'm staying.'

'No, this time of year *we* cop it, from the west. Where *are* you staying?'

'The Motor Lodge.'

'Ah, Dave and Trish — yes, they've turned that place around. Comfy?'

'So far.'

Annette followed the woman, her eyes busy. The hallway was waxed planks, yellow and wormy and twice the width of planks in a modern house. Prints and small paintings — birds and landscapes, no people — hung on the walls. The doors of what Annette took to be bedrooms were closed.

The slightly gloomy hallway didn't prepare her for the kitchen, oiled hardwood and stainless steel, and flooded with light from a perspex bubble in the centre of the ceiling. A massive table directly below the bubble was half-dissolved in the glare. Black and silver, an Aga squatted against the brick internal wall, next to it a six-burner gas stove. Racks of majolica plates stood in a leadlight dresser. A doorway to her left was a pantry, on its threshold an ancient salt-glazed crock with fresh flour on its rim. The original house had been extended. Through bay windows, Annette could see a yard sloping uphill and bare fruit trees, and in the further distance what looked like vegetable beds gone to seed, and beyond them again, its roof cut off by the tops of the windows, a low building that might once, in a house this age, have been stables. But wherever she looked, her eyes returned to the table. It was twelve feet if it was an inch, five wide planks of blond pine, initialled with knives, the edges polished by stomachs, a round scorchmark in one corner as if a cast-iron kettle had once been foolishly set down.

Cheryl Harpur was moving to the Aga. 'Tea or coffee?'

'Tea, please. I'm admiring your table.'

Cheryl Harpur raised the baffle on one half of the hotplate and slid a black kettle from the hob to the heat.

'That came from the shearers' quarters out home. Brian and I fetched it here after Mum died. Some elbow grease went into getting it just back to that.' The woman had inserted both hands into a square tin and was extracting a fruit cake.

Was the use of his name an invitation? She could be a coward, or she could ask. 'Did he … live here? Cooma.'

Cheryl Harpur had picked up a knife. She began to cut, said without looking up, 'Hereabouts.' She lifted the slice on the flat of the blade and laid it on the oval plate waiting by the board, started on another. 'I retained my maiden name when I married — which is why I'm under it in the book. Glenn, my husband, was killed in November nineteen ninety-three. By an off-duty policeman, of all people — ex-policeman, now — driving back from Bredbo drunk.' She overlapped the second slice on the first, used the knifepoint to align their edges. 'Brian came down for the funeral — he was living in Queensland. I was a mess. I had three kids, from eight to thirteen. Overnight I also had a business to run — we owned the produce store. Brian stayed a month. I couldn't have got through those first weeks without him. Mind you, we had some strange meals — not that any of us cared. Just he'd been cooking for one for years. At the end of the month he went back to Queensland, sold up and moved back here.'

The kettle was emitting a low seething. Cheryl Harpur laid

down the knife and picked up a large brown teapot with poppies painted on its cheeks.

Yesterday when Annette had rung, the woman had been going to work. A produce store would be closing at five, not opening. 'You ... still run the produce store?'

'Oh, God no.' Cheryl Harpur spoke as she poured in a warming measure. 'I do the night desk at one of the rivals to where you're staying — three shifts a week. Not for the money, just to get myself out of the house. No, I sold the business. I asked Brian first — if he wanted to manage it — he shied well away. People coming in all day he knew and who knew him.' She emptied the pot into the sink, opened a caddy, and began spooning leaf. She'd been constantly busy since entering the kitchen. Their eyes hadn't met, Annette realised, since the front door. 'Could you take the plate out to that other table, please.'

The table in the sunroom was a cabin trunk topped with a sheet of heavy glass on grommets. They sat each side in leather armchairs. It was a long time since Annette had drunk tea from a fine china cup.

'You said he told you he was from down here.'

'Yes. Numeralla, the farm.'

'You'd know also, I suppose, why he volunteered for North Teapot.'

'We got the story on day one — the poet, your father, Gorman. I've included most of that, too.'

'In this ... thing you've written.'

'Yes.' Annette began to stand, to go to her bag.

The woman put out a hand. 'No.'

Annette lowered herself again into the armchair. She couldn't decide from the tone whether the refusal was definitive or a postponement.

'Do you know his file stayed open all those years? He'd get visits from detectives just to remind him he was still "a person of interest", even in Queensland. They had a nasty habit, too, of letting people know who he was, in their not-very-subtle way, which cost him both friends and jobs. So after all that, you'd think, wouldn't you, when this mongrel admitted to it, that it might have entered some cop's head to come round here — or even just ring. "Hello Ms Harpur, a bit of good news — Brian's been completely cleared." Two minutes it would have taken.' Her eyes glistened.

'Might you go to the trial?'

'I don't ever want to see the mongrel.'

'Can I ask … is your father still living? It must have been hard for them.'

'"Hard" barely begins to describe it. No, they're both gone. The three of them are in the cemetery out there — Brian asked to be cremated and scattered over them. But yes, back then he was the front page of our paper for weeks. "Local man questioned over mystery disappearance." You can imagine the rumours that flew, the size this place was then. He's camped up in the bush with two women. Both hippies by the sound of it — the missing one surfed in the raw. Be a threesome every night, have to be. That was the sort of stuff doing the rounds. You'd probably know he left the university.'

'I ... heard, yes.'

'He wouldn't go out home. Too ashamed. I made him, took him out. But it was awful, Mum and Dad couldn't deal with it. I was here in town in a flat. This was before I married. I made him stay with me. But I had to go to work. Every day when I left I was worried sick he'd go off in the scrub with a rifle. That was the state he was in.'

Yes, I saw, Annette wanted to say. But she wanted more to keep the woman talking.

'Eventually the bouts of crying eased off to where we could have a conversation about what he was going to do. The good thing was, he retained his practical streak.' Cheryl Harpur had been directing her words at the wall, but suddenly looked at her. 'Speaking of which, I bet he had her bloody camp site up and running in a day.'

'Pretty much.'

'And feeding everyone, if he took fishing gear.'

'Yes.'

'So anyway, he had money saved from Dad paying him for round the farm. I gave him a thousand — it's nothing now but it was a fair bit back then. He bought a ute. Then he went out home and got his tools, said goodbye, and drove to Queensland. He came down for my first daughter's christening. More to see

Mum and Dad. Mum was sick. After that, it was just funerals. Eventually his.'

'Do you mind … Can I ask how he died?'

'Of cancer. The lymph glands, and then it spread.' Cheryl Harpur stood. 'I'll top up the pot.'

Annette thought to follow her, fetch the photocopy. But the confusing 'no' was still in her ears.

Cheryl Harpur's mind had not been idle either. She set down the pot and said, 'Do you have siblings?'

'An older brother. In Canada.'

'And husband — kids?' She gave a cold smile. 'I do see the ring, but it proves nothing these days.'

'I know. Half my kids' friends played musical houses. I've got two, girl and boy. She's in Adelaide, he's still at home — but between him and my husband it's more like a boarding house. My husband's a field geologist.'

'I know that feeling.'

'Could I ask you something? You mentioned earlier, years of cooking for one. He … never married?'

'I'm pretty sure my brother died a virgin.'

'You're joking! No — sorry — of course you're not.'

Cheryl Harpur regarded her calmly. 'He certainly was up to the time our mother died. We both got pretty drunk after the funeral. Sitting right here, actually, just the two of us. It got a bit teary. I asked him about … friends. I don't know why I didn't say "girlfriends", he wasn't gay, obviously. That's when he told me. That he'd never had sex. I believed him. It's not a thing you'd say lightly, even drunk.' She brought her hands together in a light clap. 'I suppose you're going to tell me now it was bullshit, he slept with you.'

Annette shook her head. 'No. We were working towards it, though. At least, I thought so.'

'You're the one who saw him, aren't you.'

She set down her cup. Cheryl Harpur didn't look poised to spring at her. 'Yes.'

'No one else would have come looking for him. The reason I can sit in the same room with you is because when he first came to me, I made him tell me whether it was true, the perving. The police here leaked it. The town did the rest. Anyway, he admitted to it. So having it come out again at the inquest didn't change anything. Just meant our name in the local rag again.'

'I've written about that, too. Not about here, about what I saw.'

'And probably very well. Except I have no wish to read any of it.'

'I'm not suggesting you do for my sake. More for his.'

'Nothing can be done any more for Brian's sake. I do, however, have a question. You might not be the best person to be asking, though, after what you've just told me.'

'Can I ask something first? Did Brian never mention me? Him and me?'

'No. The only one he talked about was her.'

'Marilyn.'

'Yes. Which is my question. Did she lead him on? Was the perving part of some game? Because it happened more than once. That's not what got said at the inquest, but it's what he admitted to me.'

'And that was my initial thought, too ... the time I saw him — them. Even then, though, I knew it was just jealousy talking. I'd spent enough time around Marilyn. Yes, she was hugely grateful to him, and she wasn't inhibited about showing it, and I think that led Brian to confuse gratitude for something more. I'm pretty certain, though, if she'd known about the perving she'd have acted to stop it.'

'So he was fantasising, you're saying.'

'Well, he had reason. She was more beautiful than the photographs show — and not just physically, as a person. And I know she continued being warm towards him when they moved up to The Ferns, because I witnessed it. He'd given her a site that was going to make her name. Right up with her husband's.'

'Which, I gather, was the problem.'

'Part of it.'

Cheryl Harpur nodded. 'Thank you. And now I'll say this, you've been brave to come here. Because, for starters, I really don't think jealousy's a sufficient excuse for doing what you did. Do you? I know you were young. But did you honestly have no inkling of the likely consequences? To Brian? Why didn't you just confront him? To his face. Shame him. He deserved it. Not put him up to the police as a *murderer*. Brian was as incapable back then of murdering someone as he is now.'

'Well, I think you're underestimating jealousy. I'm not offering that as a defence. As for shaming and consequences, you're asking the same questions I've asked myself. Yes, I did have an inkling. That's why I asked them not to record what I said — for what that turned out to be worth. All I can say is that, at the time, I thought I was doing the right thing. Which is not my thinking now.'

'"The right thing". A woman's missing, the evidence says she's drowned, and you tell the police she's been murdered, or at least strongly hint it, and my brother's who they want.'

'And I was half right.'

'And half *wrong*! Which is the half that matters to me. And I think you *are* trying to defend yourself.'

'Explain, not defend. That's why I wanted you to read the account. So you might understand how it could happen.'

Cheryl Harpur closed her eyes, shook her head. She spoke with her eyes still closed. 'I understand well enough, thanks. But I don't expect *you* to fully understand the pain your "doing the right thing" caused our family, every single member of it.' She opened her eyes, looked at Annette. 'Have you ever lived in a small town? To this day there are people who cross the street rather than meet a Harpur. I'll tell you what *you* felt — back then, *and* now — you felt "bad". That's not the same as *pain*! The kind that doesn't go away. In our family's case, for years.

That pain's *still there*! It still hurts!' She caught sight of her index finger jabbing the air level with Annette's eyes and dropped her hand to the arm of the chair. When she spoke she was calmer. 'I'm not for a second denying what you saw. It's what you *did* with it.' She sat back in the chair. 'I said you were brave. Now you know why.'

'I didn't come here expecting forgiveness.'

The tilt of Cheryl Harpur's head said plainly, *just as well.*

'That said, I'm glad I did. We all only know our own side of things until we hear the other.'

'Yes, well. Easy to say.' The woman leaned hands on her thighs and pushed herself up. 'I'll just be a minute.' She walked round the table to the room's other doorway.

Annette lifted her cup and saucer onto the tray. She *was* glad. Cheryl Harpur could choose whether or not to believe her. The visit was over. She began to stand, saw cake crumbs in the crease of her jeans, and flicked them into her palm, spilled them onto the saucer.

The woman came back holding in thumb and finger a ball of fuzz, grey and brown, with wings of what looked like feathertips, fine as hair. She raised the ball to eye level. 'This needs a short explanation. He made custom rods and flies for the local sports store. Trout fishing's big business round here. This one he tied for me, but it'll be of interest to an ex-archaeologist. It's a Bogong moth.'

She proffered it by the hook, itself little thicker than a hair.

Annette took and held it as the woman had, in finger and thumb. She'd seen the moths. One of their first field trips had been to a peak near Thredbo where the fat-rich aestivating migrants had once been brushed in their thousands from its sheltering walls, roasted, and feasted on. She could just see a juvenile moth in this confection. She moved to return it, and Cheryl Harpur stopped her hand.

'A small souvenir of him. And now, if you don't mind, I'd like you to go.'

She pushed the key into the ignition — and dropped her hand onto her thigh. It was only a little after eleven. She sat looking through the windscreen at the poplars still flailing in the wind. She'd paid for another night. She could browse the main street. Visit the museum. Sit in her room with Patricia Highsmith. Despite the tea, or because of it, her mouth was dry. She remembered there'd been a small store opposite the gaol. She picked up the moth from the passenger seat and touched a finger to the tip of the hook — and quickly off. It was sharper than a needle. She reached up to the seamed edge of the sun visor and pushed the point into the vinyl, which punctured with a tiny pop. On a surface, his confection looked real.

She bought a bottle of orange juice and drank sitting in the car. Uniformed warders came and went, one so fat Annette wondered what he'd do if a prisoner he was escorting did a runner. She would wait a few weeks till this morning wasn't so raw for them both, then mail the photocopy. Cheryl Harpur hadn't agreed to the visit so as to listen, but to be listened to. There was so much more the woman needed to know, that Annette now *wanted* her to know. But would she even read it? She might simply feed it into the Aga.

A recycling bin stood at the kerb. Annette got out and lifted the yellow lid, dropped the bottle in, and was given a nod, *good on yer*, by a young warder crossing the road. She cut him dead, in no mood to be patronised, and sat again behind the wheel. She didn't want to be a tourist. But neither did she want to return to her room.

'Go out and see where he is.'

The arms at the railway crossing pointed to the sky. She passed a straggle of boxy houses, and then was in paddocks. A fence sign brought a snort of laughter. *Lovegrass Eradication Zone.* Annette lifted her foot from the accelerator, curious to learn what Cooma 'lovegrass' was. If it was visible, it was not a weed as distinctive as dope.

The next time she slowed, it was to wipe her eyes on a sleeve, tears suddenly trickling down her cheeks.

The paddocks petered out into low hills. They were not the soft swellings she'd seen from her room, but eruptions of granite boulders, intergrown with a single species of mallee, and shrubs that looked bred to permanent winter. Annette was glad when she topped a crest and looked into blue distance. The descent was steep and winding. Halfway down, she was ambushed by the first houses, seemingly dropped in among stone and scrub. Below to her right was a river flat, willows and flashes of sand marking the actual watercourse, and, beside it, a large oval, its grass burned white, the only greens a patch around a sprinkler point and the alien stripe of the cricket pitch. She had no directions, hadn't, when she left Cheryl Harpur, even entertained coming here. But a sign beside the post office store told her to turn left for the community hall, church, and cemetery. A girl about five standing on the store verandah didn't return her wave.

The churchyard was too small. A hopeful-looking fence around emptiness turned out to be a park with swings in its far corner. Peering up driveways for someone to ask, she crept on to the last house. Thirty metres beyond it, the road became gravel. She'd missed the cemetery, but couldn't account for how — which didn't alter the fact that the village was behind her and she was again headed into bush. The roadway narrowed, ditches each side. She could only drive on towards a rise that looked like it would take her out of the valley, but showed on its crest what appeared to be a gravel dump or quarry, at least a clearing where she could turn. And from the clearing she was indeed gazing out over the next valley, but, to her surprised relief, also down on a fenced paddock with old pines and headstones.

She was the only visitor. She parked at a weldmesh farm gate in the shade of a row of pines to which the fence had been stapled. When she stepped from the car, it was into a wind less biting than in town, but still sharp, and the hammering of a pump. The pump grew louder when a gust came, faded when it passed. It took her a moment to locate the arm of water lifting and falling beyond the cemetery's far fence.

The foot entrance was an unwelcoming narrow opening split by a steel pole. There, Annette got her first clear view of the ground she had to cover. It looked to be three or four acres. The headstones were in clusters, a long way apart. If they were in denominations, there was no signage to say so. Trees appeared to outnumber the stones. The stockade of old pines in the centre of the paddock suggested they might once have surrounded a house, but all trace had vanished of a drive to its front door. There was a seeming aversion to burying anyone too near the entrance, the closest stones sixty metres to her left, down a slope. Double that distance away, a straggling line of graves ran along the right fenceline. A brown boulder with a plaque was its own island. The cluster of headstones to her left was the biggest, and appeared also to be in rows. She started down the slope.

When she began moving along the first row, Annette discovered that she was among not a denomination, but an Irish dynasty. To make sure, she walked partway along the next row. The same surname whispered to her from each marker. Choosing a gap she hoped wasn't an unmarked grave, she walked out and up again into the open. The wind dropped, bringing closer the hammering of the pump, its insistent beat making it difficult to think. Had there been Harpurs running sheep before his parents? If so, they'd have been at least a clan. Annette vaguely remembered him saying an uncle had kept watch on the farm when the family went down to the coast. A feeling rather than a reason started her towards the pines. Only when she was twenty metres from the giant solitary growing in the centre of what might once have been a lawn did she spot in its shade the pair of low headstones. The closeness of the pairing was compelling. She altered direction.

They faced east. To the Harpur at the coast, or just to the rising sun? Annette wondered as she walked round the graves and stood at their feet. The twin concrete beds were filled with grey and white pebbles, recently weeded — Cheryl's doing, she supposed — the shrivelled plants lying where dropped. The markers were cream marble, now veined orange, and bare of anything but names and dates. Why had they not given their father a line or two from the poet namesake? She'd once had an expert eye for bone, could spot the tiniest sliver. But she knew from her own father's that cremation ashes were pulverised. And the bone was calcined, not charred — two or three falls of rain and there would be no trace.

'I haven't arrived with a speech, Brian. I just wanted to see where you are.'

As she passed back through the opening in the fence, a man wearing a khaki army jumper with elbow patches and jeans faded

almost to white passed between the gateposts of the property on
the other side of the road. He was leaning against the weight of
a jerry can in his left hand, his gaze directed down at his boots.
His hair was hidden by a raw wool beanie. From the obvious
weight of the jerry can, Annette put him in his thirties. But
when he reached the road and she her car, she saw from the skin
at his throat and the purple blotching of the hand clenched on
the jerry can that he had at least twenty years on her.

He heard the jingle of keys and glanced up, and instantly
muffled his huffing. The sides of the jerry can were greasy with
old petrol. The only vehicle in sight was hers. Then she heard
the silence. The pump had stopped. She couldn't have said
when. The man hitched his near shoulder, to ignore her, or —
the more generous interpretation — to respect her privacy.

Annette looked along the fenceline. He had a carry of sixty
metres to a gate in the adjoining paddock, then the length of the
cemetery to where, earlier, she'd seen the arm of water rising and
falling. 'Excuse me? You wouldn't like to put that in the boot of
my car and I'll drive you?'

The man shot her a glance along his raised shoulder. 'No. But
thank you.' He had the trace of an accent. His muted huffing
resumed.

He was Numeralla, the only chance she would get to speak
with this place. Annette started after him.

'I *do* see you're working. But could you spare a minute?'

He halted and half-turned, but didn't lower the jerry can.

Annette saw in his face impatience and physical strain doing battle with good manners. She would need to be quick about stating her business.

'I've been visiting the Harpurs. Did you know them?'

He turned and faced her. His eyes were a deep brown. The skin of his face had, beneath its tan, a yellow cast, not the Anglo pink she expected in a man living here. Annette wanted to ask his name.

'Jim I knew quite well, Phyllis to talk to.'

The omission was not oversight. He'd judged her age. The accent was southern European, but from a long time back.

'Were they an old family? I mean, in this area.'

'It's my understanding the farm's still in the family.'

'And ... people from round here I suppose went to their funerals?'

Annette saw his jaw harden, the bristles stand up from the skin. He'd guessed where she was taking him. 'Yes.'

'And Brian's — their son's?'

The man's face flickered as if lightly slapped. 'You've been speaking to who? The hippies?'

'Briefly, yes, on the phone. But to his sister. In town — Cooma.'

'And she sent you here, the cemetery?' He leaned and, without putting it down, transferred the jerry can to his right hand.

'No. I ... that was my decision. I knew him from a long time back. You may have heard — it's been on the news — a person's

304

been charged over the remains found earlier this year.'

'We do have TV, even out here.' Annette opened her mouth to explain, that she wasn't being derogatory. An imperious whip of the hand forestalled her. 'I don't know if you're still a friend. But let me say this — charged or not, he was a murderer.' He jutted his chin towards the fence. 'Of two bloody good people. They really were. Oh, he comes and cleans the graves. It doesn't bring them back.'

Annette stared at him. 'She', he must mean.

'How far have you come?'

'Me? From Sydney.' She heard the strange croak she had for a voice. 'Sorry — *who* comes and cleans?'

'He isn't dead. But so you don't go back thinking we're *all* liars around here, I'll tell you what you might do.' The man leaned to again change hands on the jerry can, then, as his hands met, he lowered the can to the gravel between his feet. He used the blade of his left hand to carve directions in the air. 'You go back the way you came, turn left at the store, go down over the bridge, and you're on the Countegany road — you'll see the sign. A mile up, you'll come to the last farm on the right. Don't tell yourself you've missed it when you first hit scrub, that's a wildlife corridor. The name's on the gate. The hippies are in the house, he's down the back — the old shearers' quarters.' He bent at the knees and, the choice of hand quite deliberate, gripped the jerry can in his right.

'We were obviously meant to meet. I'm … just not sure if I should say thanks.'

'If anyone, thank my wife. She wouldn't let me out till I found my beanie.'

The man pivoted on the jerry can's weight and stumped away, the huffing resuming after a few steps.

She needed thinking time. She drove up onto the ridge separating the valleys and pulled into the small roadbase quarry overlooking the village. Projected on the view was Cheryl Harpur's kitchen, the woman moving around making tea, slicing cake. Much that had felt like deflection now made sense. 'Everything was props. You were in a play.' Annette was not even surprised to discover that she was more admiring than angry. The woman had devised and rehearsed a script, acted it with total conviction. Nor could Annette fault her motive. Cheryl Harpur had guessed from the first who she was. The woman owed her nothing, least of all the truth. But the fact remained, she didn't like being lied to.

She drove through the village and across the bridge onto the Countegany road. But as she jolted up its corrugations, Annette was forced to confront the possibility that she was perhaps making a very big assumption. That he knew she was here. That the 'hippies' had gone straight down to the shearers' quarters and told him. What if, instead, they'd rung Cheryl Harpur and been instructed not to? In which case, opening his hermit's door to her knock would be a massive shock. Annette couldn't just presume his mental state. Clearly, though, he was no longer the person she'd known — if his sister had 'killed' him rather than risk his meeting her.

She passed through the belt of scrub the man had warned of, and out again into pasture, with distant sheep. A steepening climb brought her to a chained farm gate bearing a tie-wired plank with *C Harpur* and the RMB number painted in rust red. She slowed to a crawl. Downhill, visible only from its windows up, was a weatherboard farmhouse with a roof painted from the same can as the sign. She made her decision. She would turn around and come back, stand at the gate for a few minutes to take in the place, maybe speak to him, then drive away. She now had his address, to use or not.

The pasture ended abruptly at a fenceline, and she was again into scrub. A gap just ahead offered a place to turn. But when she ran the nose in, the gap revealed itself to be the opening of a track running downhill parallel to the fenceline. Annette turned off the motor and got out. As she did she heard a ringing thud, dulled by distance. She cocked her head, but it didn't come again. Then, a minute later, did. Someone splitting wood. Downhill from where she stood, but not from the angle she guessed the house to lie on. The sound would be brighter, too, if coming from the house. Annette walked to the mouth of the track. Sticks and streamers of bark lay unbroken across the ruts. She walked back to the car and pushed her shoulder bag under the seat and locked the door.

She could make out the pasture through a screen of mallees

and wattles. The thuds came erratically — wood had to be picked up, positioned on the block — but each thud was louder, its ring cleaner. The track began to veer from the fenceline and into a gully. She stopped and looked behind her — the car was out of sight — studied again the angle the track was taking. She bent and pleated her jeans cuffs and drew her socks up and over.

She was ten paces into the mallees and wattles when she saw the flat ridgeline of a wide-roofed structure, its iron rusted. It had to be a shearing shed. Annette began moving from trunk to trunk, choosing where she placed her feet, the ground littered with dry leaves and sticks. If he lived alone, he almost certainly had the company of a pair of ears sharper than his own. She halted and looked for a trunk near the fence and thick enough to stand behind. There was one — with a lean, but if she knelt she'd be hidden. She moved in a crouch, keeping a stunted wattle between her and the open sky above the pasture.

When nearly to the trunk, a flash of white froze her. At the far side of the pasture, a black-and-white dog, almost certainly a kelpie, was silently harrying sheep penned against a fence, working them one way then the other. Then Annette saw that the fence was actually between it and the stupid things, the reason it couldn't go behind. But they had command of the dog's attention. She walked to the trunk and knelt and waited for a thud, then leaned to look.

The hair rose on the back of her neck. He — if it was him — but it had to be! — was at a block thirty metres from a corrugated-iron hut with a brick chimney, from which smoke was lifting, then being snatched sideways by gusts. His head was skulled in a blue-and-white beanie. There was not sufficient face to recognise or not, being mostly beard. Beneath a brown cardigan vest, he wore what looked like, but couldn't be, the same checked shirt, its sleeves rolled to the biceps as they'd been the first day she saw him. His height and build, too, were etched in her memory — and the practised ease of his swing. Annette had watched him often enough at Gorman's fireplace. He tossed the halves onto a pile beside a wheelbarrow and leaned the axe, lifted a new block onto the splitting block, then took up and swung the axe in a lazy loop that, just before the head met the timber, became a flash.

She'd wanted only to see if it was truly him. But what if she stepped through the strands of wire and walked down the paddock? He wouldn't, at first, credit his eyes. What should she say? 'Simple,' she whispered. 'Hello, Brian.' And if he reacted like a cornered animal? He was holding an axe. He didn't immediately lift the next block, stood watching the dog. He began to raise his hand, she thought to whistle it, then changed his mind. An uncomfortable thought was edging into her mind, too big and uncomfortable to keep out. *You've done this before, watched him when he didn't know.* She should leave. Her retreat back then, though, had had the excuse of youthful confusion. To do so now would be cowardice.

She'd debated for too long, the kelpie had tired of the sheep and was loping back. Annette pushed down on the middle strand of wire and bent through. She saw the kelpie see her and, without a sound, become a flat blur. She would not reach the man before the dog reached her.

'Brian! Call your dog!'

He'd split a block and was stooping to pick up the halves. He jerked upright, grabbing instinctively for the axe. Then he registered the words and turned to the paddock, fingers going to his lips. The dog braked instantly and veered into a trot towards him, but throwing her shy, hostile glances.

Annette didn't move, not really thinking its obedience would be anything less than total but wanting to be sure.

The man let his hand be licked, then patted the neck. 'All right, to your mat.' The dog gave her a last appraising glance and trotted towards the hut.

Annette began walking. He had not looked at her again, he was staring out across the paddock, the axehead resting on the ground beside his boot, its handle against his thigh. The hand she could see, his right, was a fist. He was surrounded by limbs and strips of bark, blocks lying where sawn, she had to pick a path through.

'What's its name?'

'His. Pepper.'

Annette walked round in front of him, her stomach filled with flapping birds. He glanced at her face and down. The beard was massive, years of it, grey and ginger, but she'd caught a glimpse of the left eye, the flecks of brown in the blue. Not that it could have been anyone but him — he'd answered to his name. She put out her hand.

Brian Harpur unfisted his, took hers in a limp grip.

Annette had braced for the reptilian skin he'd had then, but his palm was almost soft. 'A long time.'

Brian Harpur lifted his hands, balled the left into the cup of his right, and brought them to his mouth. He closed his eyes, sucked in breath, and began to cry. Annette's eyes filled. She stepped to him, her hands hovering, then she put them to his shoulders. He kept his hands pressed to his mouth, his elbows a barrier, but didn't shrug her off. Nor did he attempt to control his crying.

Annette glanced towards the hut, worried how the dog might interpret what was happening. He'd stood, was watching, but clearly wouldn't leave the verandah without an order.

Brian Harpur had his eyes squeezed shut. His brows, like his beard, needed trimming. The beanie, too, was in need of repair. When she thought the crying might be slackening, some thought, or image, set him off again. Annette couldn't have said how long they stood. When she heard and felt the crying truly begin to slacken, she slid her hands from his shoulders and enfolded his clenched wet hands in hers. She was no longer teary, was almost elated. She could have driven home believing him dead. Instead, she was holding his hands.

'I'm sorry, Brian, that I didn't tell you. That it was me. At the time it was too hard, I couldn't. I was jealous, and I was angry.'

She waited. He kept his eyes closed. 'You know, don't you, that she was found. And about Aled.'

'Yes.'

He pulled their hands down to his chest, tugged for Annette to let go. He reached into his trousers pocket and drew out a handkerchief and wiped his eyes, blew his nose.

'So, when did you know? That it was me.'

He sighed and opened his eyes, looked at her. His right eyelid had a droop it didn't have when she'd last stood this close to him. 'The inquest. I thought you'd be there.'

'I was in London.'

Brian Harpur looked past her. 'Better place to be.'

'It wasn't deliberate.'

He gave a lift of the shoulders, not quite a shrug.

'You might already know — I rang your sister. She told me you'd died.'

'You're not the first. It doesn't bother me as much as you might think.'

'I've spent part of the morning with her. I don't know how much else she invented.' *Your virginity, for example,* she said silently. 'She'd have made a good actor.'

He gave the same half-shrug.

'She said the police kept track of you, and told people who you were.'

'She didn't invent that.'

'Well, that's ... horrible.'

He looked at her. 'Just doing our job, Mr Harpur.' He smiled, coldly. 'You'd make a pretty good cop, yourself.'

She couldn't implicate a neighbour.

'I came out to say goodbye. She said you'd been scattered on their graves. Then I came looking for the farm and spotted the name on the gate. When I got out, I heard the axe.' Annette gestured towards the block. 'It was a bit of a shock to see a dead man splitting wood.'

She was rivalling Cheryl Harpur for invention. But he simply arched his brows, *the things you see, eh.*

'You're in Sydney, yeah.'

'Yes, but not in archaeology. I'm a librarian. She didn't tell you that?'

'No.'

'When did you speak to her?'

'Last night. She rings the house.'

'You have a bit to do with "the hippies", then.'

'A bit.'

'So you knew already I was here. From them.'

'Yeah.'

She thought to say, *They said they'd never heard of you.* But why score points? 'Actually, I left Canberra and archaeology not long after the last time I saw you.'

'Out the Cotter.'

'Yes.'

'When are you heading back?'

'Tomorrow.'

'You want to come in? This wind's not exactly warm.'

'Yes, please.'

Brian Harpur picked up three splits and stacked them in the crook of his left arm and ushered her towards the hut. The kelpie smiled and began to wag his tail. Annette spoke his name and the tail went mad, shaking the whole hindquarters. There was no step, the verandah so low. A cane armchair with a green corduroy cushion cratered in the centre spoke of where he spent his evenings. Perhaps his days. Pepper nuzzled her hand. Annette stroked along the groove in the skull, dried her fingers on the soft ears.

'Sit,' Brian Harpur said, and the dog went instantly to a hair-matted sack.

'Not on my account,' she said.

'All right, in you come.'

The dog was up in a flash, nose pointed at the door.

Brian Harpur heeled off his boots. 'You can leave yours on.'

'No, I have the same habit.'

He moved past her in his socks, turned the handle, and gave the door a push. The dog darted past her knee. Annette halted just inside and took in his 'cell'.

One room. Brick floor — old handmade bricks, worn and polished by soles. Immediately before her a square raw-plank table, two chairs. Beyond it the fireplace, a half-consumed log lying on a bed of red coals. A cast-iron camp oven on the hearth.

A bench with a double gas burner, below the bench shelves with crockery and cutlery, tea towels, soap. A standing shelf with cans in towers. To her right, against the wall, a made single bed with the addition of an opened greatcoat lying up to where his thighs would be, at the head a shelf with books and a gas lantern. A powerful torch standing inverted on the floor. To her left, a workbench with a delicate vice like a claw and racks of glass jars filled with every shade of fur and feather, but some, she saw, looking more closely, containing hooks, brass rings. More feathers, whole, tied in bunches. It was here he'd confected the Bogong moth. At the front of the bench a lathe-like device, with a belt drive, worked by a treadle. Standing in the corner, slender fishing rods, finished and blank, the finished with written tickets — *Blay*, she read on one — tied to the lowest runner.

Brian Harpur had walked round her to the fireplace and unloaded his arm onto the floor. He pulled off his beanie and lobbed it onto the bed. Annette saw now why it had fitted so snugly, the little hair he still possessed cropped to the skull. With scissors, it looked like.

He went to the stove and hefted the kettle for weight, sat it back on the burner and lit the gas. 'I've only got coffee.'

'That's fine.'

He stooped and drew out a bottle, displayed its label, Tullamore Dew.

'I think so, yes.'

He pointed her to a chair. The dog had been waiting, but

came now and crouched, chin on paws, bright eyes trained on her. Brian Harpur nodded down. 'You can see we get a lot of visitors.'

He made a plunger. Milk was tube condensed. Annette saw now what was missing — a fridge. Brian Harpur spilled oatmeal biscuits onto a plate. She hadn't seen how large were the shots he'd poured, but got an idea when she raised the mug and the fumes bit her nostrils.

She lowered the mug without sipping. 'I wasn't really a drinker back then. Or you, very much.'

'We weren't a lot of things.'

Annette heard the stirrings of anger. She had expected it eventually, the natural arc from self-pity, and didn't panic. 'We could have been. If not for events. And choices.' When he didn't speak, she said, 'You made choices, yourself, and have obviously gone on making them. I left the life I thought *I* had too, and started another one.'

'You've done a bit better, I think.'

'By the conventional measures. But I've never been on a site again.'

She waited. He dipped his head and took a swig of coffee.

'I agree that's nothing like what you've been through.'

'I knew I never touched her. Doesn't matter what anyone else thought.'

'That's not what you said that morning you came to Tate Street. You were a mess. "In hell."'

316

'Yeah, well. I got better at dealing with it.'

She opened her mouth to ask *how*, but he said before she could speak, 'What did you do with the skeletons?'

'The ske—? Oh, the fish! Threw them away.'

'At Teapot.'

'Yes. I didn't want any reminders of the place.'

He gave the unreadable lift of the shoulders he'd given earlier.

'So … you ever hear what happened? With the sites.'

'More than heard, I read the papers. Aled wrote one on the beach cave. Later our year, seventy-one, Sue and a man named Tom Sieglitz — you didn't ever meet him — they re-opened The Ferns. Their paper appeared in seventy-two. You're credited with finding the site.'

The smile he gave didn't part his lips and didn't reach his eyes. 'She stayed in archaeology, then.'

'Sue's from tougher stock than me. The last time I saw her's like you, out at the Cotter. But she did ring to tell me Marilyn had been found. Just a voice message. What about you? Did you ever consider returning to engineering?'

'I was in Queensland.'

'You could've written to ANU, got your subject credits.'

'I wasn't using my *name*, mate. Bit hard to enrol anywhere. And I didn't need a degree for what I was doing.'

'Which was?' Annette inclined her head towards the rods in the corner.

'No, that's a Cooma thing. I was on farms.' He lifted the

plunger. 'You want a top-up?'

She'd hardly touched the brew since recoiling from the fumes. 'I'm okay.'

She was surprised, even slightly shocked, at how natural it felt to be in his company. But it was time to end the dance they were doing around one another.

'Like I said, Cheryl told me you'd been scattered on their graves, which is why I went there. They'd been weeded recently. I thought that was her doing, but it was yours.'

He nodded, but didn't meet her eyes, looked instead down at the dog.

'So do you think now you can give this place up and move into town? Or go somewhere else entirely? You're free now, I'd have thought.'

'This's where I live. Where I *choose* to live.'

She heard the barb. He was watching her again to judge its impact.

'Choose differently. My father's dead, Brian, but I talk to him. Go down and talk to them. I'm no psych, but this isn't healthy, or even necessary — certainly not now — this ... obligation, punishment, whatever it is, you've laid on yourself.'

'Yeah, well, I'll be the judge of that.'

'Sure. But how does Cheryl feel, about you hiding out here?'

'It's none of her business, either.' Not a barb, but a blunt warning.

'I know I'm diving in uninvited, Brian. But I helped make

your "hell". And Cheryl made it brutally plain to me that you're very much her business. I understand how she keeps your hermetic world intact, like Moon and Saffie do. But it's going to get a jolt if there's a trial.'

'There won't be. Not the full rig, anyhow — jury, witnesses, and so on.'

'My husband reckons there will be, if the police refuse to go with manslaughter.'

He shook his head. 'And even if there is, I won't be called. Not by the cops. I'd be a "hostile" witness.'

'I think you can be forced.'

He was already shaking his head again. 'Won't happen. And how I *know* is! When they announced she'd been found, Cheryl came out wanting me to go in with her rather than the cops come and get me. I told her no. Let them waste their time and petrol. Still haven't seen one.'

'Well, I feel a bit better to know your sister didn't entirely believe you, either.'

'She at least wanted to.'

'I've said, Brian, I was angry. We both know why.'

'Enough to want it to be me.'

'I didn't *want* it to be you.'

The eruption of his hands from beneath the table and their sharp clap made her jump. 'I would never have done *any*thing to hurt her! I said so to that bastard of a cop. That she was a goddess! But he turned everything into ... into some *dirty* question! None of you — you, him, bloody inquests, even my sister … None of you would have believed me. About why I watched her. So I never said.'

He propped his elbows on the table, eyes tightly closed, hands fisted on his mouth. Then he reached under the table and brought up his handkerchief, pressed it to each closed eye.

Annette waited. He kept his eyes closed.

'So, tell me now.'

He shook his head.

'Please? If I got it so wrong.'

He shifted phlegm in his throat and swallowed.

'I wanted her to get into trouble. In the water. So I could … save her.'

They were only the width of the table apart, but Annette had almost not heard the last words.

'Brian, she was a better swimmer than any of us.'

He opened his eyes. They were wet and fierce. 'I could swim! Back then. There was a rip up that north end. That gutter. And she'd go straight down from working, into cold water. You saw how far out she'd go. A bad cramp, and she wouldn't have got back in.'

Okay, Annette, she thought. *You can nod yes. But how many more lies are you supposed to swallow today?* She looked down at the dog, was met instantly by the intelligent gaze. *He's got you. That makes no sense, but it's the only comfort I can find right now.* She looked again at Brian Harpur.

'I'd like to believe that, but I can't. I have too strong a memory of Tate Street. You made a confession to me. Which was very different from what you just said, and which'll make it next to impossible for the two of us to go on sitting here.' She slid from the chair and stood. 'So I'll leave, okay.'

He shrugged. 'Up to you. But you don't have to. Makes no difference to me what you believe. We don't have to sit — we can go for a walk.' He pushed back the chair and rose, and the dog sprang up, trotted to the door. 'I can even show you a site, a small one.' He gestured over his shoulder. 'Down at the creek.'

'Show me a site?'

He smiled, but frowning.

Annette shook her head. 'It's better I just go.'

She began to put out her hand, then stepped to Brian Harpur and embraced him, the beard like scratchy wool against her cheek and his body in her arms shocked and rigid, his arms only belatedly rising as she stepped away.

'We never did that, either, Brian.'

She had to watch her feet to navigate the scattered wood heap, didn't look back till she was at the fence. He was standing on the hut verandah, the dog against his leg. His hand remained at his side.

Habit insisted she make some gesture. She nodded, didn't wait to see whether it was returned, ducked through the wire.

*

Beside the bridge was a small parking bay. She pulled in, leaving the engine running and her foot on the brake. There were wattles along the creek's far bank. She looked at them through the windscreen, but saw his face across the table as he told her about Marilyn.

'Goddess' would have hurt once, badly. Now it was just puerile. And sad. She found herself wondering what 'dirty questions' Isles had turned the word into. She could have asked. The word was clearly a revenge on the man, and on all of them, her included, for Brian Harpur to have kept it burning in his head all these years, and to have, just now, thrown it at her so defiantly. Yet, at the same time, he'd had no desire, it seemed, to confront her. He'd known since yesterday she was in Cooma and why, knew what she would be told, that he was dead. He hadn't wanted even to see her.

So what, then, was she to make of the uncontrollable tears when she'd first walked up to him at the splitting block? And how natural it had felt to be in his company? He, too, had felt it. But, weirdly, he had not felt or understood the shift that began when he clapped, and which became more and more uncomfortable as he spoke. For her, the sensation had been almost physical, the table seeming to grow wider.

No, it wasn't weird. She'd done almost the same, with her own version of events. He'd told himself the story *he* wished to believe so many times it was now *the* story. Credible or not had ceased to matter. He'd even said as much. *Makes no difference to me what you believe.* It had not been bravado — he had, in the next breath, suggested a walk. He'd genuinely wanted her to stay.

If she was going to go on sitting here replaying everything, she should at least turn off the motor.

'No, you should go home.' *Tell reception, fetch your bag, and leave. You'll get most of the way in daylight.*

She put the selector in drive and glanced in the mirror, though not seriously expecting to see another vehicle. Then she pulled out onto the Countegany road for what would certainly be the last time.

Brent turned sixty and declared an end to fieldwork. Lucas moved out to live with the oud player.

Annette was acting head at the library, Oliver on indefinite stress leave. She arrived at work early, left late, brought files and problems home. She had almost forgotten that, somewhere, Aled sat in a cell.

The reminder came by phone. Brent poured her a wine before telling her she had a message, and that there was no need to panic when she heard the intro.

The speaker was a Detective-Constable Robert Wells. He had a light Scots burr. He was ringing on behalf of Detective-Sergeant Townshend to inform her that she would not be required to testify in forthcoming proceedings against Dr Aled Wray. It had been decided to proceed with a charge of manslaughter, and police and prosecutors were advised that a guilty plea would be entered. He thanked her, wished her a good day.

Annette hit the button, strode back into the kitchen.

'Proceeding when? He doesn't bother to say!'

'They still mightn't have a date. I can get you a number.'

'I have a number.'

'Oh?'

'You said this was what they'd do.'

Brent shrugged. 'They sometimes run murder knowing they can settle for manslaughter. Seems in this case they're not bothering.'

Her hand began to shake. She managed to reach to the table with her glass.

'How about you sit, eh.'

Brent lifted a chair to be opposite, took her hands in both of his, spoke gently into her face. 'No witnesses, no physical evidence other than her remains, and very difficult, love, to prove intent. They're probably just happy they've got a confession to go with.'

Annette learned of his court appearance only when it was over. She'd got home too late to watch the news. Brent, too, had been caught by surprise.

'He's not sentenced. That's in a fortnight. But I'd imagine the beak won't be too impressed by the lengths he went to to avoid ever facing a court.'

'Is that ... I mean, will that be open to the public?'

'The sentencing? Yes. It's part of the trial.'

'Could we … go?'

He was silent for several seconds. 'If you want.'

'I don't especially need to see him, Brent. But I need him to see *me*. Brian Harpur would be better, but *someone* at least who was there! Who he acted all that shit to!'

Again, Brent was silent. Then he said quietly, 'You can speak, you know. Even for Harpur. That's what a sentencing hearing's for.'

'I don't think I could. I'm angry now just talking to you.'

'Yes, I can hear.'

'Whatever he's given, it won't be enough.'

'Oh, I think it will, love. At his age. It will.'

They caught the bus to Hyde Park and walked up Oxford Street to Taylor Square. Annette had only ever seen the ugly sandstone building with its massive columns from a passing car. To walk through the gates and into its shadow was to be made aware of how truly intimidating it was.

Brent was more nervous than she was. For all his knowledge of courtrooms, he had never set foot inside one. His hand had gone clammy, she let go. He pulled out his phone and announced the time, then asked in a tight voice if she wanted a coffee. No, she said, an apple juice. He scooted back down the cracked bitumen road towards the freedom of the pillared gate and Oxford Street.

The first reporters and cameramen arrived. Several looked at her speculatively. Annette pretended a great interest in the traffic flowing through the square. Which was why she saw the lone man as soon as he came through the gate. He slowed, shooting sidelong glances at the immense stone façade as he walked, as if to stop and confront it was too much. Annette watched him along her shoulder. The man was in jeans and joggers and a badly cut brown leather jacket that ballooned around his torso. He'd lost most of his hair, aviator sunglasses hid his eyes. But Annette was certain it was Paul. He sensed her interest and studied her a second, changed direction. She put out her hand.

'Paul. Hello.'

'Hello, Annette.' He took off the sunglasses and exhaled the tension he'd suppressed all the way from the gate. 'Strange, the things that bring people together again.'

'Yes. Are … Do you know if any of the others might be coming?'

'I haven't seen any of them in thirty years. You?'

She'd left herself open, would have to lie. 'The same — no.'

'You quit, too, didn't you.'

'Yes. And you, by the sound of it.'

Annette was stunned when his jaw began to quiver and his eyes filled. Her own eyes prickled. He turned away, blinking, and touched the back of his hand to each lid. The smile he attempted when he turned again to her was worse than a grimace. 'I did eight months in Vietnam before Whitlam killed nasho. Might get a bit of wild justice today for that, too. Look, I need to find a toilet. I'll see you in there. And after, maybe.'

She watched him hurry towards the portico, where he was dwarfed, disappeared. Brent had to nudge her arm. He began to put the bottle in her hand, then saw her face.

'What's happened?'

'Oh, there was a man here, just now — Paul. He was at North Teapot, too.' Annette swallowed, her eyes prickling again. 'He's in a worse state than me.' Before Brent could ask, she lifted her chin towards the portico. 'He's gone in.' Annette suddenly understood that the smell that had hovered between them, and which she'd thought was the cheap leather of his jacket, was in fact spirits of some sort. 'I think he went to find a quiet corner.'

The knot of reporters and cameramen had swelled and moved closer to the building, into its shade. She saw a man in a suit appear in the portico. The man faced the square and buttoned his coat, not noticing that his tie was outside, then seeing and tucking it in. He ran a hand over his hair, then descended the steps and walked towards the reporters.

Brent, too, had seen him and picked up on his nerviness. The man had been swallowed by the knot. Then one of the reporters broke out, pulling a phone from his pocket. The knot began to unravel. A reporter obviously asked the man — a solicitor, was he, she wondered, or court officer? — to repeat to camera what he'd said, for the cameramen began jostling for position.

Brent pushed his cup into her hand. 'Back in a sec.'

He made a beeline for the man speaking on his phone and stood a metre from him, openly eavesdropping. The man lowered the phone and, Annette guessed, asked who he was, none-too-politely to judge from the jut of his jaw. Whatever Brent said, she saw the man give her a swift appraising glance before he replied. He glanced again, ticked a finger towards her, and spoke. Brent shook his head. The man dismissed him with a flick of the hand, the phone already at his cheek.

Brent walked back to her. The impassivity of his face was confusing. He lifted bottle and cup from her hands and stood them on the road, enfolded her in his arms and spoke into the hair beside her ear.

'He's been sentenced. He died half an hour ago, love. In the holding cell. They think a heart attack.'

He'd placed it on the hallway table where she would see it as soon as she came in, a small padded postbag, overnight delivery. Annette lifted it — light — turned it over. The sender was *Townshend*, the address a post office box in Batehaven. She carried it to the stool in the phone alcove and sat and unzipped her bag for her glasses.

A folded page had been folded again around two neat parcels of white tissue and sticky tape. Annette unwrapped the larger. Inside a clear clickseal pouch was a stone point. She opened the seal and slid the point into her palm. Its shape was the familiar gumtip scimitar, the stone a pale red-brown. The working edge was intact, the point broken. She placed it down on its tissue and picked up the other parcel. Compared with the first, it felt weightless.

A slim, gold wedding band. Annette reached her right little finger into the pouch and captured the ring, drew it out. She resisted the impulse to slide it down to the knuckle, instead pushed it off with her thumbnail into finger and thumb of her left hand. She knew whose ring she was holding. She angled it into the light falling through the kitchen doorway. The hallmark was too tiny to decipher. She placed the ring beside the point.

The note was on plain paper. Just the post office box address again, and the date.

> *Dear Ms Cooley*
>
> *The stone first.*
>
> *I found it in the gully after rain. Perhaps lost by one of your colleagues, but I'm more inclined to think, from where I picked it up, that whoever dropped it did so when us whites hadn't been even dreamed of.*
>
> *The ring.*
>
> *The following is not a morbid joke, but a legal opinion. We believe it extremely unlikely that there will be any appeal arising from the Wray conviction. Certain items of the physical evidence are therefore no longer required to be held.*
>
> *You will know who the ring belonged to. It was found on her.*

*I believed it should go to someone who would know best what to
do with it. A private decision, and I ask that you keep it private.
Should you wish to reply, please do so to the above address and
not to the station.*

*We've never met, but, for obvious reasons, I feel I've met you.
The events of this case affected you deeply, and, as you made clear
in our phone conversation, still do. 'Closure' is a much-overused
term. I prefer 'healing'. I hope that can now occur, despite the
burdensome faculty of memory.*

*Your honesty was at all times, then and now, greatly
appreciated.*

My best wishes
Wayne Townshend

She retained the note in her hand and picked up the ring.
The image that arrived, she didn't want — blue-gloved fingers
sliding it from bone. She touched the ring to her lips, folded her
other hand over it, closed her eyes.

Marilyn came to her not at The Ferns, but standing imperiously
beautiful against the reddening sky as Annette climbed the last
few steps up from the beach, Aled behind her with the dingo.

She opened her eyes and her hand. The band was so fine it
was only her eyes that told her she was holding anything. *So
which of your elements do I return you to, earth or water?* She
didn't have to decide now. One or the other would speak when
she got there. She pinned the ring to her palm with a fingertip

and picked up the point, and went looking for Brent.

The back of his head and shoulders were framed in the kitchen window, he was sitting at the courtyard table. He hadn't heard her, and started when the flyscreen door squealed. He smiled hello, glanced at the page number, and lay the book down.

'So, what's your cop sending you?'

Annette passed him the note.

When he raised his head, she placed first the point, then the ring on the cover of the book.

He left them there. 'They belong in only one place, don't they.'

'Yes.'

'Do you need to go on your own?'

'Probably, but I don't want to. Come, please.'

'Sure. When?'

'Soon? Even tomorrow? I can text Julie.'

'Yep. We get up early and go.' He picked up the ring, held it out to her. 'And my suggestion is, you wear this. Until it's time to take it off.'

Acknowledgements

Sharon Jones read an early draft and suggested I put it away for a while, and I thank her for the sound advice.

Roger McDonald read a later draft and found enough evidence of a novel to encourage me to keep going. I thank him for his writer's eye, his faith, and, above all, for his long and abiding friendship.

For conversations on archaeology, which gave the novel much of whatever authenticity it has, I thank Val Attenbrow, Jack Golson, Peter Hiscock, Philip Hughes, and Marjorie Sullivan. Any errors of fact or interpretation I took from those conversations are mine. As are, of course, all outright inventions.

The late John Mulvaney was foundation professor in the Department of Prehistory and Anthropology at the Australian National University. Over lunch one day in the staff club with him and Jack Golson — who had, perhaps unwisely, vouched for my ethics — I described the novel and explained that I intended to re-people the department he'd founded with fictional strangers. Although too polite to say so, he clearly thought it a dubious enterprise, but gave it his blessing, and for that I thank him.

I regret that I never met the late Ron Lampert. His papers on sites along the New South Wales South Coast are models of thoroughness and detail, and were a constant reference.

Allison Dejanovic of the Australian Museum gave me access to their holdings of material and photographs from the Curracurrang site. In return, my grateful thanks.

I thank Lyn Tranter, my agent, for her uncompromising support — and for the great good sense she talks.

It has been a privilege and a pleasure to work again with Anna Thwaites, at Scribe. Wise, funny, passionate — and tough enough to keep insisting, ever so gently, that a scene was still not quite there. I thank her as my editor, and as my friend.

Finally, to Bette, who read every draft, my love and deepest thanks. For this, and for so, so much more.